THE FOURTH MAGI

A TALE OF PROPHECY, DOUBT, AND DESTINY

BRYAN E. CANTER

TELIKOS PUBLISING, LLC

The Fourth Magi: A Tale of Prophecy, Doubt, and Destiny

Published by Telikos Publishing, LLC.
Cheyenne, WY

Paperback ISBN: 978-1-963945-04-1
Hardcover ISBN: 978-1-963945-05-8

FICTION / Christian / Biblical

This is a work of fiction. Unless otherwise indicated, all the names, characters, businesses, places, events, and incidents in this book are either the product of the authors imagination, or used in a fictitious manner.

Scripture quotations taken from the New American Standard Bible® (NASB), Copyright © 1960, 1962, 1963, 1968, 1971, 1972, 1973,1975, 1977, 1995 by The Lockman Foundation. Used by permission. www.Lockman.org

Scripture quotations taken from the New King James Version ®, Copyright © 1982 by Thomas Nelson, Inc. Used by permission. All rights reserved. www. thomasnelson.com

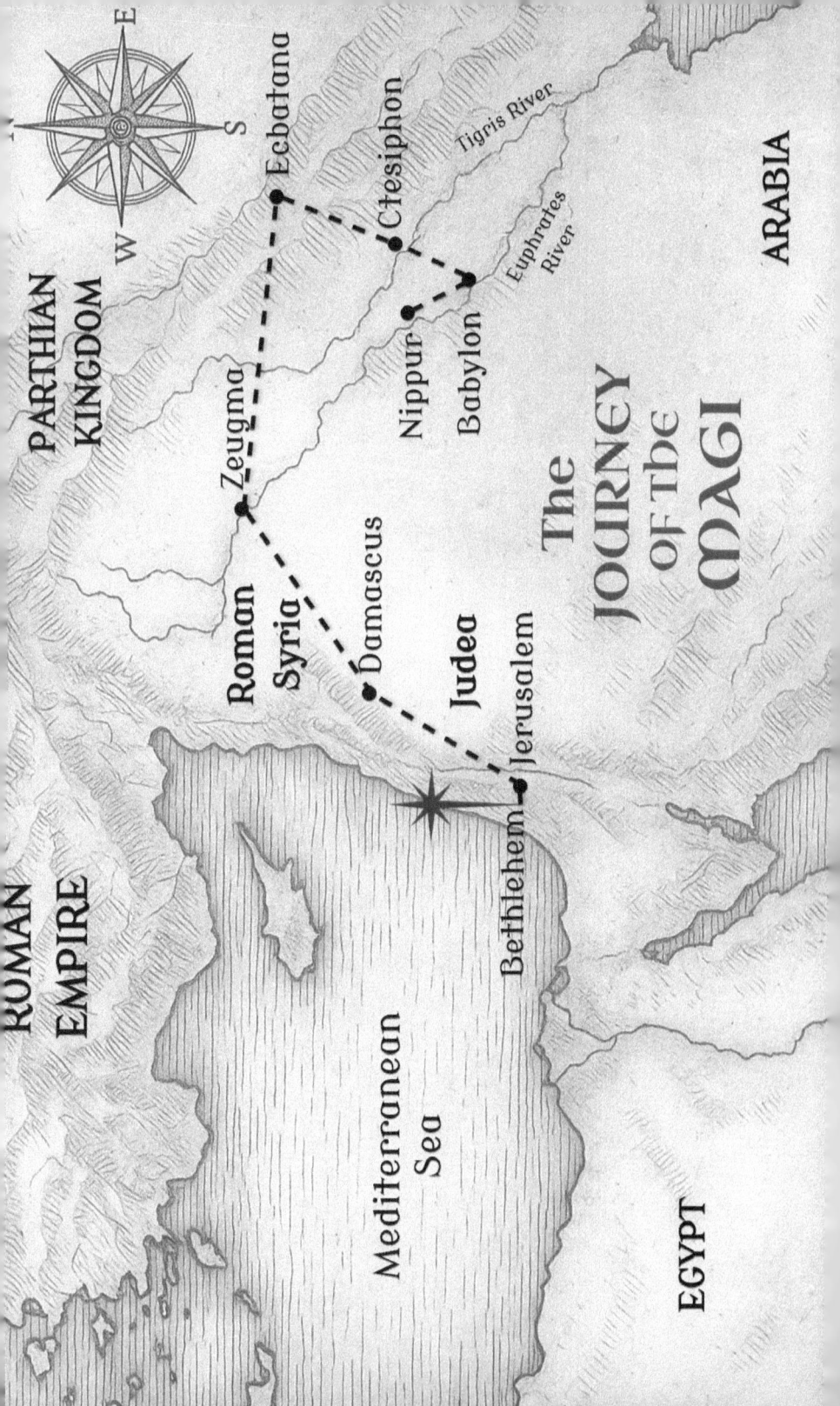

PREFACE

In the hallowed halls of palaces, temples, libraries, and observatories across the Parthian Empire at the turn of the first millennium, wise men known as "magi" searched the heavens for signs from the gods about the meaning of current events or clues to what the future would hold. They consulted vast storehouses of clay tablets, parchments, and vellum scrolls, which contained centuries of accumulated knowledge from the Babylonian, Persian, and Greek empires.

Astronomers had carefully studied the movements of constellations for hundreds of years. These well-known groups of stars traced slow, predictable paths across the night sky. They were associated with powerful gods, mythical beasts, or heroic figures that varied from culture to culture. Modern readers are familiar with some of these constellations as the twelve signs of the zodiac.

Other bright objects in the sky moved along faster, less predictable paths. Today we know these as the planets of our solar system, but ancient astronomers called them "Wanderers" because of their erratic movements.

Occasionally, strange, uncharted lights would appear, lasting for brief moments or for many months, and blaze across the night sky. These are known to us as meteors, shooting stars, and comets. The scholars, priests, and philosophers of the ancient world speculated about the nature of these sporadic celestial entities, but acknowledged that they, like the well-documented constellations and Wanderers, were manifestations of spiritual beings. Their sudden and intermittent appearance suggested great and ominous portents for the world.

The magi who served the Parthian king worshipped the single god of the Zoroastrian faith, Ahura Mazda, but also acknowledged many lesser gods and spiritual forces. While they adopted the Babylonian names for the heavenly bodies they studied, they were also familiar with the Persian, Greek, and Roman titles of these same celestial entities.

The names these magi used for the constellations and planets may sound unfamiliar to modern ears. For clarity, the more familiar Greek or Roman labels of some celestial bodies that feature prominently in the tale are provided in the key below.

- *Marduk:* Jupiter. The chief deity of Babylon. To the Parthians, this planet represented the supreme god of the heavens.
- *Ninub:* Saturn. A god of agriculture and healing. To the Parthians, it was the star of the king.
- *Nergal:* Mars. The god of the underworld and war. To the Parthians, this "Wanderer" was associated with the region of Syria and Judea.
- *Ea:* Pisces. The Parthians linked this cluster of stars to the god of wisdom, life, and creation. Pisces is the last of the twelve constellations of the zodiac that the sun passes through each year, so it was often associated with endings and new beginnings.

"Conjunctions" were times when the planets, or "Wanderers," would appear to join together. The constellation which lay behind such conjunctions helped ancient astrologers understand the meaning and significance of each occurrence.

The magi in this story discover a unique triple conjunction of Jupiter and Saturn within the constellation of Pisces over the course of eleven months. They witness a rare and ominous sign that would not appear in the heavens again for another 800 years.

And now, *The Fourth Magi*…

CHAPTER ONE

Early Spring, 7 BC
Ekur Temple Complex, Nippur, Parthian Empire

Belshazzar stared in wonder at the clay tablets lying side by side on the reading desk. *This would be no ordinary king.*

"Gondophares," he called over his shoulder. "Come. You must see this."

A slightly younger man with a light brown complexion in his late thirties stirred from his own studies and rose to the summons. There were only three scholars in the hall at that late hour, so the steps of his leather sandals echoed through the silence.

"What is it, my friend?"

Belshazzar gestured with a stylus to the tablet on his left. Shadows from the angular impressions in the hardened clay danced in the flickering light of the oil lamps. They identified the tome as one of the detailed celestial almanacs compiled for the upcoming year.

"I've been consulting the predictions for the forthcoming season to know what we might expect to see in the heavens," he replied. "Look here." He pointed to a specific line in the text.

His friend's long, flowing black beard brushed his shoulder as he leaned forward to scan the document.

"Ah," Gondophares finally said and read the words aloud, "'*Ea* moves toward its station, and two of the Wanderers, *Marduk* and *Ninib*, draw near.'" He reflected on the passage for a moment and then observed, "This must be a very rare alignment. These two move on slow and deliberate paths that seldom intersect. I don't recall ever observing it myself?"

"I searched the archives when I first noticed this," Belshazzar replied. "Their conjunction within the Swallow occurs only once every twenty years. That alone would be of interest. But there's more in this particular case."

Belshazzar shifted his attention to the other clay tablet and pointed out another passage. He waited as his companion muttered the words under his breath. A moment later, he heard Gondophares' rapid inhalation of surprise.

"Again?" he gasped. "A second meeting only three months later? That's extraordinary."

Belshazzar poked his finger at a third tablet. "Not just twice," he said in awe. "Three times."

"No!" Gondophares exclaimed. "That can't be true."

"It is," Belshazzar confirmed. "*Marduk* and *Ninib* will join together within *Ea* three times in just eleven cycles of the moon."

"That's astonishing," the younger man exclaimed. "It must presage something of incredible significance. Has such a thing ever happened before?"

Belshazzar stroked his beard thoughtfully. "That would be a worthy task for one of our young apprentices. I'll have Kidinnu search the archives."

"Have you confirmed the calculations?" A new voice interjected itself into their conversation, and both men turned to see their colleague, Artaban, approach. His erect posture, strong angular features, and straight prominent nose belied his noble Persian heritage, as did the white linen tunic, trimmed in blue silk, that he wore over his traditional Persian trousers. "If they *are* correct, I wonder why the scribes didn't note that fact when compiling the almanac."

"I questioned that myself," Belshazzar replied. "But, as you can see, since the conjunctions occur several months apart, they're documented in separate volumes. No doubt, these were recorded by different scribes in the school of Master Shuma. Each one must have thought the occurrence he logged was an isolated event."

Artaban came to a stop at the left side of the writing desk, opposite the other two men, and bent to inspect the tablets.

"Hmm," he muttered. "That could be the case. Still, I'd want to verify the accuracy of the forecasts. They could have misread the charts and confused *Marduk* or *Ninib* with *Ishtar* or *Nebo*. See here," Artaban pointed to a line on one of the journals. "This says the second alignment will occur far to the east of the first and the third. Though the Wanderers do sometimes reverse their paths, it seems unlikely that both *Marduk* and *Ninib* would follow each other so precisely."

Gondophares also leaned in and traced his finger over the passage, careful not to touch the precious tablets with his ungloved hands.

"That's definitely something we should investigate. With your concurrence, Belshazzar, I'll consult with Master Shuma after the morning ceremony."

"Of course. It would be wise to confirm the accuracy of such an extraordinary sign. Thank you, Artaban, for calling our attention to that possibility. I'm afraid I was so amazed at the implications of such an occurrence, I overlooked the prospect of its being in error."

"But," Gondophares interjected, "in the event the calculations are correct, we should most certainly consider the implications *of* such a rare and significant sign. What exactly could this portend?"

Belshazzar straightened and grasped his colleague's arm. "That, my friend, is precisely why I wanted you to see this. What might it signify when *Marduk*, the supreme god of the heavens, and *Ninib*, the star of the king, converge within *Ea*, the giver of wisdom, life, and creation?"

"Since *Ea* is the last constellation to enter the stage each year, I would expect it to indicate something about endings and a new beginning."

"Exactly," Belshazzar exclaimed. "I believe it portends the birth of a king—a new divinely appointed king."

Gondophares tilted his head to the side and gazed into the distance for a few moments, considering the idea. "That could be true," he finally concurred. "But this is *not* just an isolated conjunction. There will be three juxtapositions in a single year. That must foreshadow an unprecedented and glorious event."

"Indeed." Belshazzar stared into his friend's eyes for several heartbeats and then shifted his gaze to Artaban. "It will usher in a new world order." He spoke slowly and deliberately to emphasize his next words. "This will be no ordinary king."

As soon as he had uttered the words aloud, a tremor of profound personal responsibility washed over him. Belshazzar realized his interest in this event went far beyond scholarly excitement. This wasn't just academic curiosity. He felt like he had been carrying a burden his entire life and had finally glimpsed the possibility of laying it down.

"Where?" Artaban voiced the question that was on all of their minds. "Where will this king arise? Here? Is the Parthian Empire to receive a new heir? Will King Phraates have another son and send Phraataces to join his four brothers as a hostage in Rome so this new child king can take the throne without internal conflicts over the succession? Or," his voice took on an ominous tone, "will this new divinely appointed monarch come from the very loins of Caesar Augustus and become god-emperor of Rome?"

"Be careful what you say, Artaban," Belshazzar warned. "Such words could be construed as treason."

"I only speak of what occupies your own thoughts as well," Artaban grumbled. "If the stars point to a new world order, it's very important to know what kingdom will rule over it."

Gondophares muttered something under his breath, and then suddenly exclaimed it aloud, bringing their verbal sparring match to a momentary detente. "Judea!"

"What?" Belshazzar asked, perplexed at the outburst.

Gondophares rushed to his own compartment and sorted carelessly through stacks of clay tablets, finally selecting one and hurrying back to their sides. Belshazzar just stared at him the whole time as Gondophares' deep red cloak, fastened over his shoulder, fluttered behind him. Magi did not comport themselves in this way. Scholars did not run.

"Gondophares, gather yourself. You should treat the archive documents with more care. Here now, please don't handle them without gloves."

He reached for the fragile journal, but before he could grasp it, his companion laid it on the desk.

"Judea," Gondophares repeated. "The king will be born in Judea."

"How do you know?" Artaban interjected.

Gondophares pointed excitedly at the clay tablet. "*Nergal* will join the final conjunction. It will enter *Ea* at precisely that time."

"The star of war?" Artaban asked.

"The star of war, yes," Belshazzar intoned, "but also the star of the West. Our colleague here is correct. The new king will arise from Judea."

"Well, now. That complicates matters somewhat," Artaban remarked.

"It's better than Rome," Gondophares suggested.

"Perhaps. But Judea *is* a Roman province, after all."

"True," Gondophares replied. "But we all know the Romans really think of it as a buffer zone between our kingdom and their empire. When you cross the Euphrates, it's not exactly an abrupt transition from Parthia to Rome. That entire region is really a blend of East and West. And Judea plays a big part in that mix."

"Hmph," Artaban grunted. "Herod's a puppet of Rome. What did he do when our armies invaded Syria and captured Jerusalem?" Artaban answered his own question without waiting for a reply. "He ran straight to Augustus and convinced the Roman Senate to proclaim him 'King of the Jews.' Without the aid of Roman legions, he would never have reclaimed his throne. He's beholden to Rome."

"The way I see it," Belshazzar countered, "King Herod blows with the wind. His support of Marc Antony and Cleopatra in the Roman civil war evaporated pretty quickly after Octavian's victory at Actium. If the tides of power shift again, Herod's allegiances will, no doubt, change course along with them."

"How then could such a superficial monarch sire a king of kings who will usher in a new world order?" Artaban challenged.

"The ways of the Great God are beyond our understanding. But he writes his signs in the heavens to show us his plans." Belshazzar said.

"We have yet to determine whether the calculations are correct."

"You're right, Artaban," Gondophares conceded. "I'll confirm the accuracy of the records tomorrow with Master Shuma. If they're true, I believe we're duty-bound to bring the matter before King Phraates."

"And what if the conjunctions do not occur as predicted?" Artaban asked. "That could be just as potent a sign, but with a far different meaning."

"Might I suggest," Belshazzar intervened, "that we journey to Babylon to confer with our old mentor, Master Melchior. As we all know, he's an expert on the Jewish faith and the political situation in Judea. Perhaps he can provide additional insights that we have overlooked. If he concurs with our speculations, then we could approach the Great King at Ctesiphon with the matter before the Royal Court moves to Ecbatana for the summer. By then, the first conjunction will have occurred, and the signs will have been confirmed or negated. In either case, we can bring the appropriate message before the king."

"Assuming the first conjunction happens as forecast," Artaban countered, "there will still be two more alignments in the future. Either of them could fail and negate your proposition."

"Do you have an alternative plan to offer?" Gondophares asked. "The situation is far too consequential to disregard—and not just for kings and emperors. This could have a tremendous impact on the lives of everyday people. Our own families and friends could get swept away in the turmoil. We must do something."

After a long moment of silence, Artaban bowed and took a step backward.

"Very well," Belshazzar concluded. "We are agreed. We did not seek out this task, but our God has placed the burden on our shoulders. It is now ours to bear, for good or for ill. All glory to Ahura Mazda, our Great God."

"Praise be to him," they replied.

CHAPTER TWO

Spring, 7 BC
Bīt Mummu ("House of Knowledge"),
Babylon, Parthian Empire

A wave of apprehension swept over Artaban at the thought of seeing his *usted*, his mentor, once again. Though he had always respected Magus Melchior's deep wisdom, during his years as a student he would commonly come to different conclusions about how the ancient principles should be applied in their present context. He often wondered whether his *usted* interpreted his continual stream of questions as scholarly curiosity or as contempt.

The grand hall of the Bīt Mummu thronged with priests, scholars, and aristocrats as the afternoon purification ritual concluded. Acolytes in white robes extinguished the fire in the central circle. Its smoldering embers sent trails of smoke spiraling toward the vaulted roof, soaring to the height of twenty men, while the presiding priest led his entourage out through a passageway on the right side of the building.

Artaban gazed with nostalgic wonder as he once again took in the hall's grandeur. Statues of priests and scholars graced the alcoves. Bas-relief carvings adorned the multi-tiered supports to the roof. Murals depicting the great epochs of Babylonian, Persian, and Parthian history decorated the walls. And intricately colored mosaics of the heavenly constellations spread across the floor. His heart swelled with pride at being even a small part of the rich heritage of learning and wisdom that had created not only this structure but also the ages of accumulated knowledge that filled its walls.

Amid the dispersing crowd, the travelers eventually located their old mentor, Magus Melchior. Though his frame was thinner than Artaban had recalled, and his shoulders slightly stooped, his richly embroidered indigo robe, and the depth reflected in his dark brown eyes, gave him an air of dignity.

As the three companions approached their wizened *usted*, they raised their right hands to their hearts and inclined their heads in a gesture of respect and affection.

"Master Melchior," Belshazzar opened, "it has been many cycles since last I stood in your shadow. The years have been kind to you."

Melchior's hair was thinner and his well-trimmed beard much grayer than when Artaban had last seen him. Though Artaban was the youngest of the three companions, it had still been over ten years since he had studied under his old mentor's tutelage.

Melchior's gentle, rounded face broke into a wide grin, and he clasped Belshazzar's shoulders in his wrinkled hands.

"Ah, the Lord be praised. Wisdom and light be upon you, my sons." His eyes shifted to each of his former students in turn. "You return to me as men of great accomplishment, but always as my own. What brings you back to this ancient house of learning?"

Gondophares replied to the question as the old sage's attention shifted to him. "Belshazzar has discovered an ominous sign in the annual forecasts, Master. We seek your wisdom to determine whether our understanding is correct and your counsel on how we should proceed. The matter could be of great significance and urgency."

"Or, esteemed *Usted,*" Artaban countered, "our interpretation may be in error and the actions we contemplate might cause immense harm to our king and to all Parthia. We trust your discernment to help us know which is the case."

Melchior shifted his gaze to Artaban and smiled broadly. "Ah, Artaban, always my cautious skeptic. If memory serves, our opinions often differed in this regard during your years under my instruction. We seldom agreed on the proper course to follow, even when our understanding of the omens converged. And yet," he swept his gaze across the other two, "I'm honored that three of my most accomplished students would seek my counsel in this matter."

Melchior turned to a servant who stood a few paces behind. "Nadir, go tell Ramin to prepare a meal for my guests." Then, inclining his head to the trio, he said, "Please, enjoy the hospitality of my household. Afterwards, we shall return to my chamber here at the Bīt Mummu to discuss this sign in the stars."

The scent of clay dust, aged parchments, and flickering oil lamps filled the air in Melchior's *gizru.* After lavishing them with a midday meal of roasted lamb, saffron rice, lentil stew, herbed flatbread, cucumber yogurt, dried nuts, and date palm juice, their old *usted* led the trio through the labyrinth of halls within the Bīt Mummu complex to his personal chambers where they could converse in private.

Unlike the grand opulence of the great hall, the workspaces in the temple complex were more subdued and practical, even for a venerable scholar like Melchior. The *gizru's* thick, mud-brick walls were hung with simple tapestries for insulation—one depicting the zodiac wheel and the other embroidered with a menorah. A small window at the far end allowed a cool breeze to waft through the room and provided a limited view of the sky for quick observations during nighttime hours. The distinguished astronomers of the Bīt Mummu would, of course, conduct more comprehensive studies of the heavenly bodies in the many well-equipped observatories situated along the rooflines of the temple complex. But the little portal allowed the room's occupant to view a small, manageable portion of the celestial tapestry while never forgetting the enormity of all the heavens might reveal.

A flutter of wings in the corner caught Artaban's attention. He chuckled softly and raised a finger into the air. "Simur," he exclaimed as the starling landed on the temporary perch he offered, "you're still here."

"Yes, indeed," Melchior said. "Our little bird with big ideas has yet more knowledge to impart to the old scholars of this esteemed institution."

Melchior settled down on a reed mat and leaned back against some deep red cushions, variously embroidered with cypress trees, stylized lotus blossoms, and pomegranates. He gestured for his guests to join him.

"Now," he prompted, "tell me of the mystery in the stars that brought you to seek an old man's counsel."

Belshazzar pushed up from his reclined position and leaned forward toward their mentor. Artaban could tell that he struggled to maintain his scholarly composure and to control his excitement.

"The almanacs predict a conjunction of *Marduk* and *Ninub* within *Ea* in just a few days."

"Yes," Melchior responded. "It's a phenomenon I last observed twenty years ago—a somewhat rare occurrence and a subject of interest..." he paused before continuing, "but not of such importance that it would warrant an expedition of three distinguished scholars to the Bīt Mummu to consult with their onetime *usted*. I'm not—"

"But what if," Belshazzar interrupted, in an almost disrespectful display of enthusiasm and impatience, "there was not just one such conjunction, but three meetings of *Marduk* and *Ninub* in less than eleven months?"

The old sage straightened up a bit and raised an eyebrow. "Three times, you say? All within the *Ea*? And within a single year?"

"Indeed," Belshazzar confirmed, and looked expectantly at his mentor.

"Well, now, that *would be* truly remarkable."

"Brack. Truly remarkable," Simur parroted from his perch on Artaban's finger.

"You discovered this in the almanacs?" Melchior inquired.

"Yes, Master," Belshazzar confirmed, unrolling a star chart and pressing it flat on a low table beside them. "The three instances are documented in separate volumes, so the different scriveners must not have noticed the correlation. But I have consolidated the three convergences here on this diagram."

"Hmm," Melchior murmured. "I've often pondered the wisdom of compiling the almanacs chronologically rather than by subject matter. I fear we may miss many such threads that run through the currents of time. Fortunately, your diligent investigation has brought this important circumstance to light."

Belshazzar straightened, as if struck by a sudden realization. "My father..." he muttered almost breathlessly, his fingers absentmindedly touching a signet ring on a chain at his throat.

"What is it?" Melchior prompted.

"On his deathbed, my father told me about the alignment in

the stars that marked his own birth. He felt as if our Great God had chosen him for a grand purpose, but he would not live to see it fulfilled."

"I knew your father well," Melchior said, laying a hand on Belshazzar's shoulder. "He was a remarkable scholar with a noble heart. His death was a blow to us all. He would be proud of what his son has discovered this day."

Belshazzar's voice grew heavy with the memory. "He said his calling would pass to me... that I would be the one Ahura Mazda would use to serve His divine plan." He swallowed hard. "My whole life, I've wondered what that might mean," he said, gesturing to the astronomical chart. "Now I know."

Melchior patted his shoulder twice. "That may well be true." He paused for a moment and then tapped on Belshazzar's sketch of the stars. "Let's consider this revelation from our Wise Lord more fully. Have you confirmed the calculations?"

"Yes, Master, at Artaban's insistence," Gondophares replied. "The projections are valid."

Melchior stood, prompting the three former pupils to rise as well. He began pacing back and forth across the small study, muttering to himself. "Hmm... Ea... transitions... a new beginning?" He shook his head. "No... no, more than that... a new era... a new order..." Suddenly, he stopped pacing, straightened up, and raised a finger in the air. "A king. A king will arise," he proclaimed with confident assurance. "A great king!"

"Brack. A great king," Simur echoed.

"Yes, Master," Belshazzar affirmed. "That's exactly what we concluded. Your affirmation is a welcome relief."

The wizened philosopher seemed not to hear Belshazzar's words. Instead, he hunched over and resumed pacing, once again lost in thought. He murmured, almost under his breath, "But from where... from where?"

"Judea." Gondophares' voice cut through the momentary lull.

"The king will arise in Judea. It's why we came to consult with you."

Melchior halted and spun to face Gondophares. "Judea?" He gaped at his former student with an expression of shock. "Why Judea?"

Gondophares seemed somewhat taken aback by the intensity of his reaction. He hesitantly replied, "Master, please forgive my interruption. It's just... we are perhaps too enthusiastic about this discovery and all it might portend."

"Yes, yes." Melchior waved a hand for him to go on. "Why Judea?"

"During the third and final conjunction of *Marduk* and *Ninub*," Gondophares explained, "*Nergal* will also enter within *Ea*. Though it will not fully converge with the other two, its presence within such close proximity must surely be of consequence."

Melchior sighed, as if pieces of a puzzle were falling into place. "*Nergal*. Of course. It's all starting to make sense now. I knew we must be getting close. But this... this may well be the sign we've been seeking to tie it all together."

The three younger magi looked quizzically at one another but were reluctant to interrupt their mentor's internal deliberation. He went on pacing and muttering to himself for some time.

Finally, Simur broke the tense silence. "Brack. *Nergal*. A king from Judea. A king from Judea."

"Yes..." Melchior said, his voice taking on a tone of conviction. "Yes, it's all beginning to come together."

"What is it, Master?" Gondophares prompted. "Is there more to this situation than we've understood?"

"Perhaps," he replied. "Perhaps a great deal more." He motioned to a group of scrolls stacked on a nearby table. "Over the past several weeks, I've been reviewing some ancient Hebrew prophecies about the long-awaited Jewish messiah.

This omen in the stars might be related to those predictions. If so, it could provide missing pieces about the timing of their fulfillment. I think perhaps your visit here is quite propitious."

"What is this messiah, Master?" Artaban asked.

"Ah, yes," Melchior responded. "I often forget that most magi have not immersed themselves in the ancient Hebrew writings, as have I. Well, the Jewish messiah is much like the *Saoshyant* of our own faith."

"A deliverer, then, who will lead us in the final battle between truth and evil?" Gondophares asked.

"Just so," Melchior replied. "In Hebrew lore, their god raised up a man named Moses who performed great miracles to deliver the people of Israel out of bondage in Egypt and lead them to their promised land—the land they now possess in Judea. Their prophets told of another such deliverer, one like this Moses, who would once again rescue their people from a similar situation of bondage. Many of their scholars, and even many common people, hope for this promised messiah to come free them from Roman oppression and restore the glory of their former days under Kings David and Solomon."

"Could this Jewish messiah be the same as our *Saoshyant?*" Belshazzar asked?

"Be cautious, Belshazzar," Artaban interjected. "Such talk could be considered blasphemous."

Melchior placed a hand on Artaban's shoulder. "Not necessarily. The truths revealed to us by the great Ahura Mazda may have imperfect echoes within our sister cultures. The Hebrew scriptures may indeed contain distorted shadows of the spiritual realities of our faith."

"Do you mean the spirits of light have spoken to the Hebrew prophets?" Artaban contested. "What then are we to say of the Roman beliefs or the Buddhist faith—or any others who deny the One True God?"

Melchior replied to the challenge with the calm restraint of wisdom. "When the Father of Light reveals his will, it is like a stone thrown into a pond. The truest understanding is for those to whom it was revealed. But the impact ripples out across the surface with diminished strength. Those nearest the center will have the purest comprehension, and those farthest away, the most degraded. Yet we can discern a reflection of the original in them all."

"That may be so," Artaban countered, "but the greatest lie contains the most truth. Leaders of other faiths, like the corrupt Roman priests and emperors, use half-truths to effect great evil."

Melchior, with a hand still on Artaban's shoulder, squeezed it warmly. "Unfortunately so. What the Wise One reveals is his prerogative. What use men make of it is our responsibility. And he will one day hold us all to account."

"You speak wisely, Master," Belshazzar interposed. "Let us make the most of what our Great God has given us." He gestured toward the scrolls. "Tell us more of what the Hebrew scriptures reveal about our signs in the heavens."

Melchior gave a slow nod and looked toward the remaining scrolls on the table. "I have only a portion of the Hebrew writings here in my chamber. If we are to fully comprehend what the heavens are proclaiming, we must consult the sacred archives."

He crossed the chamber and struck a bronze chime that hung beside the doorway. Moments later, a young apprentice appeared. "Samid," Melchior directed, "return these scrolls to their boxes and take them to the Chamber of Foreign Wisdom. Place them in my alcove and then locate the two scrolls we consulted from the writings of Beltashazzar last week. Do you remember the ones written during the reign of Darius, the king of Media? One described the vision of the beasts and the other recorded the prophecy of the seventy sevens?"

The young man bowed slightly. "Yes, Master. I remember

them. I shall retrieve them for you." He moved to the table and began gently rolling the delicate parchment documents in reddish-brown leather sheaths and placing them in cedar boxes, engraved with their appropriate labels.

"Come. The texts we need are kept in a special repository beneath the main library. They're stored separately from our own astronomical tablets and require particular care, because the parchment is more delicate than clay. I believe you'll find the words of these ancient Hebrews most enlightening. If the stars are truly declaring the birth of the Jewish messiah, then the voices of their prophets may yet speak to us across the ages."

Artaban felt as if they had descended into the very bowels of the earth. He remembered going into the special collection archives only a few times during his apprenticeship under Melchior. The musty smell of parchment scrolls, even sealed in their protective cedar cases, was quite different from the dusty odor of the cuneiform clay tablets he used to record and study astronomical data. Melchior's fascination with Hebrew culture had brought Artaban to these catacombs occasionally, but never often enough for him to navigate the dark and twisting passages with confidence. He was much more at home in the rooftop observatories, gazing into the night sky.

Melchior had claimed a study cubicle for himself off the main floor of the archives, where hundreds of scrolls lined the shelves, all carefully cataloged by subject matter, culture, and era.

"Ah," Melchior said as the light from his oil lamp illuminated the interior of the room. "I see Samid has brought the scrolls from my study. We can begin with these, but the other documents I asked him to retrieve are most relevant to the issue at hand. I expect him to arrive with them shortly."

"Master," Artaban began. "This place is a bit dank and dreary."

"Brack. Dank and dreary," Simur squawked from his perch on Melchior's shoulder.

Artaban continued, ignoring the bird's interruption. "Do you ever wonder if the Father of Light is absent from these catacombs—that the Dark One actually rules here, over the false writings of false prophets inspired by false gods?"

As soon as the statement was out of his mouth, Artaban regretted his impertinence. But he was so overcome by the foreboding sense of this place that he had momentarily forgotten his normal scholarly restraint.

Yet Melchior seemed to take no offense. "Not at all. The Creator is present in all parts of his creation. Without light, there can be no shadows. Sometimes, when we seek to discover the realities that are hidden from our view, we can discern their outline in the images of darkness they cast around us. There is much we can learn from the ancient writings in these archives."

Their wise mentor donned a pair of gloves and gently lifted a scroll from its case. He held it up before his former students.

"This is from the writings of a Persian nobleman named Belteshazzar, who rose to prominence under the Babylonian king, Nebuchadnezzar, almost six centuries ago. Even though Babylon eventually fell to the Medes and the Persians, Belteshazzar continued to hold senior positions in the governments of Darius the Mede and Cyrus the Great of Persia."

"Master Melchior," Belshazzar asked with a quizzical expression, "I thought this archive was for the scrolls of foreign prophets. Why would Persian government documents be included within this collection?"

Melchior smiled. "You see, this particular nobleman was

once a Hebrew slave, taken captive by King Nebuchadnezzar during the siege of Jerusalem in the first year of his reign."

"A Hebrew slave?" Artaban exclaimed.

"Yes. A slave. But also a Judean aristocrat," Melchior replied. "The Babylonian king planned to educate a cadre of young Jewish noblemen in the Chaldean ways and then send them back to govern Jerusalem as his representatives."

"That seems like a wise practice for a conquering king," Belshazzar observed. "But how did this slave's writings end up in the Bīt Mummu's Chamber of Foreign Wisdom?"

"It turns out this Judean slave happened to be a prophet of the Jewish god. As part of the enculturation process, the Babylonians gave him the name Belteshazzar, but his Hebrew name was Daniel, which means 'god is my judge' in their language. This Daniel was an interpreter of dreams that no one else could explain. He himself also received many visions from his god that foretold the future with uncanny accuracy. His wisdom elevated him to positions of great authority, first in the Babylonian court, and then in those of the Medes and Persians."

"An interesting tale," Artaban intoned, impatient to move matters along. "But what does this have to do with the upcoming conjunctions of *Marduk* and *Ninib*?"

Melchior removed the parchment scroll from its box, unwrapped the leather sleeve, and ran his finger across its length, apparently searching for a specific section. As he scanned the document, he explained its context.

"Daniel penned ten different scrolls. The first one tells the story of how he was taken captive and entered into training for service to the king. Most of the rest discuss various visions that Daniel either interpreted for others or that his god revealed to him. These revelations had a consistent and intriguing theme. They outlined an interesting future for the world—a prophecy that has since played itself out with remarkable accuracy."

"In what way?" Gondophares asked.

"Well, take for example the account documented in this scroll. King Nebuchadnezzar had a dream that greatly disturbed him. He called his diviners together to tell him what the dream meant, but they could make no interpretation for him."

"Hmph," Artaban grunted. "My experience with court mystics is that they'll always provide some explanation, regardless of whether they received it from a god or conjured it from their own imaginations."

Melchior glanced up at him with a grin. "The king shared your skepticism. So he required the seers to first recount the vision itself before expounding on its meaning."

Artaban chuckled, "A wise king after all. I expect that baffled them."

"Yes," Melchior confirmed. "It stymied all of them except Daniel. He sought an audience with the king, claiming that his god had shown him not only the dream, but its interpretation."

"And..." Belshazzar prompted.

"Daniel said the king had dreamt of a great idol with a head of gold, belly and arms of silver, torso of bronze, legs of iron, and feet of iron mixed with clay. The king confirmed the accuracy of what Daniel described and asked to hear the explanation. This is the fascinating part," Melchior observed. "Daniel said the head of gold represented King Nebuchadnezzar and his kingdom. But then he predicted that Babylon would eventually be supplanted by another kingdom, inferior in quality but superior in strength."

"The empire of the Medes and the Persians!" Belshazzar exclaimed.

"Precisely," Melchior confirmed. "But that was not the end of the vision. Daniel declared there would be two more such transitions—"

"A bronze kingdom," Belshazzar broke in again. "It had to symbolize the empire of Alexander—the kingdom of the Greeks."

"Followed," Artaban said with an edge of disdain in his voice, "by the iron empire of Rome."

Melchior nodded. "Correct."

Artaban reflected on that for a moment, and the significance of the prophecy slowly solidified in his mind.

"That's... remarkable," Artaban breathed. "You say all this happened during the reign of Nebuchadnezzar? Rome was nothing more than a collection of villages dominated by the Etruscans at that time. No one could have predicted the eventual rise of the Roman Empire in those days."

Melchior lifted his gaze from the scroll and straightened. "So you see, my cautious skeptic, how ripples of truth might emanate even from the shadows?"

Artaban bristled. Yes, Melchior was venerable and wise. And yes, the old scholar had once been his *usted*. But that did not justify such condescension. And yet, he could not allow his aggravation to show in front of his peers.

"I do see, Master Melchior. I can't deny the remarkable accuracy of Daniel's prophecy if, in fact, this account is genuine and reliable."

Melchior remained nonplussed. "A worthy question indeed. My own studies of Daniel's writings, as corroborated by other historical records of the Babylonians and Persians, have convinced me of their authenticity. But I'll allow you to settle the matter in your own mind."

He bent back over the parchment and continued searching through the document, tracing his finger over the faded words on the yellowing material, across stitches where separate pages had been sewn together. Finally, he pointed to a particular passage.

"Ah, here it is," he said, reading the words aloud. "'In the days of those kings, the God of heaven will set up a kingdom which will never be destroyed. It will crush and put an end to all these kingdoms, but it will itself endure forever. Just as you saw that a stone was broken off from the mountain without hands, and that it crushed the iron, the bronze, the clay, the silver, and the gold, the great God has made known to the king what will take place in the future. So the dream is certain, and its interpretation is trustworthy.'"

Though the phrasing was somewhat arcane, Artaban was well-versed in the Aramaic language and clearly understood the words Melchior quoted.

Belshazzar was the first of the three to link this prophecy to their own situation. He spoke up. "A kingdom that will crush all other earthly kingdoms... Such a ruler would be no ordinary king." He took a deep breath. "Might this oracle, in fact, predict the coming of our *Saoshyant?*"

Melchior raised an eyebrow, and there was a gleam in his eye. "Ripples in a pond. Glimmers of truth among the shadows." He nodded slowly, knowingly. "The Hebrews believe this pagan king's dream describes the coming of their messiah."

"And the triple conjunction..." Gondophares jumped in. "If it foretells the rise of a divinely appointed king, then Daniel's prophecy might now be approaching its fulfillment. The iron kingdom of Rome was the last of the four great empires in the vision, correct?"

"Wait!" Artaban exclaimed. "I feel as if we're rushing ahead into a dark chasm without a lamp to light the way. This all sounds very enticing. But should we base such a significant assumption on a single, ancient story from a foreign slave who knew nothing of Ahura Mazda, the One True God? If this prophecy is accurate, what would it mean for Parthia and our own King Phraates?"

"Artaban is correct," Melchior glanced toward the others. "With issues as consequential as these, it is important to confirm our assertions with multiple sources." He shot an impatient look at the door. "I had expected Samid to bring us some additional documentation by now. I wonder what's keeping him."

As if on cue, the door opened and the young apprentice appeared, breathing heavily. He wore an agitated expression, and blurted out between gasps, "They're gone, Master. The scrolls... they're missing."

"Are you certain? The scrolls from Beltashazzar's writings during the Babylonian and Persian periods?"

"Yes, Master," Samid confirmed. "The ones you were studying last week. I returned them to the archive when you finished with them, but now they're gone. In fact, the entire collection is missing."

"The whole collection?" Melchior asked with a surprised voice.

Samid shrugged. "Even so, Master. I rechecked the archive index to ensure I was looking in the right location. The entire set of Beltashazzar's parchments is missing. Perhaps another researcher is consulting them."

"No." Melchior shook his head slowly. "I know every scholar with a special interest in the Hebrew prophets. I can't think of anyone who would have drawn this collection of writings from the shelves. There were multiple copies of some scrolls. Are those gone as well?"

"Yes, Master. The whole collection is missing."

"Brack. Very odd. Very odd," Simur squawked.

"Yes," Melchior opined. "Very odd indeed."

Belshazzar interrupted. "What was in those documents, Master Melchior? Was there more material about this vision of a mighty kingdom that will crush all others?"

Melchior sighed. "Indeed. Much more. I did take a few personal notes. They're back in my chamber. But a careful study would require access to the original texts."

"Well, the most important question for our purposes," Artaban interjected, "is when this heavenly kingdom will appear. The description in this scroll does not stipulate how long the Roman Empire will remain before it's crushed by the stone. Rome is still quite young on the scale of history, depending on when you identify its origins. It could last for another thousand years before this new king arises."

"Quite true," Melchior said in resignation. "There was more specific information in the seventh, eighth, and tenth scrolls, which are now all missing. But if I recall correctly, the visions recorded in those documents repeat the same sequence of empires but with different symbols and with substantially greater detail. Alas, my memory is not sufficient to the task. Without the parchments, I'm at a loss. But perhaps—"

He cut his words short and cocked his head in thoughtful reflection.

"What is it, Master?" Belshazzar finally prompted.

The three waited in tense anticipation until Melchior finally replied. "The ninth scroll!" he exclaimed with renewed exuberance. "I had almost forgotten about it. It's quite different from the rest."

"How so?" Belshazzar asked.

"The ninth book doesn't repeat the sequence of kingdoms like the others do. Instead, it describes a visit to Daniel by a heavenly messenger named Gabriel."

"Are you saying that a *yazata* was sent to this Hebrew slave?" asked Artaban in disbelief.

"The ancient Hebrews referred to them as *malakim*, and the Jews of our day more commonly use the Greek term 'angels.' But yes, such messengers are generally comparable with the *yazatas* of our faith."

"So," Belshazzar steered the discussion back on track, "what was this angel's message? Did it have something to do with the final empire of the other visions?"

"In a way," Melchior replied. "As I mentioned before, King Nebuchadnezzar had besieged Jerusalem and taken the Jews into captivity in Babylon. But this angel's visitation occurred after Babylon had fallen to the Medes and the Persians."

Melchior began pacing back and forth in the little room as he searched his mind for the details of the ninth scroll.

"Daniel had been studying the writings of an earlier Hebrew prophet named Jeremiah, who predicted that the Jews would be released from captivity after seventy years. In Daniel's calculations, that time was almost at hand. He prayed to his god for a sign that their promised deliverance was nigh. The angel Gabriel came with a response to this prayer—an answer that told of the coming messiah."

"But the kingdom of the Medes and the Persians was only the second in the sequence from the other visions, correct?" Belshazzar asked. "I thought their messiah would come to establish the fifth and final kingdom."

"Gabriel's answer addressed both their deliverance from captivity and the eventual coming of the messiah. It was as if Daniel's god was telling him, 'The deliverance of your people from captivity in Babylon is coming soon, yet an even greater deliverance will come through the messiah at the end of the age.' But here's the interesting point for us now," Melchior said. "The message contained very specific timeframes for both of the events."

"It gave actual dates?" Gondophares asked with unveiled excitement. "And you remember the details of this scroll? You remember those time predictions?"

"I studied that passage extensively," Melchior said. Then his voice took on a peculiar tone he used when quoting sacred texts. "'From the command to restore Jerusalem until messiah the prince, there shall be sixty-nine sabbatical years.' So that means—"

"Wait," Gondophares cut him off. "I know the Jews observe a weekly Sabbath, but what is a sabbatical year?"

Melchior smiled. "There are, in truth, two Sabbath cycles.

The first is the weekly Sabbath that you are no doubt familiar with. The second is an annual Sabbath. The Hebrew god commanded them to allow their fields to lie fallow every seven years. In the seventh year, they were to refrain from planting crops and to live off whatever grew on its own. It was a test of their faith in god to provide for their most basic needs."

"So Daniel's prophecy referred to this cycle of seven years, not to the weekly Sabbath?" Gondophares asked.

"Even so," Melchior confirmed. "And by my calculations, that timeframe of sixty-nine sabbatical years points to our present age."

Artaban shifted uncomfortably. "You're certain of that?"

"The angel's prediction was very specific," Melchior confirmed. "He identified the period as four hundred and sixty-three years beginning from the Persian decree to rebuild Jerusalem." The old sage's eyes gleamed with conviction. "Which brings us to now."

"But wait," Gondophares interrupted. "If I remember that period of Persian history correctly, there were actually several decrees—"

"Brack. Too many details," Simur interrupted, ruffling his feathers impatiently.

Melchior grinned up at the little bird. "Our feathered friend is correct. I could expound on the intricacies of these prophecies for hours. But the precise chronology matters less than the fact that multiple sources—our star charts and Hebrew prophecy—seem to correlate with one another. Though we can't know the exact date with certainty, I think we can be confident that the time is near."

"And that means—" Gondophares began.

"That means the triple conjunction of *Marduk* and *Ninib* could very well point to the fulfillment of this prophecy and the coming of the Jewish messiah," Belshazzar exclaimed.

"*Could!*" Artaban hastened to interject. "It *could* imply that.

However, it might mean something altogether different. This is a very speculative determination. We need to be cautious about reading too much meaning into events that may or may not have any true association with each other."

"Artaban, why must you quench every flame?" Belshazzar shot back. "Every time we uncover a kernel of truth, you're determined to crush it under the weight of skepticism and doubt before it even has a chance to sprout and grow."

"I'm just being—"

Melchior halted the budding quarrel with a raised hand. "Caution is prudent in such situations. These are weighty matters of great consequence. Artaban is right about the dangers of rushing ahead without due diligence."

Belshazzar shrank back from the chastening.

"However," Melchior continued, "the timing of the circumstances and the will of the great Ahura Mazda in bringing this matter to our attention demand some urgency." He looked back at Belshazzar and extended a hand of invitation. "If our supposition is correct, and we have been given a sign in the heavens that confirms this ancient Hebrew prophecy, then we should take a moment to consider the implications for our own kingdom. What do you suggest we should do with the knowledge we have received?"

Belshazzar stepped forward, gesturing with outstretched hands to emphasize the importance of each point. "This will be no ordinary king. It will be critical for Parthia and our Great King to initiate positive relations with this new monarch as soon as possible. We need to establish ourselves as friends and allies early in his rise to power. And to that end, we must bring this issue before King Phraates and his council immediately, so he can send a diplomatic envoy to Judea to honor the birth of the new king."

"Those are bold measures," Melchior began.

"Extreme measures, I would say," Artaban cut in.

"Master Melchior," Belshazzar pressed on, leaning forward with desperate intensity, "the more I think about it, the more I'm convinced this conjunction isn't just something I discovered by chance. My father always said the Lord of Light doesn't waste the gifts He gives." Belshazzar's voice cracked slightly. "My father was marked by the stars at his birth but died before fulfilling his purpose. And now, I'm determined to follow through on his calling."

Artaban felt a chill. The weight of a father's legacy was a burden he knew all too well. But where he bore an inheritance of failure and shame, Belshazzar carried the pressure of an unrealized sacred calling.

"The will of the Wise Lord always prevails," Melchior acknowledged and then moved on. "Gondophares, what is your appraisal of the situation?"

"I concur with Belshazzar's assessment. In my opinion, the actions he recommends are not rash. The triple conjunction is well documented in the almanacs, and we have confirmed the accuracy of the calculations with Master Shuma. We have observed the approach of the first conjunction, and its culmination in just a few days will validate the astronomical signs. The additional information you have provided on the prophecies in Hebrew scripture, imperfect reflections of truth though they may be, adds credible support from a completely unconnected source. When multiple independent signs point to the same conclusion, it adds great legitimacy to the premise. Therefore, I have much confidence in our thesis and suggest that we act without delay."

"So you—" Melchior began, but Gondophares cut in.

"Forgive me, Master, but there's something else I feel I must say. We..." he paused to gather his thoughts. "We keep talking about our duty to inform the king and the Court."

"It is our responsibility, is it not?" Melchior raised an eyebrow and tilted his head.

"Of course," Gondophares replied. "But we, and indeed the king himself, also have a duty to the people."

"In what respect?" Belshazzar asked.

"About twenty years ago, my uncle saw omens in the stars about a drought that would devastate the region around our home in Sakastan. He confirmed these revelations with other observations of magi who studied patterns in the weather. The elders didn't want to panic the people unnecessarily, so they waited for the signs to be confirmed."

"I'd consider that a prudent course of action," Artaban observed. "What happened? Were the magi correct?"

"They were right about the events," Gondophares replied, "but wrong by several months in the timing." He shook his head. "When the rains continued, contrary to the predictions of their advisors, the elders chose not to alert the people or to prepare for a coming famine. Instead, they actually sold their surplus grain to Bactrian merchants. But the drought eventually did come…" His voice trailed off.

"I remember that time," Melchior said. "The entire region was affected for three years or more, if memory serves. The resulting famine was terrible. Many people starved to death, from what I understand."

"They weren't just people," Gondophares lamented. "They were my people. My friends and relatives." He straightened his shoulders, and his voice grew heavy with conviction. "Do you see why we must not ignore signs in the heavens… why we cannot fail to act when our God warns us of a coming crisis?"

An awkward silence hung over the group for a long moment. Artaban empathized with his friend's remorse, and yet he also had to contend with the ghosts from his own past and his father's failed interpretations of omens in the stars. He struggled with how to chart a course between the two paths of peril.

Finally, Melchior shifted his gaze to Artaban. "You have

already expressed some of your doubts, Artaban. Perhaps you can take the opposing view and articulate the risks we take if the analysis is incorrect. Then please identify what actions you would propose."

Artaban appreciated the opportunity to voice his concerns, but felt as if the stars themselves were aligned against him. He took a deep breath and then proceeded to make his case. "I agree that the triple conjunction is accurately predicted in the almanacs and that the calculations are valid. Yet I'm not fully convinced about our interpretation of its meaning and significance. I'm also concerned that if the conjunction fails to occur as expected, it might convey a completely different message. Recommending that our Great King send a diplomatic envoy to Judea poses enormous risks. Such an action could be interpreted as a provocation and shatter the tenuous peace between Parthia and Rome, ushering in a new age of war and strife. Our recent history shows that we would likely end up on the losing side of any such conflict. It could spell an end to the freedom of Parthia and make us all vassals of the Roman Empire."

Belshazzar jumped in unbidden. "If Daniel's prophecies have any ring of truth, then Rome's fate is already sealed in the courts of heaven. It seems more prudent to risk being subservient to Rome than creating an adversarial relationship with a divinely appointed kingdom that will ultimately dominate the whole world."

Melchior raised a hand again to quell the dispute. "Let's allow our companion to finish making his case. Artaban, what course do you recommend? Would you advocate for inaction— that we do nothing with this information we have uncovered? Or do you believe we should take the matter to King Phraates?"

"We must proceed with caution," Artaban replied. "We should confirm the first conjunction before taking any action at all. A reversal of the Wanderers would imply a much different situation. I do agree we need to approach our Great

King with this information, but I strongly oppose recommending a diplomatic mission to Judea. The risk of inciting Rome is too great, and we certainly don't want to experience the wrath of the Empire's legions. If a new king does, in fact, arise in Judea, there will be plenty of time to choose sides as events unfold."

"Well then," Melchior asserted, "I believe we have achieved concurrence." Their old *usted* looked at each of them in turn.

The three former students glanced variously at him and at each other in confusion.

Melchior continued. "We all agree we should observe and confirm the first conjunction, correct?"

They all nodded in assent.

"And we all agree we have a responsibility to inform King Phraates and his council about this sign in the heavens."

Again, they nodded in affirmation. But then Belshazzar spoke up.

"Surely, the Great King will ask for our assessment and recommendation. How shall we reply?"

"Of course he will ask," Melchior concurred. "And we shall present the two assessments we have articulated today—the option to send a diplomatic mission to Judea, as well as the risks of angering the Romans. It is the duty of magi to advise. It is the prerogative of kings to decide."

"Brack," Simur squeaked. "Inform the king. Inform the king."

"So we are in agreement?" Melchior concluded. It was more of a statement than a question.

The three bowed slightly in deference to the decision of their master.

"If that is our course," Gondophares hastened to add, "then we must act soon. The spring thaw of winter snow has swelled the rivers and delayed the move of the Court to the summer palace at Ecbatana. But I hear King Phraates is eager to escape the growing summer heat and has commanded his officials to prepare for departure. If we are to address the Court at Ctesiphon, it must be soon."

"Hmm," Melchior muttered thoughtfully. "I had not considered that point. You are quite correct, and time is of the essence. We must seek an audience as soon as possible after the first conjunction."

Artaban felt as if they were imprudently rushing matters as it was, and oppressive memories from his childhood weighed heavily on his mind. Images of Roman soldiers tearing through his family's home searching for prophetic documents flashed through his thoughts, and he shuddered. What terrified him most was not the legionary's burning eyes glaring from beneath his bronze helmet, nor the glimmer of light on his steel *gladius*, but the impassive disdain in the priest's expression as he stood in his pristine white toga, trimmed in gold.

Artaban trembled at the vivid memory and raised his voice. "It can take weeks to arrange an appearance at court. Surely the Great King will be far too occupied with preparations for the move to receive a delegation of scholars with such a speculative concern. Perhaps we should wait until we have done more research and have more conclusive evidence. We could petition the King at Ecbatana in less haste."

"No," Belshazzar shot back. "This issue is of far too much consequence to delay. Master Melchior, you know people at the court who could intercede for us, do you not?"

Melchior took a deep breath and looked thoughtful. Finally, he nodded. "I know someone who could help, if he will."

He reached out a hand to clasp Artaban's shoulder. Artaban felt the depth of his probing gaze, as if his old mentor was searching deep within his soul. "Artaban, my son, I hear your concern. I, too, wish we had time to conduct more extensive research. But our Great God has revealed this omen to us at this moment for a reason. It would be imprudent not to act on the insights with which we have been blessed. Have faith." Artaban felt a gentle squeeze. "The Divine Will shall direct all paths to his desired end."

Melchior turned to address his young apprentice, who had been standing in the doorway as the drama unfolded.

"Samid, I have some additional research to do but no time to complete it here. I need you to gather some specific scrolls for me to take on our journey."

Samid looked at him with a shocked expression and started to speak, "But—"

Melchior cut him off. "I know. It is not... shall we say, customary, for scrolls to leave the Bīt Mummu library. But extraordinary times demand extraordinary measures."

Artaban heard Simur's squawk echo down the deep dankness of the archive halls. "Brack. Extraordinary times."

CHAPTER THREE

Early Summer, 7 BC
Ctesiphon, Parthian Empire
Location of the Royal Winter Palace

"Vahman, my friend, we appreciate your assistance with this situation," Melchior said. "I know it is no small thing to arrange an audience with the Great King under such circumstances. We also thank you," he added, "for your hospitality in providing accommodations on such short notice."

Vahman lifted a hand in reassurance. "It's my duty to my Lord the King to bring such matters to his attention. I only wish it were a less weighty burden to lay upon the royal throne." He took a deep breath and shook his head slightly, the sharp, angular features of his face revealing signs of the strain of his office. "A Jewish messiah… a king of kings… This is not an idea many rulers would want to consider, in Parthia or in Rome. I'm only thankful that it came to my attention through an old and trusted friend."

"Are we well received?" Melchior inquired.

"The Chamberlain was naturally reluctant to add something more to the Court's busy agenda. But I was able to convince him of the potential importance in this case. His Eminence takes omens from the heavens quite seriously. Not all monarchs are so wise or so pious."

"And the Great Houses...?" Melchior prompted.

Vahman stretched his mouth in a wan, thin smile. "This is the Royal Court after all, and palace intrigue is a matter of course, I'm afraid. It's rarely possible to know the motivations that may stir within the Great Houses. Be wary of allowing anyone to bait you into an unwise position. I will make the introduction." He glanced at the other three magi. "There should be no reason for anyone except Magus Melchior to speak."

"My Lord," an assistant entered the room and bowed, "we have received the summons. The Court awaits your arrival."

Vahman appraised the four petitioners briefly, nodded his approval, then turned to lead the way.

As the junior-most member of the delegation, Artaban took the last place in line. It gave him a good vantage point from which to observe their procession.

Vahman led off, garbed in the formal regalia of his office—a richly dyed, deep blue robe, trimmed at the hem with gold-embroidered stars and belted at the waist with a sacred cord fashioned from seventy-two silk threads. He was crowned with the traditional conical felt hat of the magi class, though some-what taller than most to emphasize his status as a royal advisor. He carried his staff of office in his right hand—a long cypress shaft banded with silver and topped with a stylized golden sun set with lapis lazuli at its center. Artaban also recalled seeing the amulet Vahman wore on a chain, which identified his position as the Royal Astronomer. It was engraved with the royal insignia of King Phraates IV, featuring a partially encased bow, a star, a crescent, and an eagle.

Master Melchior was next in line. His deep indigo mantle, crossed by a yellow sash embroidered with a scroll and tablet, identified him as an elder of the Bīt Mummu. Belshazzar, Gondophares, and Artaban were clad in similar robes, but without the rank insignia and with less elaborate trim. Each one favored a different color for his outer garment—deep crimson, forest green, and earthy brown, respectively. For appearance at the Royal Court, they all donned the conical felt caps of the magi, though in less formal circumstances, Gondophares preferred a turban, while Artaban frequently let his hair hang free.

Their entourage garnered little attention as they processed through the streets. Under normal circumstances, perhaps more of the city's residents would have paused to observe a group of distinguished magi parading toward the palace with a contingent of guards. But Ctesiphon was a city in transition.

Everywhere he looked, Artaban saw a buzz of activity in preparation for the Great King's move to the summer palace in Ecbatana. The markets thrummed with unusual energy as merchants sought to unload their perishable fruits and vegetables before the Royal Court departed, along with its host of attendants, advisors, and retainers. Craftsmen rushed to finish work on royal commissions. Work crews loaded long wagon trains with large wooden crates. Stable hands groomed teams of camels and mules. Lines of grumpy-looking tradesmen formed at the tax collectors' booths to settle their accounts. Messengers and couriers scurried in and among the crowds. Cavalry troops exercised their horses on the parade ground. And a squadron of advanced guards filed out of the city gate to secure the route. Artaban again marveled that Melchior had been able to coordinate this last-minute audience with the Court.

As their group approached the palace complex, Artaban craned his neck to view the immense brick walls rising to the height of seven men. The city's massive walls, with their heavily guarded gates and imposing watchtowers, seemed defense enough. But the palace added yet another layer of protection—a fortress within a fortress, built on the city's highest point.

Artaban approached this place with trepidation. His father had once served as a junior court advisor under the Royal Astronomer, but that was when Artaban was very young. He himself had never appeared before any senior royal official, let alone the Great King. With a salute to Vahman, the guards parted to let their group pass. They proceeded in silence, as dictated by protocol and their purpose. They were here as advisors to the Great King, not as visiting guests.

Artaban noticed the blending of cultural influences throughout the palace grounds. Ancient Babylonian and Persian elements mingled with Hellenistic design and Parthian additions. Their group advanced down a wide pathway lined with palm trees alongside Persian-style *paradisos* gardens. The gardens featured exotic flowers, plants, and shrubs arranged in geometric patterns, interlaced with water channels and pools fed by the nearby Tigris River. The melodic tones of lutes and lyres mingled with the laughter and light banter of women gathered somewhere out of sight under a pergola or shade tree, their casual leisure standing in stark contrast with the hectic activity outside the palace complex walls.

As Vahman led the group up the stone steps, Artaban sensed a blend of imperial power and ancient sacredness. The broad ochre facade projected authority, its entrance dominated by double cypress doors studded with bronze and bound with iron. Sacred flames burned in bronze braziers flanking the doorway, while glazed brick mosaics of celestial motifs adorned the perimeter. The guards, brandishing sturdy spears, snapped to attention as Vahman passed them by.

Cool air greeted them as they entered the vestibule, a relief from the outdoor heat. The rich fragrance of incense mixed with floral scents, wafting in from the gardens through latticed windows. Sunlight and shadow danced across the mosaic floors as they proceeded down a long arched hallway, where the Chamberlain met them before the entrance to the throne room.

"Venerable Magi," the Chamberlain greeted them. "When we enter the Great King's royal presence, I shall announce the Royal Astronomer. Follow the lead of Magus Vahman as you approach the throne. You shall all prostrate yourselves at each position marked with an eight-pointed star on the floor. At the invitation of the Great King, Magi Vahman and Melchior may rise to stand. The rest shall remain in a kneeling posture throughout the proceedings. When you are dismissed, you will rise, bow, and back toward the doorway."

The visiting magi nodded their understanding, and the Chamberlain signaled for the guards to open the doors.

Artaban realized he was holding his breath as he got his first glimpse of a sight that very few people ever observed. And he was not disappointed. The vaulted ceiling soared over the throne dais, drawing his eye upward and his thoughts to the divine power behind the throne. The curved ceiling, painted a deep lapis blue and flecked with golden constellations, shimmered faintly in the flickering light. The stars of *Ea* gleamed just above the dais, joined by those of the Lion and the bright figure of *Marduk*. A shaft of sunlight angled down through a small window near the apex, catching wisps of incense smoke and casting an ethereal glow on the raised throne platform.

The throne itself, carved from a solid block of black granite, sat atop seven steps representing the seven emanations of Ahura Mazda and the divine right by which the Great King ruled. Lion paws formed the armrests, while the high back bore an engraving of the symbol of divine glory—a winged disk with a bearded man at its center. Below it were inscribed the foundational Parthian virtues of good thoughts, good words, and good deeds. Flames rose from bronze braziers on either side, sending the scent of myrrh and sacred cedar curling into the still air, while the eternal flame danced on a golden altar supported by four winged lions.

Behind the throne, carved into the wall itself, seven golden medallions bore the symbols of the Amesha Spentas—fire, water, earth, plants, cattle, metals, and good thoughts.

Artaban's eyes shifted to the guards lining the walls. They stood silent and unmoving in polished scale armor, with red cloaks draped over one shoulder, brandishing silver-tipped spears.

As Artaban continued to take in the overwhelming grandeur of the throne room, the Chamberlain's ceremonial staff struck the granite three times, the sound echoing through the vast space like distant thunder.

"By the grace of Ahura Mazda and the will of His Majesty Shahanshah Phraates, King of Kings, Chosen of the Wise Lord, Protector of Parthia and Sovereign of the East. His Royal Astronomer Vahman, Keeper of the Celestial Mysteries, Servant of the Sacred Flame, presents before the Golden Throne learned magi from the ancient seats of wisdom. He hereby commends Magus Melchior of Babylon, Elder of the Eastern School, Keeper of Ancient Counsel; Magus Belshazzar of Nippur, Scholar of the Heavenly Wanderers and Master of the Tablets; Magus Gondophares of Sakastan, Keeper of the Ancient Calculations and Recorder of Stellar Movements; and Magus Artaban of Ctesiphon, Watcher of the Western Skies, Disciple of the Way of Wisdom. They come bearing urgent tidings written in the stars themselves. May the Wise Lord judge the truth of all words spoken."

The king raised a hand, summoning them forward.

The magi began their measured approach down the processional aisle. Two hundred paces of polished black granite stretched before them, drawing the eye inexorably toward the distant throne platform. The pathway was inlaid with golden constellations, and Artaban recognized the familiar patterns— the Fish-tailed Goat gleaming beneath his sandals, the Twins holding hands in eternal embrace, the Archer-Centaur with his bow drawn toward the heavens.

Stories of conquest and glory surrounded them on every side. To his left, a blood-red tapestry, stitched with gold thread, depicted the victory at Carrhae in meticulous detail. It showed Parthian cavalry raining arrows down on fleeing Roman legionaries and captured eagles being presented to Parthian nobles. The artistry was magnificent, and the message was unmistakable. The kings who sit on this throne have humbled Rome itself.

A massive silk tapestry on the opposite wall reiterated this sentiment. It depicted the recapture of Mesopotamia in three vivid scenes. The first showed Parthian siege engines breaching the walls of Babylon while Roman eagles were lowered in defeat. In the second frame, magi rekindled sacred fires in temples that had been defiled during the Roman occupation. The third portrayed a Roman legate in a white toga surrendering the keys of his fortress to a seated Parthian noble, while grateful civilians brought offerings of bread and wine.

At the first prescribed stopping point, Vahman halted, and the magi prostrated themselves as protocol demanded. Artaban's forehead touched the cool granite, and for a moment he stared at the golden constellation beneath his face—*Ea*, the very sign that had brought them here. The irony was not lost on him. After the appropriate amount of time, Vahman rose, and they all followed his lead.

At this distance, Artaban could see Great King Phraates

more closely as he sat motionless upon his celestial throne. His presence was both commanding and subtly diminished by the overwhelming grandeur surrounding him. The royal diadem, a thin gold band with two hanging silk ribbons, encircled his brow. He wore a long robe of deep crimson, its hem and cuffs embroidered with interlocking lions and winged bulls that symbolized strength and divine sanction. His broad shoulders bore a mantle of fine wool, dyed in royal purple and fastened at the collar with a sunburst brooch inlaid with lapis and carnelian.

As they continued their reverent advance, Artaban became acutely aware of the watching eyes from the side galleries. Court officials in richly dyed robes observed from raised platforms, their faces carefully neutral. He could feel their gazes like unseen spears—cold, piercing, and potentially lethal. They were courtiers, scribes, royal counselors, and the heads of the Great Houses. These men would tally every word, every glance, and every hesitation. A voice inside him whispered that the true power in the room was not on the throne, but in the shadows above it, clothed in silk and silence. Artaban kept his gaze forward and his face composed, but a chill ran down his spine. It came not from fear of what their delegation might say, but from what those in the galleries might choose to hear.

At the second stopping point, they prostrated themselves again. This time, Artaban found himself studying the repeating eight-pointed star patterns etched into the floor. Everything had meaning, he realized—every symbol, every pattern, every carefully calculated distance between throne and supplicant. They were not merely seeking an audience. They were taking part in an elaborate ritual designed to portray the cosmic order with the Great King at its center. Again, after the appointed interval, they rose and continued their procession.

As they approached the final position before the throne platform, Artaban's eyes were drawn to a ceremonial table beside the royal seat. Upon it rested the king's famous bow in its ornate leather case, decorated with pearls and rubies, along with a crystal orb that contained what appeared to be sacred fire, frozen in glass. Vahman came to a halt, and the magi performed the deepest prostration, remaining with foreheads pressed to the granite until the king should acknowledge them.

In that moment of absolute submission, breathing in the scent of roses and incense while the eternal flames crackled softly behind the throne, Artaban felt the full weight of what they were attempting. They had come to tell their own sovereign monarch about a sign in the stars that proclaimed another king's birth, a king whose dominion would overshadow all other earthly kingdoms. The madness of their mission weighed heavily on his shoulders. He whispered a word of thanks that he would not have to present the thesis and pleaded that Melchior would be given wisdom.

After a long moment of silence, a new voice broke the stillness and echoed through the audience hall. "Arise, learned magi, and address your King."

Following the Chamberlain's earlier instructions, Vahman and Melchior stood to their feet, while Artaban and his fellows rose to a kneeling position. Artaban looked for the speaker whose voice he had not recognized. A man dressed in robes almost as elaborate as those of the king stood at the monarch's right hand. Artaban assumed him to be the Grand Chancellor. He understood that the Chancellor and the heads of the Great Houses were the only few men who might speak during a royal audience.

Vahman bowed his head briefly and then began the introduction. "Most Divine King of Kings, I present before Your

Majesty's throne Magus Melchior, venerated scholar of the Bīt Mummu in Babylon, student of the sacred writings of many nations, and my own esteemed colleague in the celestial arts. For an entire generation, he has served the pursuit of wisdom, interpreting the movements of the wandering stars and the prophecies of ancient seers. His learning encompasses the traditions of Babylon, the wisdom of the Hebrews, and the sacred knowledge of our Zoroastrian fathers."

Melchior bowed his head to the king. Then Vahman gestured toward the other three.

"These distinguished magi have journeyed from their distant observatories at his counsel, bearing observations of the heavens that may touch upon matters of great consequence for Your Majesty's realm. Magus Melchior seeks permission to lay before the Golden Throne the signs they have witnessed among the stars, that Your Majesty's divine wisdom might discern their true meaning."

"We know of you, Magus Melchior," the king's voice boomed, as if the vaulted ceilings echoed his words from the heavens. "Your wisdom is highly esteemed throughout our land. Your counsel is welcome in this Court."

Melchior began his address. "May the blessing of Ahura Mazda, the Wise Lord, shine ever upon Your Majesty's reign. We do not come with the words of men, nor from ambition or favor, but as those who have studied the signs set in the heavens —signs not written by human hand, but placed by the will of the Creator. If it pleases the Great King, I will speak now of what has been revealed."

Artaban saw the vaguest twitch of the king's finger, and then the Chancellor prompted Melchior to proceed.

"Wise King, the Court knows of the meeting between the Wanderers, *Marduk* and *Ninub*, in the presence of *Ea* just this past evening, for on this account the royal procession to the summer palace has been delayed."

The king nodded.

"Mighty One, my companion, Magus Belshazzar, has discovered from the almanacs at Temple Ekur that these two Wanderers—the star of the Supreme God, and the star of the king—will likewise meet before *Ea* twice more within the space of a single year."

Artaban heard a collective gasp from the courtiers in the gallery, for even these earthly-minded nobles apparently recognized the rarity of such an encounter.

"And yet, Great King," Melchior continued, "there is more. During their final encounter, these celestial luminaries will be joined by a third, *Nergal*, divine patron of war, and guardian of the West."

An immediate hum of murmurs arose from the galleries, which were just as rapidly quelled by the raised hand of the Chancellor.

"These projections have been reviewed and validated?" the Chancellor asked.

"Yes, Lord Chancellor. Magus Shuma, Master Astronomer at Ekur Temple, verified the accuracy of the calculations, and we have since confirmed them with Nabur-Yahim, Senior Scribe of the Star Tables at the Bīt Mummu."

The Chancellor and the King conferred in hushed tones, and then the Chancellor again addressed Melchior.

"This would seem to be a rare occurrence and a very potent omen..."

He paused, and Melchior must have assumed he was waiting for confirmation of the fact. Artaban feared Melchior might be speaking out of turn as he rushed to expound on the issue.

"It is indeed an exceptionally uncommon event, Your Majesty. The most esteemed scholars at the Bīt Mummu estimate that such a conjunction might occur only once in a thousand years."

Another gasp from the assembled nobles punctuated the

statement, again revealing their perception of its potential significance.

Melchior continued. "The addition of *Nergal* likely makes this a singularly unique phenomenon in all the history of gods and men. As near as we can calculate, such a convergence of celestial luminaries has never occurred before and will, quite likely, never happen again."

This time, a stunned silence filled the hall. Incense wafted through the air, its pungent fragrance adding a sacred gravity to the moment. But no voice was raised. No one stirred. No murmur arose from the galleries.

Finally, the Chancellor spoke with some apparent annoyance in his tone. "Yes, well, we shall have the Royal Astronomer look into the matter in further detail."

He looked as if he intended to go on, when the Great King lifted a hand and drew all attention to himself.

"Learned Magus, we commend you and your companions for discovering this omen in advance and bringing it to our attention. No doubt, the astronomers in all our institutions would have noted the signs as they occurred. But to have foreknowledge of the harbinger, and to understand both its rarity and gravity, can bring us much esteem in the eyes of our Great God. It shows that we are attentive to His signs and heed His warnings. Your service to the crown is acknowledged and appreciated."

The magi all bowed deeply, and Melchior replied. "You honor us, Great King. We are your humble servants."

The king continued. "Since you have detected this sign and brought it to our attention, we would also now hear your interpretation of its meaning and significance."

Artaban cringed. He had expected the question but had hoped they could leave the task of interpretation to the king's other advisors. He saw Melchior also hesitate before responding. But the gauntlet had been thrown down. The conjunction they presented to the king was simply a matter of facts. There was no speculation involved. But the interpretation was highly subjective, and opinions on the meaning would vary widely among scholars. This would be the arena where they could all come under fire from fellow academics and, most significantly, from Court officials.

"Mighty King, we are but humble scholars of history, the heavens, and sacred knowledge. You alone, Wise Lord, receive direct revelation from the throne of the Great Ahura Mazda to chart the path of your kingdom on earth. Who are we to suggest the meaning of such a potent omen in the stars to one such as you?"

Artaban knew this statement was merely a formality of the Court. Such deprecation was necessary and appropriate when addressing one of the most powerful rulers in the world. As Melchior had said, their role was but to advise. The Great King would bear the burden of deciding how to receive their counsel and what actions to take.

"Nevertheless," the king prompted, "we would know your explanation of the sign and its significance for our realm."

"As you will, Lord King. When *Marduk*, the supreme god of the heavens, and *Ninib*, the star of the king, converge within *Ea*, the giver of wisdom, life, and creation, it is commonly believed to have special relevance to the kings of the earth. And since *Ea* is the last constellation to enter the stage each year, the convergence should indicate something about endings and a new beginning. So we believe this conjunction portends the birth of a king, a new divinely appointed king."

The Chancellor interjected. "This is no great revelation. Our Great God raises and deposes all kings. It is He who has ordained the heir to the Royal House of Phraates to reign as King of Kings. New divinely appointed kings are born as a normal course of events."

"It is as you say, Wise Chancellor," Melchior demurred.

"And yet," the king continued, "this interpretation would be true for a single conjunction, one such as we witnessed this evening past. We have not heard your explanation of the triple conjunction or the joining of *Nergal*. Please continue, Magus Melchior."

"As you command, Your Majesty," Melchior acknowledged. "*Nergal* is the patron of war, but is also strongly associated with Judea and Syria in the West. This Wanderer's entry into the convergence could signify the rise of a new king through warfare, though as the wise Chancellor has correctly noted, this is a common occurrence in the affairs of men. In this instance, we believe *Nergal's* presence points more to the location of this king's rise than to the method by which he gains power. It could, of course, imply both."

As Artaban listened to Melchior's explanation, he realized his old mentor was feeding the exposition out in small, easily digestible fragments. Such a tactic would dampen the shock of the full revelation. But eventually, the whole truth would be revealed in all its fullness, and the astonishment, muted though it may be by the process, would ultimately emerge with all its horrific implications.

"And the significance of the triple conjunction..." the king prompted, beginning to show some annoyance at how the response was being drawn out.

"The significance of such a rare event cannot be overstated, Great One. This would be no ordinary king."

The king remained silent as he reflected on the information. Finally, he spoke, almost to himself. "A king to challenge the Roman Emperor? An Eastern king, appointed not by Caesar, but raised up by the Holy One, himself? I wonder..."

"Sovereign Lord," the Chancellor interjected. "The interpretation offered by our esteemed scholar is, learned though he may be, highly speculative. It could lead to rash conclusions that might be of great consequence to your realm. Your Majesty, in your great discretion and wise judgment, no doubt sees the prudence of seeking opinions in this matter from other sage counselors."

The king appeared to ignore his Chancellor. Instead, he gazed intently at Melchior for a very long moment. A low din rose from the galleries as the nobles discussed the issue in hushed tones among themselves. They all quieted down again as the king finally raised his voice.

"Magus Melchior, we understand you are knowledgeable in the history and culture of Judea and Syria. How might the rulers in those lands interpret these signs? We must consider not only what our Great God reveals to us, but also the reactions of the kings of Judea and Syria, and even the Roman Emperor himself. Scholars throughout these lands will surely observe the manifestations as they occur. How will they counsel their lords?"

Artaban hoped his internal apprehension at this question did not show in his demeanor. He silently prayed that Melchior would temper his response with appropriate discretion.

"Your Majesty honors my life's work of study in service to the kingdom. The archives of history are vast, and I fear I have but extracted a mere cup from an ocean of knowledge. Still, I will offer what little insight I can. The sacred writings of the Hebrew faith might be of particular interest to the king of Judea. They point to the coming of a messiah, or 'anointed one,' who will deliver their nation out of bondage and into prosperity much in the same way their patriarch, Moses, led them out of captivity in Egypt and into the land they now inhabit. The prophet Daniel, in particular, foresaw the rise of the messiah at a time which is now imminent, according to my humble understanding of his predictions."

"And," the king prompted, "what shall be the nature of this messiah? Will his influence be upon Judea alone? Or will his rise have a wider impact within the region?"

Melchior cast his eyes to the ground in a visible sign of

deference and humility. Artaban wondered if the spokesman of their delegation would tactfully back away from this volatile and precarious path or press forward without prudent restraint.

"Great One, I offer only what I have read in the histories and archives. You alone, Wise One, can rightly ascertain the virtue and pertinence of my insights to the present situation." He paused and took a deep breath. "Daniel's visions were quite vivid. He foresaw the messiah being given an eternal kingdom that would grow until it filled the whole earth." Melchior halted and bowed his head.

The galleries once again broke into a clamor, but with even greater intensity. Artaban furtively lifted his eyes to gauge the king's reaction. To his surprise, the monarch appeared, at least externally, to be unperturbed. The Chancellor was another matter. He once again inserted himself, unbidden by the king.

"What nonsense is this, esteemed Magus? Shall the Great King and his Council now heed the words of foreign mystics who know not of our One True God? Shall ancient myths and fables now dictate royal policy?"

This was the backlash that Artaban feared. The Chancellor was not the kind of man they should provoke. As second in power only to the king, he was most certainly not a man they would want as an enemy. But Artaban had no means to intervene. He could not whisper warnings in Melchior's ear. Nor was it his place to speak out.

"I beg your forgiveness, Wise Chancellor," Melchior demurred. "I would not presume to direct the interpretations of His Majesty the King or the Royal Court in this regard, but merely to address the king's concern of how foreign monarchs might understand the omens. Perhaps you would allow me to correct a previous error on my part. I failed to note that the Hebrew prophet Daniel also served as a senior official in the royal courts of Babylon and Persia under Kings Nebuchadnezzar, Darius, and Cyrus the Great. The history of our land knows him by his Babylonian name, Belteshazzar."

Grumbles and mutterings again filtered down from the galleries.

"Be cautious, Magus Melchior, in your words to this Court," the Chancellor hissed. "Need we remind you that our Great King rules under the divine right and authority of the One True God, Ahura Mazda? Though we inherited our land and customs from the Babylonians, Medes, and Persians, Ahura Mazda does not speak through false prophets or worshippers of idols, regardless of which royal courts they may have served."

He paused to take a breath, and a murmur of assent echoed from the onlooking elders. He might have said more, but the king interposed with a raised hand.

"Magus Melchior, we have heard your interpretation of the sign and how it might be perceived in Judea. Tell us now what course of action you would advise. If this is indeed a rare and portentous sign from the heavens, what might our Great God expect from us in return?"

Artaban stifled a groan. Why had he allowed the others to lure him into this snare? He felt as if the King was coaxing Melchior deeper into the Chancellor's trap, adding brush to the raging fire of his deputy's wrath. In sealing his own fate, would Melchior implicate them all? A simple act of duty had taken a perilous turn, yet his old *usted* appeared oblivious to the danger.

"Far be it from me, a humble servant of Your Highness, to advise this Council in any way, for to you alone is wisdom granted from on high. If this truly is an omen from our Great God foretelling the birth of a divinely appointed king in Judea, the implications are significant. The Supreme Ahura Mazda is God over the people of that land, whether they acknowledge him or not. Your Majesty alone would know if it might be wise to send a diplomatic envoy with gifts to honor the birth of such a king, as a gesture of friendship to a future ruler who might rise to oppose Rome."

The reaction that rippled through the Great Houses threatened to violate protocol and break out into shouts of incredulity. Artaban sensed both Gondophares and Belshazzar stiffen at his side. The Chancellor's jaw drew into a tight line. The eternal flame hissed and spat in the brazier beside the dais. Only the king and Melchior remained composed.

The Chancellor's voice cut through the palpable tension in the room, and his words sent a wave of shock through Artaban's mind.

"Artaban, son of Nazar, you know well the consequences of rash counsel to the royal throne." His piercing gaze forced Artaban to lower his eyes to the ground. "What say you in this matter?"

Artaban's blood ran cold. How did the Chancellor know who he was, and why would he invoke ghosts from the past in this way? What would prompt the man to call him out in this situation? He was the most junior member of the delegation and the least qualified to offer any advice to the Court. As these questions raged through his mind, another voice rang out in his defense.

"If it please His Majesty and the Royal Council," Vahman spoke up for the first time. "Magus Melchior and these learned scholars have ventured here out of duty to their king to alert the Court of a sign they observed in the heavens. Might I suggest that the royal counselors take the matter under advisement for further investigation, for such weighty matters are due more than the consideration of a moment."

"Indeed," the Chancellor retorted. "And to weigh the matter

rightly, we should hear all perspectives." His voice echoed with the tone of command. "Artaban, son of Nazar, what say you?"

Artaban felt the massive brick walls and the high, vaulted ceilings closing in on him. His breath quickened, and a bead of sweat trickled from his brow and down the side of his cheek for all to see. He could demur and allow his elders to intercede on his behalf. Or he could support the majority consensus of his companions and briefly concur. He heard Vahman's earlier warning ringing in his ears. "Be wary of allowing anyone to bait you into an unwise position." But he couldn't just ignore the Chancellor's veiled attack on his family name.

"My Lord King," Artaban heard himself say, before he could restrain himself. A hush filled the grand hall. "My Lord King," Artaban repeated with more conviction. "The good Chancellor urges us to explore all perspectives. I concur with my esteemed companions, who are wiser and more experienced than I, that the predicted conjunction is most rare and portentous. It is worthy of Your Majesty's consideration. And yet, the final message from the heavens is still uncertain. If the predicted convergences do not occur as expected, then the meaning could be far different and even more auspicious."

Artaban had said much more than he should, but recognizing that this might be his one and only chance to voice his concerns, he pressed on. "Furthermore, Wise King, caution in dealing with Rome seems always a prudent course. The current peace is tenuous, and unnecessary provocation could have severe consequences."

Artaban had spoken with his eyes downcast, but risked a furtive glance toward the throne. He noticed with relief that the Chancellor was actually smiling. The murmurs in the background sounded similarly less severe. He breathed a sigh of relief. Perhaps his words had defused the growing tension within the Court, even if it might have annoyed his compatriots.

The king lifted his hands from the arms of his throne and

touched his fingertips together, while the din in the hall buzzed all around them. Artaban saw him discreetly motion the Chancellor to silence, and so the whole assembled audience waited for an indication from the king to proceed. Eventually, his hands parted, and he tapped lightly on the arm of the throne. The Chamberlain, standing a few paces behind the delegation, struck his staff three times, and the whole chamber grew silent.

The Great King's voice boomed. "Let it be known throughout the Court that the sign which has appeared in the heavens shall be weighed with diligence and care. The matter is not light, and the path of wisdom requires many counselors.

"The royal household shall now proceed, as ordained, to the summer seat in Ecbatana, where the mountains raise our thoughts close to the divine will. There, the deliberations shall continue in due order.

"Messengers shall be dispatched at once to Syria and Judea, that the Court may be informed of movements and matters of consequence in the western provinces. We search for signs not only in the skies but also in the affairs of men.

"As for the wise magi who brought these matters to our attention, they are charged to watch the heavens, to consult the sacred tablets, and to weigh the words of the prophets. Let them return to the Court in six weeks' time, on the forty-sixth day hence, under the rising of the third moon, there to present what has been revealed.

"Thus speaks Phraates, King of Kings. Let this word go forth and be upheld. May Ahura Mazda grant wisdom to Our deliberations and prosperity to Our realm."

As their delegation first bowed low and then rose to back out of the audience chamber, Artaban could not quell the rising sense of dread that they had set in motion a series of events that could not be stopped. They were being swept away in a crisis of their own making. He saw a vision of himself walking down the same precarious path his father had taken, and perhaps to the same tragic end.

CHAPTER FOUR

Mid-Summer, 7 BC
Ecbatana, Parthian Empire
Location of Royal Summer Palace

"Brack. The scrolls are missing. The scrolls are missing," Simur squawked from his perch.

"This can't be mere coincidence," Belshazzar grumbled. "First Babylon, now Ecbatana." His voice was tight with frustration. "The same scrolls from Daniel's writings, gone from both collections."

Artaban had to agree. The Temple of Anahita maintained one of the most comprehensive archives outside of Babylon itself. The royal decrees, sacred texts, and prophecies it housed were all meticulously preserved and cataloged. Documents of this importance didn't simply vanish.

The four magi had gathered on a terrace outside their temporary residence at the Temple of Anahita complex within the city walls of Ecbatana. They continued their studies of ancient prophecies during the day and observations of the stars at night in preparation for another audience with the king. The Royal Court had settled into the summer palace and resumed official business many days ago, but no meeting had yet been scheduled. Vahman had used his influence as Royal Astronomer to arrange quarters for them and was awaiting word from the Chamberlain of a summons from the king.

"The chief archivist said he had no record of anyone removing the scrolls, so someone must be attempting to deny us access to them," Gondophares offered. "Master Melchior, you said you have notes from your own previous studies, correct? Will those serve our purposes here?"

"They could assist in our research," Melchior replied, "but we would need the actual documents to support any case we make to the Royal Court."

"What about the other scrolls you brought from the Bīt Mummu? Will those suffice?" Gondophares prompted.

"They can certainly give us insights into how the Judean scholars might interpret the celestial signs, but as Artaban is fond of reminding us, they are the writings of Hebrew prophets who do not serve our Great God, Ahura Mazda. I fear the Chancellor may be of the same mindset, along with the heads of the Great Houses. They will not likely place much credence in oracles written over six hundred years ago by followers of a foreign god."

"Master Melchior," Belshazzar asked, "what can you share from your personal notes that might be useful?"

Melchior shuffled through some parchments in a box. These were not like the ancient documents that required special care in handling. Eventually, he withdrew one, unrolled it, and spread it out on a nearby table. The others gathered around.

Melchior traced over the scroll, written in his own hand, until he found the specific section he was looking for.

"Here," he pointed. "You remember King Nebuchadnezzar's vision about the metal idol?"

They all nodded in affirmation.

"That same progression of kingdoms reoccurs in several other prophecies. In his seventh scroll, Daniel recorded a vision he personally received from his god. It involved four strange beasts rising up out of stormy waters that represented the same four kingdoms from King Nebuchadnezzar's dream."

"Those were Babylon, Medo-Persia, Greece, and Rome, correct?" Gondophares interjected.

"Exactly," Melchior confirmed.

"And those kingdoms were all crushed by a giant stone that fell from heaven, if I remember correctly," Gondophares added.

"Indeed," Melchior confirmed. "A similar thing occurs in the vision of the seventh scroll, but with some subtle and very significant differences. Fortunately, I have copies of the important sections from both visions in my notes." Melchior tapped the parchment with his finger. "Here's a small portion from where Daniel described the king's dream." He read the words aloud in Aramaic.

"You watched while a stone was cut out without hands, which struck the image on its feet of iron and clay, and broke them in pieces. Then the iron, the clay, the bronze, the silver, and the gold were crushed together, and became like chaff from the summer threshing floors; the wind carried them away so that no trace of them was found. And the stone that struck the image became a great mountain and filled the whole earth."

"Here is the explanation Daniel provided to the king." Melchior continued quoting from his notes.

"And in the days of these kings the God of heaven will set up a kingdom which shall never be destroyed; and the kingdom shall not be left to other people; it shall break in pieces and consume

all these kingdoms, and it shall stand forever. The dream is certain, and its interpretation is sure."

As he heard these words, Artaban felt his gut tie itself in a knot. He had tried to remain apart from the others during the travel to Ecbatana and their studies here, observing from a distance. But he had to raise his concerns at this point. He could not remain silent as they drug him, and potentially all of Parthia, deeper into this pit.

"Belshazzar... Gondophares... Are you paying any attention to those words?" He rushed on without waiting for a reply and emphasized his exclamation with upraised hands. "This doesn't just say a king will be born in Judea—even a great king who might oppose Rome. This says the god of heaven will send a conqueror to overthrow all earthly kingdoms! What are we contemplating here? We can't take a message like that to King Phraates."

Belshazzar leaned over the table, confronting Artaban's outburst. "Don't we owe our Great King the truth? If such a thing is written in the stars, isn't it our duty to inform our lord?"

"And," Belshazzar added, "shouldn't Parthia seek an alliance with such a mighty monarch?"

"Is it truly written in the stars?" Artaban shot back. "Is it? Or are we just speculating about what a predicted conjunction might possibly mean?"

"Artaban," Gondophares countered, "we all watched the first conjunction, and we all verified the forecasts in the almanacs. This is not just idle speculation. This is a uniquely significant sign from heaven, which we have an obligation as magi to study and announce—not just to King Phraates, but to our people."

"But these words," he thrust his finger at the scroll, "are not a warning from our God—"

Melchior lifted his hands and gestured for them to calm

down. Still, it took several moments for the three of them to back off.

"Magus Artaban," he began, using his title in a rare show of respect, "your caution is noted and, I might say, quite warranted. Such a message would indeed be a difficult one for the ears of any monarch. Please remember why we consult these scrolls. It's not to discover the will of the great Ahura Mazda, but to help understand the mind of the Judean king. The sign in the stars is a powerful omen, which we have already shared with the king. We need not worry our lord with the details of these ancient prophecies. But it is important for us to study them to inform our own understanding and observations. Is that not the sacred duty of a scholar?"

Artaban fumed, and he wanted to object, but then realized the foolishness of such a response made in anger. "Very well," he finally replied. "But I strongly urge caution in how we address the matter in an audience with the king. You saw the reaction of the Chancellor and the nobles of the Great Houses during our last encounter with the Court. We're on dangerous ground."

"Brack. Dangerous ground." Simur's cackle reverberated before drifting away on the breeze.

"Perhaps," Gondophares suggested, "we can finish reviewing the materials in Master Melchior's notes."

"In the context we just discussed," Melchior confirmed, "they could prove to be quite instructive."

Resignedly, Artaban stepped back a pace and waved his assent.

"Now," Melchior gestured back at his notes on the table, "we will see a repetition of the same themes from King Nebuchadnezzar's dream in another prophecy. Daniel received this next vision directly from his god, approximately fifty years later. It depicts four mythical beasts rising up from stormy seas, one after another. They represent the same progression of empires we noted a moment ago. Then there is a remarkable scene, which I believe could be very pertinent to our interests here." Melchior rolled the scroll forward and gestured at the appropriate section of his notes. "Again we start with the vision itself and then proceed to the interpretation." He read aloud from the scroll.

"I kept looking
Until thrones were set up,
And the Ancient of Days took His seat;
His garment was like white snow
And the hair of His head like pure wool.
His throne was ablaze with flames,
Its wheels were a burning fire.
A river of fire was flowing
And coming out from before Him;
Thousands upon thousands were attending Him,
And myriads upon myriads were standing before Him;
The court sat,
And the books were opened."

Melchior pointed to the passage on the scroll. "Notice how Daniel wrote this entire section in poetic verse. Such a practice was common within Hebrew prophecy. The poetic form emphasizes the direct nature of the communication from their god. This next section is especially relevant here and echoes what we read from the previous scroll.

"I kept looking in the night visions,
And behold, with the clouds of heaven
One like a Son of Man was coming,
And He came up to the Ancient of Days
And was presented before Him.
And to Him was given dominion,
Glory and a kingdom,

That all the peoples, nations, and men of every language
Might serve Him.
His dominion is an everlasting dominion
Which will not pass away;
And His kingdom is one
Which will not be destroyed.

"Now I'll skip down to the explanation of the vision, which was provided to Daniel by a heavenly messenger."

"The court will sit for judgment,
And the dominion of the fourth kingdom will be taken away,
Annihilated and destroyed forever.
Then the sovereignty, the dominion,
And the greatness of all the kingdoms under the whole heaven
Will be given to the people of the Highest One;
His kingdom will be an everlasting kingdom,
And all the dominions will serve and obey Him."

Everyone was silent for several moments as they reflected on the words of the prophecy. For Artaban, it only deepened his apprehension. He worried not only about how their own king would receive such ideas, but also about the reaction they might provoke from the Roman Emperor. Whether or not they were true revelations from heaven made little difference. Either monarch would rightly fear that these notions could incite the Jews to rebellion. If unrest broke out, it would be critical for Parthia to stay out of the conflict.

"As you can see," Melchior's words pulled Artaban's attention back to his companions, "this later prophecy and its interpretation repeat the same themes from the earlier dream. Hebrew scholars associate both of these visions with the coming of their messiah. It's not hard to imagine the impact in Judea if the conjunctions we've observed in the heavens are taken as a sign that the messiah has come. It would portend great changes for the kingdom of the Jews and, perhaps, great changes for us all."

"This is a vision of divine judgment," Belshazzar exclaimed. "It portrays the triumph of truth and justice over falsehood."

"It says the fourth beast is judged," Artaban almost shouted. "It says *Rome* is judged. We need to be very careful about flaunting this prophecy in the face of Rome."

"Actually, the way I read it," Gondophares offered in a calmer tone, "all nations are judged. Under this righteous king, the common people will finally be delivered from persecution and tyranny."

"That's exactly why we need to be very careful about how we handle such ideas," Artaban insisted. "These notions could prompt civil unrest and perhaps even riots, not only in Judea, but anywhere people feel they are being treated unjustly by their rulers." He left the implication unstated that such sentiments could incite social upheaval even in their own kingdom.

"This prophecy," Belshazzar interjected, "depicts the outcome of the final battle between righteousness and evil. The man… the king in the clouds," he exclaimed, the intensity rising in his voice, "*must be* the *Saoshyant!*" He jabbed a finger at the words on the parchment. "It's absolutely critical for Parthia to align itself with this rising monarch as soon as possible. We must end up on the right side of the greatest battle in human history."

"I agree," Gondophares began, but Artaban cut him off.

"This is *not* the revelation of our Great God. These are the dubious words of an ancient Hebrew prophet. We—"

"Brack," Simur's screech cut through the air. "Extraordinary times. Perilous times."

Melchior reached down and began rolling up the scroll. "You see, my sons, how volatile ideas can be, even among the sincerest of friends. We must tread with great care on the path the Lord of Light has opened up before us."

"But we *must*—" Gondophares interrupted.

Melchior stilled him. "We must," he concurred, "walk that path with faith and courage. Our Wise Lord wrote the signs in the stars and brought them to our attention. He did not reveal them to other equally worthy servants of wisdom and knowledge. He chose *us* and sent us to advise his servant, our Great King. We have set our hand to the plow and must commit to seeing it through."

"Esteemed Magus," the messenger addressed Melchior, "Lord Vahman requests your presence with utmost haste. He asks all four of you to meet him inside the western portico of the temple. He insists the matter is of some urgency."

They had just finished a hearty midday meal and were preparing to convene at the temple archives to search for documents that might shed more light on the triple conjunction. The night before, they had been at the observatory tracking *Marduk* and *Ninub*, whose movements they'd followed since the first convergence six weeks earlier. Thus far, the two Wanderers had diverged as expected and were following their predicted paths through the heavens.

"What's the purpose?" Melchior asked. "Does the Royal Astronomer require an update on the status of our research? Shall we bring some of the significant documents we've uncovered?"

"My apologies, Master Melchior," the messenger replied. "My lord gave me no additional information. He bid me only to find you and relay the message to meet him right away. He said the matter was of some urgency but gave no other instructions."

"Very well. Please inform him we are on our way."

Melchior dismissed the messenger with a wave of his hand. The young man bowed and disappeared through the arched entrance of the veranda.

"Well," Melchior addressed his fellows, "I suppose our afternoon research plans have changed. Let us go meet Lord Vahman."

He rose slowly from the cushion behind the low table, his age revealing itself in his focused, deliberate movements.

"Isn't this summons a bit odd?" Artaban spoke up. "What could be the reason?"

"I agree," Melchior said with a shrug. "Master Vahman is normally quite meticulous in his planning and spurns rash actions. It has always been his way. So this kind of last-moment request must imply an unexpected situation of some significance. I suggest we proceed promptly to the portico."

Unlike the crowded streets of the markets and residential districts of the city, the temple complex was much more subdued. Artaban was surprised to see Vahman already waiting for them at the portico. Men of his position did not arrive early and wait for those of lesser rank. Artaban was also somewhat disconcerted to see Vahman garbed in the formal attire of his office, though perhaps he had been engaged in official duties when this unexpected situation arose. The four magi, by contrast, were dressed in much more informal clothes.

"Lord Vahman," Melchior greeted his old colleague. "We responded as soon as we received your message. What prompted such urgency?"

"Come, friends. There is little time. I'll explain as we go."

No one else attended Vahman, and that too was rare. A small entourage of clerks, scribes, apprentices, and aides always accompanied members of the Court, especially those like the Royal Astronomer. Yet Vahman alone led them down a colonnaded walkway overlooking the inner garden courtyard of the temple complex. Overhead vines and rows of cedar trees made it feel as if they were passing through a tunnel of vegetation.

"There has been a great deal of contention among the Great Houses and members of the Court about the omen you reported to the king." Vahman began.

"I was beginning to wonder if the whole issue had been forgotten during the move," Melchior remarked.

"Far from it. There are many strong opinions about what should be done. As you can imagine, the various parties' perspectives differ widely."

"Is that why we're here now?"

"I can only speculate. All I know for certain is that the king himself requested a private audience with us. I don't know whether he wants additional information, or if he has decided on a particular course of action."

"An audience with the king?" Artaban blurted out without thinking. "We aren't prepared or attired appropriately."

Vahman looked mildly annoyed at the junior magi's outburst. "You will find that protocols are more relaxed on such occasions. The grand display of the Court is set aside in favor of more pragmatic issues. Your appearance will be of no concern to the king. And I must assume your additional research over the past weeks has more than fit this delegation to address the king's concerns."

"Do you know who else might be present for this meeting?" Melchior asked. "Would you expect the Chancellor, the Chamberlain, or any members of the Great Houses?"

"For a private audience like this, we'll likely only see the king's most trusted associates. The Chamberlain," he said with a wave of dismissal, "is merely a protocol officer for formal business. He won't be present today. As for the Great Houses... The king has some loyal supporters, but there are also those who oppose his policies, either openly or behind the scenes. It's difficult to know who to trust within those circles. No," Vahman concluded after a moment of reflection, "I would not expect to see any elders from the Great Houses in attendance."

"And the Chancellor?" Melchior prompted.

"I've been in a protracted debate with the Chancellor over the diplomatic envoy you suggested during your previous appearance. Just yesterday, he reiterated his opposition to such an action. He's mindful of the disastrous defeat our kingdom suffered in the Syrian province at the hands of the Romans thirty years ago and is determined not to disrupt the tenuous peace we have struck with Caesar Augustus. King Herod is a thorn in that particular situation, and the Chancellor is adamant that we remain as separated as possible from Judea."

"Would he go against the will of the king in such a matter?" Melchior asked.

Vahman sighed. "Politics in the Court is complex. Everyone has his own interests to protect. Most have private sources of information and a network of agents to carry out their will."

"That was a very… hmm, shall we say, diplomatic response, my friend," Melchior said. "Now you're sounding like a politician. What we really need to know right now is who might oppose us. Tell me about the Chancellor. Do you trust the man?"

Vahman stopped and turned to face Melchior. Then he glanced at the other three magi.

Apparently reading his friend's thoughts, Melchior added, "These men are true and loyal to their god and to their king. I will personally vouch for each one."

Vahman frowned thoughtfully and finally said, "Very well. No, I do not trust the Chancellor. He's not a devout man. He views the king's piety as a weakness and thinks his faith undermines his judgment amid the power struggles both within the Court and with our neighboring kingdoms." Vahman gazed at the four magi with a look of stern warning. "The Chancellor will perceive your influence with the king as a challenge to his own authority, which," he emphasized with a pointed finger, "is quite formidable. I caution you not to underestimate him. He can be a very dangerous man."

Artaban saw the look of chagrin on Melchior's face. He himself marveled at the corruption which apparently ran rampant within the circles of power. Parthia was supposed to be a realm devoted to the Zoroastrian faith and its principles of truth and justice. The king himself ruled under the authority of their Great God, Ahura Mazda. To hear of such deep moral decay within the highest levels of their government was disturbing.

"I don't understand," Artaban interjected. "During our last audience, the Chancellor expressed his outrage that we would consult ancient scrolls from prophets who do not know or serve our Great God. Yet you say he is not a pious man."

Vahman gave him a look of incredulity. "Don't be naive. Men like the Chancellor use religion as a political tool. He will profess belief if it serves his ends. Don't trust his words, but watch his actions."

The rebuke stung, and Artaban bit back an angry response.

Vahman, for his part, resumed their procession toward the private audience with the king, while Artaban fretted over his words and what they might portend. A short distance later, they turned a corner and proceeded deeper into the sheltered perimeter of the palace complex and farther away from prying ears.

Melchior dug more deeply into the Royal Astronomer's revelation about Court intrigue. "We tried to access some ancient Hebrew scrolls in the temple archives this past week. The entire collection was missing. Could the Chancellor have anything to do with that?"

"Perhaps. Or some member of one of the Great Houses." Vahman waved a hand in a gesture of resignation. "Almost anyone with the influence or the coin for a bribe could keep those documents out of your hands."

Melchior grunted. "I suppose I shouldn't be surprised," he said. "The same thing happened to a similar set of scrolls in the archives of the Bīt Mummu. That seems to be an unlikely coincidence. But I can't see how anyone in the Court could have been aware of our findings at that point in time."

"Don't assume anything," Vahman cautioned him. "There are eyes and ears everywhere. And if your conjecture is true about a Jewish messiah, then signs in the heavens won't be the only factors at play. There may well be events unfolding in Judea itself which would raise interest in ancient Hebrew scrolls."

"Interest here? Within the Great Houses?" Melchior asked in astonishment. "How would they even get word of such events?"

"Don't be easily deceived, my friend," Vahman replied, shaking his head. "Money and influence have a long reach when it comes to protecting power."

Vahman continued to lead them down the long pathway, which, by this point, almost completely concealed their presence. At the far end of the promenade, they turned aside to an old wooden gate, overgrown with vines. It almost disappeared into the surrounding shrubbery. Oddly, it appeared to have no handle or latch.

Artaban peered up through the thick jasmine canopy woven overhead and glimpsed shimmers of gold from the innermost of Ecbatana's seven concentric city walls. He realized they were standing just outside the palace complex itself.

Vahman paused briefly at the gate. "This is a private entrance to the palace gardens, used only by a few trusted advisors. You must never speak of it to anyone."

Artaban and the other magi nodded their understanding of the warning.

Without further action on their part, the door opened from the other side, and they were ushered through by a guard clad in mail with a sword at his hip and a spear in his hand.

"My Lord, your escort awaits," the gatekeeper said, gesturing toward two similarly equipped soldiers. One led the way, and the other fell in behind the group of scholars.

The guards led them through a narrow maze of dense cedar hedges. After following a circuitous route, with numerous intersections and a dizzying array of twists and turns, the group finally broke out into a lavish secluded garden. Geometric flower beds burst with the late summer blooms of purple irises, yellow narcissus, and red tulips. The beds formed intricate patterns between narrow water channels lined with polished stones. Towering cypress trees framed a panoramic vista across a patchwork of agricultural fields to the rugged peaks of the Zagros Mountains beyond. The four main garden sections featured beautiful fountains at their centers, while polished basalt sculptures of griffins and winged lions guarded the corners. A cool whisper of wind moved through the space, bearing the sacred scents of jasmine and myrrh that seemed to sanctify this hidden refuge within the royal complex.

The main pathway opened onto a wide platform with a domed pavilion at its center. Honey-colored limestone columns crowned with lotus blossoms supported its wide eaves. Water cascaded down a back wall and flowed into a square pool in the middle of the pavilion, where a central stone pillar held a bronze brazier burning with myrrh and cedar chips.

While they were still taking in the scene, the guards snapped to attention and a few men entered through a similar break in the hedge on the far side of the square. Artaban immediately recognized the king and instantly dropped to prostrate himself on the ground. He could see his companions doing likewise through the corner of his eye. No sooner had his forehead touched the ground than he heard the king's own voice addressing them.

"Rise, honored guests. We have need of your counsel, and time is of the essence. We do not desire the formalities of the

Court to hinder our discourse. Therefore, we bid you be candid in your replies to our inquiries with no concern of reprisal."

The king was accompanied only by a steward, a scribe, and one other man. He walked over to a raised dais on the far side of the central pool, and his steward poured him a chalice of chilled date juice from a silver eagle-headed ewer. The scribe took a seat on a cushion beside a low stone table several paces behind the king and withdrew a wax tablet to take notes of the proceedings. The other man remained standing at the king's right hand, while the guards positioned themselves outside the two entrances through the hedgerows. Artaban could not help but notice the absence of the Chamberlain, the Chancellor, and any representatives of the Great Houses.

They all followed Vahman's lead in rising and then took up positions opposite the King across the flowing stream. Vahman bowed and addressed the King.

"Your Majesty recalls the esteemed magi from their last appearance at the Court. We are honored by your trust in our counsel and stand ready to serve Your Highness in any way you deem appropriate."

"You are a valued advisor to the Crown, Lord Vahman. We thank you for bringing these scholars and their observations to our attention. Magus Melchior," the king turned his attention to Melchior as the spokesman of the delegation, "in the days since your appearance before the Court, we trust you and your colleagues have conducted further research on the sign in the heavens. Have you learned anything that would change your initial assessment?"

"Great King, may wisdom and light attend your reign," Melchior began, apparently not yet comfortable addressing the king with informal dialog. "We have indeed explored the issue in great depth, knowing its critical significance to the Crown, and our findings only affirm our previous assertions. The preeminent Wanderers, *Marduk* and *Ninub*, continue along their expected paths, precisely as forecast in the almanacs. We have increased confidence in the predictions of the noble Persian lord, Belteshazzar, about a divinely appointed king who will restructure the current world order. These prophecies were repeated in three successive visions over a period of fifty years."

Melchior did not mention that the Daniel scrolls had mysteriously disappeared from two separate archives. Perhaps he feared distracting the king with matters of intrigue when larger issues were at stake. Even though Artaban still doubted the conclusions and recommendations of the others, he had to agree with the wisdom of keeping the king focused on the topic of primary importance.

"Furthermore," Melchior continued, "Beltashazzar's prophecies are reinforced in multiple instances throughout the Hebrew scriptures."

"What of our own sacred writings?" asked the king.

"Wise One, the predictions about the *Saoshyant* in our own faith are remarkably similar to the prophecies about the Jewish messiah. When a profound truth is revealed to us by the Great Ahura Mazda, would not a faint echo of that same truth ripple throughout other religions, especially those which share our own cultural roots?"

"So this sign in the heavens may point to the coming of the *Saoshyant* and the end of the age?" The king retorted with a hint of skepticism in his tone. "That's a bold claim indeed. Are we to protect the succession of Phraataces to our throne by sending his older brothers to Rome, only for the *Saoshyant* to come and subjugate even our own realm to his reign?"

The sound of flowing water filled the silence that followed this rhetorical question, for which there was no wise response. Despite the king's earlier admonition for them to speak candidly, Artaban seriously worried if Melchior had gone too far. But his old *usted*, apparently nonplussed, eventually resumed the dialog.

"My Lord King, there is much debate among scholars about the coming of the *Saoshyant* and the nature of his activities. All agree that the Lord of Light will appoint him and determine the timing of his appearance. Yet, while many believe he will subject all earthly kingdoms to his rule, others assert he will actually lead the kingdoms of righteousness in a great final battle of truth against falsehood. In such a case, the succession of the Parthian throne would be in no jeopardy, for surely there is no more righteous kingdom than the Parthian realm and no more worthy monarch than the one who sits on its throne. Such a faithful one would, no doubt, welcome the Saoshyant with gestures of friendship and goodwill."

Artaban watched the scribe feverishly scratch all these words onto his wax pad. He could only hope that the slate would eventually be wiped clean without the record being transcribed to permanent clay tablets, which would forever stand as a testament to their actions this day. His father's own words, so many years ago, eventually came back to condemn him for rash advice that had cost the kingdom dearly. Artaban himself continued to shoulder the burden of that error.

"Your conclusion, then, Magus Melchior…" prompted the king.

"Mighty King, the significance of the convergence in the stars cannot be overemphasized. Such a conjunction, unfolding three times in a single year, has not graced the skies in a thousand years. The ancient records of Babylon and Persia speak with one voice. When *Nergal* joins *Ninub* and *Marduk* within *Ea*, the constellation of wisdom and rebirth, a king will be born in the land of Judea who is destined to alter the course of empires. Our own sacred traditions foretell the rise of a righteous one at the end of the present age, a restorer of truth, whose coming shall be heralded by signs in the firmament. So these three witnesses—the heavens, the ancient records, and the prophetic scrolls—all converge upon this truth. Thus we, ourselves, conclude from all our observations and study, and we offer it now to the wise discretion of our king." Melchior paused momentarily, and Artaban wondered if it was for emphasis or for fear of the implications. "A divinely appointed king shall surely rise in the West. The Hebrews call this one 'messiah.' We might call him '*Saoshyant.*' Perhaps they are one and the same. But the sign from our Great God is portentous and must not be ignored."

"And the actions you recommend in response to this revelation by the mighty Ahura Mazda are still the same?" asked the king.

Melchior bowed before responding. "They are unchanged, Your Majesty. We humbly suggest you consider sending an official delegation on behalf of the Parthian Kingdom to Judea as an expression of friendship with this new king. We think the omen most likely points to a newly born son in the house of King Herod, though that is uncertain. The stars in the heavens have not yet revealed the patronage of this rising king. Perhaps more will be shown in the future."

The king grunted. "And what would come of our gesture of friendship should this messiah turn out to be a challenger to Herod's throne?"

Melchior pressed forward with his case. "Surely the royal envoy chosen by Your Majesty would be wise enough to read the mood of the Judean court and to maneuver appropriately."

Artaban strained to see the king's reaction. Perhaps it would be better for Melchior's counsel to be dismissed than for the king to take an impulsive action that might later provoke the anger of the Jews or the wrath of Rome. He could discern no shock or concern in the king's demeanor, only a look of cold calculation.

"Perhaps I should go on this mission myself, if the situation is of such importance and yet so uncertain," the king mused, apparently thinking aloud in a somewhat disconcerting display of transparency. "No," he muttered. "That would set the Great Houses on fire, and then someone else would be sitting on the throne by the time I returned."

The scribe paused in his work, and the others waited wordlessly as the king thought through the issues and options aloud.

Finally, the king gestured at Artaban, and his heart froze.

"What say you, son of Nazar? I seem to recall you had a different perspective in our last audience from that of your elders." He lifted his chalice and took a long draft before continuing. "My father was a fool, and yours provided rash counsel to his king. Perhaps we have both learned from our sires."

Artaban hesitated, hoping that Vahman or Melchior would come to his aid, but no one interposed on his behalf.

"Well…" the king prompted.

"Wise King, I have the deepest respect for my fellow magi and acknowledge their great wisdom in interpreting signs and omens. Their depth of experience far outpaces my own. I seek only to humbly offer a different perspective—one that favors caution over reward."

"Yes, of course." The king gestured for him to move on. "What is this more cautious advice to your king?"

Artaban sensed he was on perilous ground but had no other option than to press forward. "Your Majesty, I suggest the signs in the heavens be confirmed at each stage before further action is taken. If the Wanderers deviate from their predicted paths, it could significantly alter the meaning of the omen."

"But if the signs are validated, then you concur with the recommendations of your esteemed fellows?"

Artaban bowed. "In this regard, I also urge caution. A grand gesture of outreach to a client kingdom of Rome might jeopardize the hard-won peace we presently enjoy."

"Even if it risks the future disfavor of the *Saoshyant*?"

Artaban felt as if he were teetering on the edge of a precipice. Was the king intentionally baiting him into a trap of some kind? Again he bowed, more deeply this time. "You alone, Great One, have the wisdom to discern the right course for your realm. I remain but your humble servant."

King Phraates rose from the cushioned dais and turned to gaze past the city to the fertile valley and the mountains beyond. He lifted his goblet and motioned toward the dramatic vista.

"This is an ancient land, far more ancient than either Judea or Rome. And we are a people more noble than any other. Do I not rule under the authority of the Father of Light? And yet we stoop before Rome—before her legions and her lifeless gods, as our Great Houses bicker tediously among themselves, and my own wife plots treachery behind my back."

He turned back to face the magi. "Did my father not once wrest the whole province of Syria from Rome's grasp? And yet, that victory proved to be short-lived. It was as if we had but kicked a sleeping bear." He waved his chalice at Artaban. "You know that all too well, do you not, son of Nazar?" Not waiting for any reply, he went on. "Are we to repeat that same mistake? Or were we simply too early in that first attempt? Is now the true prophetic opportunity to ally with the *Saoshyant* and crush Rome once and for all?" He gazed down into his cup. "I wonder."

The king straightened up. "I've received word from our agents in Judea. Herod has executed his two eldest sons on charges of treason. The common people chafe under the yoke of Roman oppression, even as the priests and aristocrats thrive from the relationship. Some separatist sects speak of a coming messiah, but most fear to even hope for a deliverer. If their scriptures do indeed predict their messiah will rise soon, few have taken heed. The rulers are shrewd, and the people are cowed."

The king gestured to the scribe, who again grasped his stylus and hovered over the wax tablet, preparing to take down the king's next words.

"Thus is our decision in this matter," he declared. "It shall not be written as a formal decree nor announced to the Court. But those here gathered shall know this proclamation as an expression of Our Royal Will."

He looked forcefully at them to emphasize his words, and they all bowed in acquiescence.

"We shall send a delegation to search out and pay tribute to the rising king announced by the extraordinary signs in the heavens. It will be a delegation of scholars rather than of diplomats. You three magi, to whom the Great Ahura Mazda revealed the sign, shall be Our emissaries."

Artaban sighed with relief that he was left out of the proclamation, but then almost gasped aloud when Melchior dared to break in.

"Your Majesty certainly refers to my three esteemed colleagues, correct? For I am aged and unfit for such a journey."

Perhaps the king truly did allow for informal discourse in this private setting, for he showed no anger at the interruption.

"You shall go, Magus Melchior, for your wisdom and knowledge of the Hebrew scriptures will be crucial to the success of the endeavor. Our Great God will give you strength for the task."

"Yes, my Lord King. Your will be done. But which of the four shall then not attend?"

"You shall all venture forth. Magi Melchior, Belshazzar, and Gondophares shall be Our emissaries. And the son of Nazar shall be Our voice of caution."

Artaban's blood ran cold. What did that even mean?

The king continued the proclamation. "You shall proceed thus, with measured discretion, for neither the Chancellor nor the Great Houses shall know of this mission. You shall take letters of introduction and safe passage, signed under the hand of Our Royal Astronomer. You shall proceed to Zeugma and await confirmation of the second conjunction before crossing the Euphrates River into Roman territory. Then journey to Damascus and await confirmation of the third and final conjunction before continuing to Jerusalem. When you have witnessed the third conjunction, send a message to our agents in Jerusalem to arrange an audience with King Herod."

Artaban and the others stood in silence. Even Vahman did not speak. The notion was so unexpected and so fraught with implications that a myriad of questions swirled in Artaban's mind, but failed to take discernible shape.

The king seemed to be waiting for a reply of assent. Eventually Vahman broke the silence. "Wise King, this is an ingenious plan, given to you by the Father of Light, for it extends the hand of friendship to the prophesied one without provoking the anger of Rome. A delegation of holy scholars would not be perceived as a threat, like a royal diplomatic envoy would. And the measured steps ensure the correct interpretation of the omens."

"My challenge now," the king replied, "is to determine the nature of the gift we present to the newborn king. It must be something of value without appearing to be tribute."

"Your Majesty," Melchior interjected, "I think I have an answer that will address these concerns."

The king leaned forward, almost eagerly. "Go on, Magus Melchior."

"The Hebrew scriptures speak of the messiah as fulfilling a unique triple role of prophet, priest, and king. One specific passage from the writings of the prophet Isaiah predicts that kings of the East will honor the messiah with gifts of gold and myrrh. These would align with the roles—gold for the king and myrrh for the prophet."

"You mentioned three roles. Should there be a third gift as well?"

"Indeed, Wise One," Melchior replied. "I recommend we

bring frankincense to honor the role of priest, for such the Jewish priests burn at the altar in their temple."

"My Lord King," Vahman again broke in. "Such an offering would be a sign of the utmost respect to a Jewish messiah because of the symbolic value, but would be viewed merely as insignificant tokens by anyone else. These gifts would honor the messiah while offering no offense to Rome."

"So shall it be written, so shall it be done," replied the king. He turned and gestured to the man who had stood silently at his right hand. "Rostan is a special assistant who handles discreet matters on Our behalf. He will coordinate everything you will need for your mission."

The magi bowed in acknowledgement.

The king set down his chalice and raised his hands to commission them for their solemn duty.

"If this sign in the heavens is as portentous as we believe, then you hold the very fate of our kingdom in your hands. May our Great God, Ahura Mazda, see you safely along your way and grant you success in your mission. Be wise as serpents and innocent as doves. You carry with you the respect and gratitude of your king."

As they bowed and backed out of the king's presence, Artaban wondered about the dubious honor bestowed upon them. If all went well, perhaps they would indeed receive recognition and reward for the task they undertook. But the secrecy under which they proceeded would allow them to disappear without regard if aught went awry. And no one would be the wiser.

CHAPTER FIVE

Mid-Autumn, 7 BC
Zeugma, Parthian Empire

Artaban stared at the pontoon bridge, stretching out before him like a serpent of cedar and pine. Long, weathered planks lay across a hundred heavy barges, each moored to anchors straining against the current upstream. A cacophony of sounds arose from a parade of camels and carts, all laden with trade goods and spaced out along its length. As he took his first few steps, Artaban could feel the structure shifting beneath his feet—an unsteady reminder of the boundary they crossed between the kingdom of Parthia and the empire of Rome. Once on the other side, they would be fully committed to this dubious mission.

"Why these unsteady pontoons, Master Melchior?" Gondophares asked as he grasped the old man by the elbow to steady him. "Surely two great kingdoms, like Parthia and Rome, could construct a proper stone bridge at their busiest thoroughfare of trade."

"If this span over the river is unsteady," Melchior replied, "the tenuous peace between the two powers is even more so. Stone bridges are difficult to dismantle should the fragile truce break down into war. The pontoons make the task of separation much simpler."

They had arrived at Zeugma several days before the second conjunction. Since their mission was to be kept as inconspicuous as possible, they had dressed in the travel garb of religious scholars and camped among the trade caravans outside the city walls. Their party numbered eighteen in total—the four magi, eight soldiers, a caravan master, a cook, a steward, two animal handlers, and, of course, one rather vocal starling, along with twelve horses, four camels, and four mules. Even the soldiers had taken measures to conceal their identities. Though their arms and armor betrayed the nature of their trade, their plain tunics, without the emblems and insignia of the king, marked them more as bodyguards for wealthy nobles than as soldiers of the royal army.

Rostan's guidance for the group came by direction of the king. "A large party would draw suspicion. A small one would be too easily robbed. The group should therefore travel in modest dignity, with eight men for protection, a few to serve their needs, and beasts to carry what is required. No more."

They had considered a more innocuous crossing point at Thapsacus, but decided it was sometimes easier to hide in a crowd. Zeugma was the busiest transit point by far, and they should garner little special attention as they mingled with the steady stream of trade caravans.

Their transit across the Euphrates had been delayed by several days because of rainy season weather. On the night of the second conjunction, a heavy storm kept the magi sheltering in their tents. Though the rains abated by the next morning, the skies remained overcast for three more days.

Finally, on the fourth evening after the predicted conjunction, the four scholars rode with Captain Vakshuvar and another guard to a remote hillside away from the city's lamps and torches, where they could get a clear view of the sky. The two Wanderers, *Marduk* and *Ninub*, appeared where expected if the conjunction had occurred on schedule.

Artaban wondered how he should react to the situation as the king's "voice of caution." As they gazed into the crystal clear night, he decided to raise his concerns to his fellows.

"The Great King's guidance was explicit. We're not to proceed unless we confirm the second sign in the heavens. Surely our Great God intervened to obscure our view of the event so we could not be certain of its consummation. If the Mighty and Wise Ahura Mazda wanted us to continue our mission, he would have cleared the skies to give us an unobstructed view of the meeting."

"What unsound reasoning is this, Artaban?" Belshazzar shot back. "We've watched the Wanderers follow their predicted paths for weeks. Now we see them exactly where they should be after their second meeting in the skies. Just because we didn't witness the event doesn't change the fact that it occurred. No other course is possible."

"That's not true," Artaban insisted. "The Wanderers commonly make strange and unexpected shifts in their routes. Even during this overall sequence, *Marduk* and *Ninub* have both reversed their paths in mid-course. It's what made the second conjunction possible at all. How are we to know that one or the other didn't deviate, even by the smallest degree, so that the meeting never happened? Such an occurrence would be a potent omen indeed. We can't be certain of the truth. We can only speculate. And the King's guidance was clear. Unless the sign is confirmed, we must not proceed."

"I have to agree with Belshazzar," Gondophares interjected. "The most likely conclusion is that the conjunction occurred exactly as predicted. Any other theory is pure speculation and bears the burden of proof. We'd be foolish not to act on what the evidence clearly shows."

"Wise brothers," Melchior intervened as the three younger men faced off in the stillness of the night. "Artaban is true to the role assigned to him by the King. His caution is valid. We cannot know what we have not observed. The All-Knowing One could indeed have raised the storms to obscure our view of the heavens at just the right time."

"Are we then to abandon our commission from the King because of a rainstorm?" Belshazzar countered. "Such a course is the height of folly."

Melchior raised a hand to halt further argument. "We shall assess the risks and weigh the options according to the long-established ways of wisdom," he said. "What are the risks if we turn back here and abandon the mission?"

"The risk," Belshazzar replied in an adamant tone, "is that Parthia should anger our Great God by failing to respond to the rare and portentous warning he wrote across the heavens above. The risk is that the mightiest king in history should arise to lead the ultimate battle of truth against error, and our kingdom shall be found on the wrong side. The risk is that a mere turn in the weather should prevent us from taking a firm stand in the weightiest matter of all time."

"Well said," Gondophares concurred.

Turning to Artaban, Melchior then prompted, "And what are the risks if we proceed?"

"We risk the very real and very imminent wrath of Rome," Artaban declared. "A generation ago, we lit a fire we could not extinguish. We thought we'd won a victory over Rome in the very region we now approach. We captured Syria and Judea. We installed a compliant king, loyal to the Parthian throne. And then we were decimated in the backlash." Artaban shook his head in frustration. "The present peace is hard-won and very fragile. If we provoke Rome a second time, it could prove to be devastating to our king, our country, our families, and everything we hold dear."

"And what of the omen?" Gondophares asked. "Our Great God grants knowledge to those who can act on it," he added with intensity. "When my uncle warned the authorities in Saskatoon about the drought he saw written in the stars, they ignored his counsel, and hundreds starved. Failing to act on what our God reveals to us can have tragic consequences, not only for kings but for mothers and fathers and children."

"*Rome* is a present and real threat. Our interpretation of the omen in the stars is merely conjecture. How presumptuous are we to claim to know the mind of God?" Artaban countered.

Captain Vakshuvar, who had been listening from a discrete distance, stepped forward. "Pardon my interruption, Magus Melchior. I know little about signs in the stars or ancient prophecies, but I know a great deal about military operations. I'm afraid I have to agree with Magus Artaban. Now that Rome has consolidated its power, the Parthian army could not stand against it in a major engagement. I suggest we tread cautiously in any dealings that might provoke a military response."

"Thank you, Captain, for your insights," Melchior replied. "The matter is weighty indeed. Either course could lead to a tragic end. It's not possible to be absolutely certain about our path ahead. But," he continued, "there remains one more waypoint along our journey. If we proceed from here, we still have another opportunity to turn aside. The third conjunction is yet to come."

"Brack," Simur cawed, tilting his head toward Artaban. "Wait and watch."

Artaban eventually conceded the point, under the condition that they would await the final conjunction before meeting with Herod, just as King Phraates had directed. And so now they stood on this wobbly bridge, preparing to cross a veritable line in the sand, and Artaban could not shake the feeling they were stepping over a precipice from which there would be no return.

After the group had gone a dozen paces toward the Roman province on the far shore, an official from the Parthian border security detail hurried up to Melchior.

"Begging your pardon, Magus," the man blurted. "Captain Baraz respectfully requests that your party return to the processing area. He has received an urgent message from the palace."

It was one of the rare times Artaban had ever seen a flicker of annoyance cross his old mentor's face. They had just spent almost a full day completing the border inspection process and had finally obtained clearance to proceed. The tedious process undoubtedly frustrated Melchior, and it would likely be even more wearisome on the Roman side of the river. But the old sage recovered his composure so quickly that few probably noticed the reaction at all.

Melchior glanced toward the rest of the retinue. "Wait here. I'll go see into the matter and return shortly."

"With all due respect, Magus," the official cut in, "Captain Baraz has directed the entire company to return to the shore. A large trade caravan has just completed processing, and your group would block its path across the bridge. I'm sure the matter will be resolved quickly, and you can be back on your way."

Artaban watched Melchior struggle to suppress a sharp reply and to refrain from grumbling. He heard his old instructor's words echo in his memory. "*Patience is a virtue of the wise. Cultivate it diligently.*" Artaban observed his old *ustead's* internal battle to put his own words into practice.

"Very well," Melchior relented. "Tabor, please turn the support train around and take the animals to the holding area. Captain Vakshuvar, kindly accompany us to the administrative office." He gestured to his companions. "Shall we see what news awaits from Ecbatana?"

The magi and the captain of their security detail turned control of their horses over to the support staff, then followed the messenger off the bridge and back to the River Gate. They approached a stout stone outpost with slotted windows and iron-banded doors. The building functioned as a security checkpoint, a border registry, and a customs house. As they entered, Artaban heard the din of the busy milieu they had just left not so long ago—merchants haggling with tax collectors over the appraised value of their wares, pilgrims seeking passage to holy sites in Syria, messengers insisting that their passes be expedited, clerks cataloging all traffic crossing the border in both directions, and a host of local businessmen selling food and drink to the weary travelers.

The messenger led them through the crowd to a station on the far side of the large hall to where his superior officer awaited.

Melchior got straight to the point. "Captain Baraz, what seems to be the issue? We just recently finished validating our travel clearance here and hoped to make it through Roman customs by the end of the day."

"Forgive the interruption, Esteemed Magus, but I received a message this very moment, directly from the Chancellor himself. It instructs me to recall your party and pass the word that your mission on behalf of the Royal Astronomer has been canceled. See here," he displayed the parchment scroll, "it bears the Chancellor's official seal."

Melchior scanned the document. "This is very odd. The Chancellor offers no further details or explanation for why a journey with such a long period of preparation should be abruptly terminated."

"A regrettable situation," Captain Baraz replied, "but, as you can see, the message directs your party to return to the capital for further consultation."

"But our letter from the Royal Astronomer," Belshazzar began, uncapping the leather scroll tube which contained the document authorizing their travel.

"Unfortunately," the captain cut him off, "this directive from the Chancellor supersedes the Royal Astronomer's authorization. I'm afraid my actions are bound by the seal. Unless the king's own sign is laid before me, I cannot allow your party to pass."

"But our mission—" Belshazzar began, but was quickly cut short by Melchior's light touch on his arm.

"We understand your situation, Captain," Melchior offered. "You are quite right to proceed as duty demands. We shall withdraw and seek some redress with the Royal Court. Perhaps we will be able to clarify the matter in a way that allows us to resume our journey with the appropriate clearances necessary for our passage."

Captain Baraz bowed his head slightly in acknowledgment. "May fortune favor your efforts."

As they turned away from the captain's cubicle and headed toward the exit, the next man waiting to conduct his business with the officer caught Artaban's eye and flashed the hint of a smile. Artaban only saw a brief glimpse of the man's face—narrow, angular features with a thin, tightly groomed mustache, a small, pointed beard, and striking hazel eyes.

In the next moment, Melchior's hushed words stole his attention back. "We must all be mindful of the king's admonition to keep our mission distant from his person. Though we operate under a royal commission, the very success of our task requires that our expedition remain concealed from the forces that would oppose it. It appears our anonymity may have been compromised."

After escaping the busyness of the administrative center, they drew aside to discuss their options.

"So are we to abandon our cause?" Gondophares asked.

"The real authority behind our mission is not even the Great King," Belshazzar interjected. "Our true mandate comes from the Lord of Heaven, himself. If indeed we serve the divine throne of Ahura Mazda, we must not turn aside."

"And just how, exactly, do you propose we go about doing that?" Artaban countered. "It's not as if we can simply swim the Euphrates on our horses and camels. Even if we did, I doubt the Roman guards on the other shore would welcome our incursion with open arms."

"We had originally planned to cross at Thapsacus," Belshazzar suggested. "Perhaps that route yet remains open before us. We still have our letter of authorization from Lord Vahman."

"Truly, Belshazzar," Artaban stepped forward to confront him. "You would have us openly defy the Chancellor? In an open confrontation, do you really think the king would come to our defense? Do you imagine that even Lord Vahman himself would not withdraw from the fight? Would it be worth sacrificing his position in the Court to protect us? Surely you are not so naive as to believe we would have any defenders in the capital."

"Brothers," Melchior began, "let us not quarrel among ourselves. If our charter is indeed from the great Ahura Mazda, then let us appeal to his divine authority to clear the way before us."

In that moment, the man Artaban had seen at the border post, with the thin beard and the piercing hazel eyes, brushed past. He tilted his head sideways slightly and grinned. "Kind regards from Rostan," he declared as he pressed on and disappeared into the milling crowd.

"What—" Gondophares began as he watched the man's retreating form, but was cut short by the voice of the official who had first approached them on the bridge.

"Magus Melchior," the man called out, waving them down. "There has been a change in the situation." He handed Melchior a rolled document with the official stamp of the border security detachment. "Your transit is approved. You are free to cross the bridge at your convenience."

"What exactly—" Belshazzar began, but was hushed by a sharp glance from Melchior.

"Our thanks to your captain," Melchior said with a nod. "We greatly appreciate his efforts on our behalf. Please express our gratitude to him." He dismissed the officer, who bowed slightly and turned away.

Melchior grinned at his companions. "We submitted ourselves to the divine will of our Great God, and it seems he has sent us a champion through his servant, Rostan, to clear the path ahead." He lifted his hands in a gesture of thanks. "Praise be to the Author of Light and Wisdom."

"Praise be to his name," the others echoed.

As they turned to locate the rest of their company, Captain Vakshuvar walked up next to Melchior. Artaban thought he seemed more watchful and guarded somehow but couldn't determine exactly why. Perhaps it was something in the commander's posture or demeanor.

"Magus Melchior," Captain Vakshuvar said in low tones. "I expected to run into the typical kinds of dangers on a journey like this—bandits, thieves, and the like. And I knew we might face some limited opposition from Rome. But I was not informed of potential threats from our own people. I get the idea this is more than just a scholar's errand. The Chancellor is a powerful man. That changes the security situation considerably."

His statement confirmed Artaban's own apprehension and

made him wonder how much more dangerous this ill-fated mission had just become.

"Papers," the Roman border guard demanded from Tadmor. He eyed the party closely as the caravan master produced the letter of authorization from Lord Vahman. The letter read as follows:

> To the Governors and Officers of the Eastern Provinces of Rome, Peace and honor in the name of King Phraates IV, Sovereign of Parthia.
>
> The bearers of this letter—Melchior of Babylon, Belshazzar of Nippur, Gondophares of Sakastan, and Artaban of Ctesiphon—are scholars of Parthia, being learned in the arts of astronomy and ancient wisdom. They are charged by our royal authority to observe and interpret rare celestial events.
>
> Their journey includes consultation with learned men in the land of Judea who are knowledgeable in the sacred writings of the Hebrew people, and, with favor, a brief audience with Herod, King of the Jews, as a formal courtesy of visiting dignitaries. They bear small gifts to King Herod as tokens of respect on behalf of the Parthian Court.
>
> Their party includes personnel appropriate to meet their security and support needs during a journey of this nature.
>
> In Service of Wisdom,
> Vahman, Royal Astronomer of Parthia
> Ecbatana, in the 41st Year of the King's Reign

It was late in the day, and the sun was already setting behind them. The delay on the Parthian side of the border had cost them precious time. Artaban hoped they could pass through the Roman customs checks quickly and travel well beyond the Roman military outpost before they would need to stop for the night.

"State your business," the officer directed.

Though Melchior was the senior member of their party, and though all the magi understood the Greek language fluently, still they allowed Tadmor, as caravan master, to speak on behalf of the group.

"As you can see in the letter, the Parthian Royal Astronomer commissions these distinguished magi to consult the learned men of Judea on a matter of ancient prophecy and celestial events. Nothing more."

The officer inspected the seal on the scroll. Vahman's insignia would be much less common on documents of transit than that of the local satrap, who would typically authorize trade caravans to do business in the Roman provinces. After a few moments, he looked up to scrutinize the party members more closely.

"Your scholars come heavily guarded for a philosophical discussion," he grumbled.

"The road is long," Tadmor replied, "and we travel alone, without the company of a large caravan."

"Hmph," the officer grunted. "Wait here," he directed and disappeared into a small building, leaving them under the watchful eye of a squad of Roman soldiers who stood ready to enforce the often contentious decisions of the centurion who managed operations at the border checkpoint.

After a long moment, during which the group waited in restless silence, the officer returned.

"We'll need to see a full travel manifest for yourself and the servants as well as the armament permits and sponsor seals of your guards. However, operations are closing for the day, so you will be required to camp in the containment area for the evening. We will continue processing your party in the morning."

"But surely—" Tadmor objected.

"Soldier," the official cut him off, gesturing to a nearby member of the Roman squad. "Escort these men to the outer compound. Notify the decanus on duty to hold them until their documents are reviewed."

Artaban heard Belshazzar whisper to Melchior, "Can't we do something? Further delays might jeopardize our arrival in Damascus prior to the final conjunction."

"My understanding of the Roman authorities," Melchior replied, "is that argument simply makes the process longer and more complicated. Bribery may be an effective method to expedite matters, but that is not the way of the Lord of Truth and Light."

"Of course," Belshazzar agreed. "My only concern is for the success of our mission."

"I suggest we cooperate as best we can. It has been a very long day, with many unexpected turns. We are freshly supplied from our stay in Zeugma. A hearty meal and a good night's rest would be the best preparation for the next leg of our journey."

"As you say, Wise Master," Belshazzar conceded.

They followed the soldier to the designated area. Another small party had already pitched their tents in the holding compound, though the large trade caravan they heard about at the Parthian checkpoint was nowhere to be seen. Apparently, that group had passed through with no issues.

After erecting their own camp and finishing a hasty meal of flatbread, dried fruit, goat jerky, hard cheese, and nuts, the magi all retired to their tents. Artaban lay on his mat, listening to the animal handlers grooming the beasts before bedding down for the night.

Eventually, the stillness of evening settled over the compound, but sleep would not come for Artaban. He tossed and turned all night, wrestling with memories from his childhood and an ominous feeling of dread from being held in bondage at a Roman military outpost. Why were they encountering all these obstacles on their journey? Was the Lord of Wisdom and Truth trying to stop them from making a terrible mistake? Or was the Enemy attempting to block their path and divert them from completing their divinely inspired mission? Was their interpretation of this omen even correct at all?

His biggest question was how he had become embroiled in the whole affair. This was not his chosen path. He had not advocated for a diplomatic delegation to King Herod. He had advised caution at every juncture. And yet fate had set him wandering blindly down the same path his father had trod. Would he meet with the same end?

At some point, amid the swirling turmoil of his thoughts, he mercifully drifted into a restless sleep.

Artaban jolted awake at the sound of marching feet and a string of barked orders. "Everyone up. Out of your tents." The commands were in Greek.

Images flashed through Artaban's memory of an immense golden eagle glaring in the sun, and iron-shod sandals clattering on the cobbles, as soldiers in chain mail shirts and bronze helmets stepped over his body on their way to his father's chambers. A cry escaped his throat, "Father, nooo," before the specters of his dreams slowly faded and he was able to refocus his attention on the present situation.

He poked his head out of the tent. The sun edged up over the horizon, casting a pale orange glow over the rolling hills outside the compound. A squad of Roman soldiers in light armor, wielding short *gladius* swords, stood at the ready. A sense of foreboding swept over Artaban. This didn't look like a farewell party to send them happily on their way.

"Tadmor of Dura, show yourself," the officer bellowed.

Moments later, Artaban saw Belshazzar emerge from his own tent and approach the commander.

"What's the problem, officer?" Belshazzar asked.

"Are you Tadmor of Dura?"

"No. I'm Belshazzar, a magus of the Ekur Temple in Nippur, and one of the scholars appointed by the Royal Astronomer of the Parthian Court to confer with our Hebrew counterparts. Tadmor is escorting us to Jerusalem. Perhaps I can be of assistance."

"We will indeed need to question you further about your purpose in visiting Jerusalem." The officer signaled to one of the soldiers. "Take this man to the detention area. Treat him with respect, but ensure he's separated from the others until he's questioned by the centurion."

"Excuse me—" Belshazzar protested, but was silenced by a gesture from the officer that prompted the guard to escort him away.

"I need the following men to report here, now: Tadmor of Dura, Magus Melchior of Babylon, Magus Gondophares of Sakastan, Magus Artaban of Ctesiphon, and Captain Vakshuvar of Susa. The rest of you stay in this compound. You will be summoned if needed."

Artaban ducked back inside his shelter and hastily wrapped himself in a traveling robe and trousers while slipping soft leather sandals on his feet. He barely had time to cover his head with a simple scarf before he heard the officer again shouting for them to present themselves immediately.

The officer addressed the men when they finally assembled. "You are to be detained for further questioning about the nature and purpose of your travel in the Roman territories. You will be held separately until you appear before the garrison commander. Your escorts will treat you with the respect due your station and endeavor to meet your immediate needs. Once you are cleared, you will be permitted to return to this compound and await approval of your departure."

"I must protest, Optio," Tadmor blurted. "These men are dignitaries appointed by the Parthian Court—"

The officer waved him off. "Protest to Centurion Varro. You'll see him soon enough."

With that, soldiers stepped forward to escort each of the men across the compound and into a nearby building. Before he was ushered away, Melchior handed Simur off to Burzoe, the caravan's steward. The bird fluttered his wings and squawked, "Brack. Looks like trouble."

A guard led Artaban to a small room where a cushion rested on the floor beside a low table. On it sat a jug of water, a cup, and a platter laden with flatbread, dried dates, and pistachios. His escort posted himself outside the door, but left it open. Apparently, they did not want him to feel as if he was being held prisoner. But Artaban would have preferred to be chained to a wall in a barred cell than to be held under the watchful eye of a Roman soldier. He sat down on the rough stone floor. Though his stomach grumbled, he ignored the food on the table. Instead, he leaned back against the wall and wrestled with the dark shadows of his past.

The sun's early rays shone through a small window, leaving a spot of brightness on the floor. Artaban barely noticed it slowly creep across the unused cushion and eventually disappear as morning pressed on to afternoon. Still, no one came to summon him.

At one point, he heard a new soldier come to relieve the guard outside his room. Shortly thereafter, a servant arrived with fresh water and more food, but seeing that the previous meal remained untouched, he left without a word. Otherwise, there was no activity to interrupt Artaban's worried rumination over a future course of events that had been taken entirely out of his control. He need not have concerned himself about how the Romans might perceive the magi's visit to King Herod's court or their search for a Jewish messiah, for now it appeared they would never make it past the Empire's border.

Though he loathed the notion of interacting with the guard in any way, nature's call eventually forced Artaban to ask if he could leave the room to relieve himself. The soldier just gestured to an earthenware pot in the far corner of the room.

Finally, as the darkness of evening cast its pall over his little cell, a messenger arrived and announced that the centurion was ready to speak with the magus. The soldier motioned for him to stand and then guided him down a maze of hallways to a closed wooden door. After he knocked three times on the wooden frame, a bold, resonant voice replied from within.

"Enter."

"*Domine*, I've brought the detainee, as ordered."

"Wait outside. I'll call when I'm finished." He gestured for the soldier to leave.

"I am Centurion Lucius Aelius Varro, commander of this garrison. I have questions about your traveling party and your purpose in visiting Jerusalem. I've already spoken with the rest of your companions, and I trust your responses will be consistent with what I've learned thus far. You magi are dedicated to the principles of truth and justice, are you not?" He continued without pausing for a reply. "So, I would expect nothing less than the truth from one commissioned by the Royal Astronomer of the Parthian Court."

Artaban remained silent. He wondered what suspicions this man harbored, and what consequences would follow if he disclosed their mission's true intent. The centurion was correct. He would not lie, even to save his own life. But in truth, they didn't actually know what the signs in the heavens might portend. They had theories, but they wouldn't know for certain until their journey was complete. If this man wanted the truth, that's precisely what he'd get. Artaban saw no reason at all to share what was merely speculation at this point.

"You are…" he glanced over to a scribe who was scratching notes onto a wax tablet.

"He is Magus Artaban of Ctesiphon, *Domine*," the clerk replied.

"Ctesiphon…" the officer muttered, almost to himself. "The winter capital." He paused briefly before continuing. "Are you, Artaban of Ctesiphon, a nobleman? Is your family part of the Parthian Court? One of… What do you call them? Ah yes, one of the Great Houses?"

Artaban's blood ran cold. Did this man know who he was? Could he somehow have discovered his family background? Had an agent of the Chancellor disclosed his identity to the Roman authorities? He fought to prevent his hands from shaking and to keep a tremor from revealing itself in his voice.

"No, Centurion Varro. I'm from a family of scholars, not statesmen. My father was a minor servant to the Parthian Court —no one of any distinction."

"Hmm," Varro grunted. "How is it that you have been chosen to represent the Royal Astronomer on an important liaison mission with the Jews?"

Artaban glanced nervously around the room. The accoutrements reflected a mix of Roman practicality and power. Centurion Varro sat behind a stout oak desk, with clean lines and a dark stain. His bronze helmet, with its red plume, sat on a small table in the corner where his personal *gladius* rested. The unit standard hung on its staff, held upright in a wooden base. A large map of the border region dominated the wall. Below it, a marble bust of Emperor Augustus sat on a shelf, as if to emphasize who ruled over this territory.

"Well…" Varro again prompted.

"As you may be aware, Centurion, I'm the junior member of

our group. I commonly collaborate on celestial research with Magus Belshazzar and Magus Gondophares. I was only included with this company because of my association with these men."

"And what exactly is the purpose of your journey?"

"As our appointment letter from the Royal Astronomer states, we plan to confer with our Hebrew counterparts on issues concerning—"

"Yes, yes," he cut Artaban off with a dismissive wave. "I'm well aware of what your commissioning letter says. But why consult with the Jews? Why not go to Rome? We have many more accomplished astronomers in the Empire's capital city."

Artaban rarely thought quickly under pressure. He could reason through complex issues very well when given time, but would often struggle to provide solid answers in the midst of a conversation. There were many occasions when he would look back after the fact and regret a poorly framed response. And though he had expected this very kind of question when confronting Roman officials about their mission, in this moment he could not think of a suitable reply.

"Well..." he stammered, "we intend to consult them on the religious meaning of celestial signs, not on the movement patterns of astronomical bodies. We share similar monotheistic faiths and have noticed common themes in the writings of their prophets and ours."

"A single god," Varro muttered, shaking his head. "You'd better be careful with that nonsense. You never know what other gods you might offend when touting those notions."

Artaban had no response, so he waited silently for the next question in the assault.

"What can you tell me about the other scholars in your party? Do you know them well? Do they have any commercial interests in the Syrian province?"

Commercial interests? That question took Artaban by

surprise. But he could again provide a completely candid response with no regrets.

"I have known these men for over fifteen years. Magi Belshazzar and Gondophares are research colleagues at the Ekur Temple, and we are all former students of Master Melchior. I am confident that none of them has commercial interests in any Roman territory."

"What about your caravan master?"

"Tadmor?" Artaban asked. When the centurion nodded in affirmation, he continued. "I had never met him before we started preparing for this journey. He was contracted by an administrator of the Court in Ecbatana."

"Has he mentioned any business ventures? What trade goods is your caravan carrying for barter in the Syrian province?"

The topic of commerce again caused Artaban to wonder. Was there some hidden issue in this regard? Or was it a questioning tactic to throw him off guard?

"We've brought only provisions to meet our own needs and enough currency to resupply when we run low. That's all declared in our documentation. We have no goods for barter or trade. As for the caravan master, I've not spoken to him extensively. I know he's led several other excursions to Damascus and Jerusalem. It's why he was chosen to be our guide. But I don't know anything about his other ventures. As I said, I only met him shortly before we set out."

"I see," he muttered thoughtfully.

The man was very matter-of-fact in his manner. He didn't raise his voice or gesture much at all. He appeared to be somewhat stoic and very calculating. To Artaban, this was very disconcerting. He would prefer to deal with someone who was brash or arrogant or even hostile. He knew such people almost always acted out of insecurity, putting up a facade of bravado to cover over internal anxiety or fear. But Artaban wondered if this military commander's calm, almost indifferent demeanor might mask something sinister or dangerous beneath the surface.

"What can you tell me about the commander of your guard detail?" Varro continued after a moment of thoughtful reflection.

"Not much, I'm afraid. I did chat with Captain Vakshuvar briefly one evening around the campfire. He's from a region in northeastern Parthia where he's served primarily as an escort for trade caravans and diplomatic missions along the eastern trade routes to Bactra and Sogdiana."

"Is that all?" Varro prompted.

"He told me a story about a time when he led a small band of six men across the salt desert to recover a nobleman from one of the Great Houses who was being held for ransom by bandits near Herat. He returned with five of the soldiers and the hostage, for which he was rewarded with rank and honors."

"Hmm," the centurion murmured. "I wonder why a soldier who earned a reputation in the East would be assigned to guard a convoy heading west into Roman lands, where he knows neither the people, the languages, nor the customs."

When Artaban remained silent, Varro raised his eyebrows, inviting a response.

"I'm afraid I wouldn't know. I didn't ask, and he didn't volunteer a reason."

"You don't seem to know the people you're traveling with as well as one might expect, especially when you're relying on their skills and trustworthiness to see you safely to your destination."

"I rely on my God," Artaban replied, perhaps a bit too adamantly.

"Ah, yes. Your God," Varro mused. "That brings me back to my original question. What specific theological matters do you intend to discuss with the Jewish scholars in Jerusalem? What signs in the heavens did you observe that prompted this expedition?"

Artaban hoped that by being overly technical in his response, it would either confuse or bore the centurion, so he framed his answer in that way. He also used the Parthian names for the celestial bodies instead of their Greek or Roman counterparts, with which Centurion Varro might be more familiar.

"My colleagues and I discovered a prediction in our almanacs about a triple conjunction of the Wanderers, *Marduk* and *Ninub,* within the constellation of *Ea.* These conjunctions were all projected to occur within a period of less than twelve months. During the final conjunction, *Marduk* and *Ninub* would be joined by *Nergal.* This is a rare occurrence, which we felt warranted further investigation."

Varro just stared blankly at him for several moments, then finally asked, "And what does this have to do with the Jews?"

"We brought the matter to the attention of our mentor, Magus Melchior, and he felt the writings of ancient Jewish prophets might provide insights from similar conjunctions in the past. One particular Hebrew prophet who commented on these types of issues also served in the Babylonian and Persian courts. We had access to copies of his writings from approximately six hundred years ago, but were uncertain as to the exact interpretation. When we raised the issue with the Royal Astronomer, he suggested we consult with experts in Jewish theology."

"And what exactly is the meaning of this rare sign in the heavens?"

"That's the problem. We don't really know. It's the reason we're traveling to Jerusalem to consult with others who might have deeper knowledge of the subject. Depending on what we learn from our Hebrew counterparts, we may next request to confer with the Roman scholars you mentioned a moment ago. We simply felt the sign was too rare to ignore."

Artaban was relieved to see that Centurion Varro did, in fact, look somewhat bored with the whole affair. Hopefully, he would perceive no threat to Roman authority from such a banal visit.

"One final question," he said. "What about the gold, incense, and spices? Those are controlled commodities."

"Yes, Centurion. They're token amounts to be presented as gifts of courtesy if we're granted an audience with King Herod. They're declared in our transit documents, as required, and are not for barter or sale."

Centurion Varro looked at Artaban long and hard, apparently judging him with the studied eyes of a soldier who had stared down formidable opponents on the field of battle. After a long moment, he called to the legionary who waited outside the door.

"Return this man to his caravan in the holding compound." Turning his attention back to Artaban, he finished up, "You and your companions will await my decision regarding your travel permit."

He dismissed the two with a wave of his hand.

Back at the caravan, Artaban discovered that the other magi and the captain of the guard had undergone similar questioning.

"Our caravan master is the only one who still hasn't returned," Melchior commented, poking a stick at a fire their steward had kindled in the center of their impromptu camp. "I expect he'll appear soon and recount an experience similar to our own."

"They're asking the right questions and taking detailed notes," Captain Vakshuvar observed. "This isn't routine border screening. Someone's specifically interested in your mission.

Believe me, Roman soldiers couldn't care less about a bunch of scholars doing academic research. So something must've gotten their attention."

"Well, what do we do?" Gondophares asked.

"If our Great God has indeed called us for this mission, the Romans will approve our travel and we'll be on our way," Melchior answered.

"Albeit," Belshazzar cut in, "with a delay that may very well prevent us from reaching Damascus in time to observe the final conjunction."

"Patience, my friends," Melchior counseled. "I've lived long enough to learn that Ahura Mazda's plans cannot be confounded, no matter the obstacles that may arise. I believe he gave us the signs in the heavens, and he has guided us thus far. If that's true, then he'll likewise prepare the path before us. When Tadmor returns and our transit is authorized, we must be prepared to strike out."

But three days passed, and Tadmor never returned. Neither was there any word from the Roman authorities. At that point, even Melchior's patience was wearing thin. Artaban followed him as he approached the guard on duty.

"Soldier," he began, "I would like to speak with your centurion. We have been held here for over three days now. We are on an official mission on behalf of the Parthian Court, and it's of utmost importance that we proceed with all haste. In addition, our caravan master was taken away for questioning and hasn't returned. We need some answers."

The guard appeared to be unfazed by the old man's state of distress. "My orders are to hold your party here until the commander makes his decision. He directed us to ensure you have access to the necessities of food, water, and firewood while you await a determination in your case. However, he has refused any additional audiences."

"I must insist—"

The soldier shook his head, cutting him off. "You may go back to Parthia at any time. Other than that, I have my orders to detain you here."

Just then, a stocky man with a confident bearing emerged out of a nearby doorway, glanced around the compound, and then proceeded over to where Melchior and Artaban were speaking with the guard. As he approached, he reached out a hand and touched Melchior lightly on the arm—a gesture of familiarity that shocked Artaban, but to which Melchior did not react.

"Greetings, friends," he said in fluent Aramaic, a language the soldier was unlikely to know. "Might I have a word with you and your companions? I bring news of the garrison commander's deliberations."

"Who—" Artaban began.

"Please," the man gestured calmly toward the other members of the caravan. "I can address your questions when we've joined the others."

Artaban watched Melchior appraise the man, then nod and step off toward the caravan.

As they walked, the man said, "My words might best be reserved for the scholars in your party. I presume the others will take direction from you, correct?"

"Yes," Melchior confirmed. "Artaban, would you kindly ask our fellows to join us?"

Soon thereafter, the four magi had gathered some distance apart from the rest of the caravan. The others, especially Captain Vakshuvar, watched with obvious irritation that they had been excluded from the conversation.

"I have just spoken to the garrison commander," the stranger began.

"Wait," Belshazzar interrupted him. "Who exactly are you? How do we know your information is reliable?"

As the man replied, Artaban noted his appearance. He

looked to be about forty years of age, of medium height and stocky build, with thinning brown hair. He was clean-shaven in the Roman style and wore a leather tunic with bronze fittings. Artaban was struck by the man's sharp, calculating eyes that seemed to miss nothing.

"I am Lucius Volusius Niger of Hierapolis, about forty miles from here. My patron is a man of some influence in this region. He finances trade caravans and holds some important supply contracts with the military. He was notified of your mission and sent me to monitor your border crossing to ensure it was unimpeded."

"He was informed of our mission?" Belshazzar once again jumped in where Melchior should have been speaking on behalf of the group. "By whom?"

"Let's just say that he and Rostan have a good working relationship. They assist each other on either side of the river."

"Very good," Melchior resumed control of the conversation. "We appreciate any assistance you can provide with our current situation. You said you bring information from the centurion."

"Yes," Volusius replied. "I'm afraid your caravan master has been detained by the authorities for tax and trade violations from his previous travels into the Syrian province. He has been charged with some rather serious crimes. Unfortunately, your association with him has brought all the members of your party under the highest scrutiny."

"We must resume our travel immediately," Belshazzar again inserted himself. "We need to be in Damascus by the end of November—"

"To observe the final conjunction," Volusius finished Belshazzar's thought. "Yes, I know. I was able to convince Centurion Varro that you and the rest of your party share no culpability with your caravan master's crimes. He has agreed to issue writs of transit for your company. Regrettably, Tadmor won't be able to accompany you on the journey."

"It's imperative that we have our caravan master to proceed," Belshazzar insisted. "We don't know the routes. If he owes some sort of back taxes or fines, I'm certain we can arrange for those to be paid."

"If it were only the tax issues, their remittance, plus certain administrative fees, might resolve the problem. But Tadmor is, sadly, implicated in a larger illicit trade ring. I expect the authorities will try to pressure him to betray the more influential parties involved. There's simply no chance you'll be able to retain his services."

"You said your patron is involved in financing caravans. Would he be able to locate a replacement caravan master for us?" Melchior inquired.

"For the right price, I'm certain we could find a suitable man for the job."

"How soon?" Belshazzar interjected.

"It's a long journey, and this is short notice. The best guides are contracted months in advance by very lucrative trade caravans. But we could probably arrange for a qualified leader within two or three weeks."

"No," Belshazzar lamented. "No, that won't do. We don't have that much time."

Volusius shrugged. "I'm afraid that's the best I can offer. And even that's not a guarantee. I'd need to do some searching."

Artaban had been reticent to join the conversation, but felt he had to raise an issue they may've overlooked. "Are we missing something here?" he began, and they all looked at him. "First, we had trouble with the Chancellor's message on the other side of the river. Now, our caravan master has been detained for criminal activity. Perhaps Ahura Mazda is trying to get our attention and turn us away from a ruinous path."

Belshazzar almost pounced on Artaban in return. "No! The omens in the heavens are clearly a message from our God. The prophetic writings affirm our course. Even the Royal

Astronomer and our Divine King endorsed the mission. These obstacles have been placed in our path by the forces of darkness to dissuade us from our purpose. The Father of Light surely allows these hindrances in order to test our resolve. Beware, Artaban, with which side you align yourself."

Artaban bristled at the accusation, and he struggled to retain his bearing. "How exactly do you propose we proceed without a caravan master?"

"I say we press on without Tadmor. We trust in our Great God to guide us. He'll provide a light to illuminate our path," Belshazzar quipped.

"That's well and good for spiritual guidance. But we need to know which direction to travel through a desert. That's an altogether more pragmatic issue."

"Brack," Simur crowed from his perch on Melchior's shoulder. "Find a guide. Find a guide."

"The road is well traveled, is it not?" Gondophares offered. "Surely we can follow in the path of the trade caravans that traverse this route. I've spoken with our husbandmen. Both of them have traveled this way many times."

"We can't delay any longer," Belshazzar declared. "Every day we waste here, we risk making Damascus in time for the final convergence. The stars will not wait for us."

Gondophares nodded. "The road lies open. We have provisions, guards, and the stars. Tadmor was useful, yes, but not indispensable. Tabor knows the routes well enough."

"Tabor is a competent animal handler," Artaban shot back, "but he's not a caravan master. That road is longer than you think, and less forgiving. Will the stars guard us from a well gone dry? Or guide us past the tribes who'll slit our throats to steal our horses?"

Melchior stroked his beard thoughtfully. "The concerns of both sides have merit. Artaban's caution is wise. The desert is unforgiving of poor decisions. Yet Belshazzar's urgency is also justified. The conjunction approaches whether we are prepared or not."

"I'm not the right man to consult on matters of faith," Volusius remarked. "But I would urge caution when striking out along this route. The road to Damascus is well traveled, but conditions are unpredictable, and bandits grow bold. And you carry valuable gifts that will attract attention."

"What would you counsel?" Melchior asked.

"Travel light and fast. Hire local guides at each major stop. Keep your identity concealed. Perhaps claim to be consulting physicians. Wealthy scholars present too tempting of prey," Volusius suggested. "There are great perils in undertaking such a journey, but you have significant support in your party, so it is possible."

"You see," Belshazzar said. "This man knows the risks and still believes we can succeed."

"Not exactly," Volusius countered. "Magus Melchior merely asked what counsel I would offer if you choose to go forward. But I do believe the dangers are very great."

"We have a sacred mission," Gondophares insisted. "We swore an oath before King Phraates to complete this task. Would you have us return to Ecbatana as failures, bearing news that we abandoned our duty at the first sign of difficulty?"

"I counsel caution, not failure," Volusius corrected. "There's a difference."

Artaban lifted his hands in exasperation. "Gondophares, you speak of sacred missions while ignoring basic prudence. We are four aging scholars with a handful of guards, traveling through territories where Roman authority grows thin."

"Brack," Simur squawked, his cry cutting through the tension in the air. "Who do you trust?"

Melchior gestured the arguing men to silence. "I've spent my life studying the movements of the heavens and the words of ancient prophets. Never in all my years have I seen such a clear convergence of signs. The stars themselves cry out that a momentous time has come." He paused, his voice taking on the weight of deep conviction. "But more than astronomical calculations compel me. I feel deep down inside that we stand at a turning point of the ages. The great Ahura Mazda has set us on this path. To turn back now would not be mere prudence, but faithlessness."

Artaban shifted uncomfortably. "Master, your wisdom is profound, but—"

Melchior placed a reassuring hand on Artaban's shoulder. "Do you think the Wise Lord brought us this far to abandon us now? Did he not provide Rostan's agent to secure our release? Did he not guide us past the Parthian border guards and through Roman customs? Have we so little faith in his protection?"

Artaban sighed deeply. "I can't deny the signs we've observed. But still I fear not only for our safety, but for that of our kingdom."

"Your caution has served us well," Melchior assured him. "Continue to be our voice of prudence. But don't let prudence become paralysis."

Volusius nodded. "If you proceed, I can provide letters of introduction to reliable contacts in Damascus."

Belshazzar looked around the group. "Then we are decided. We continue to Damascus."

One by one, they nodded—first Gondophares, then Melchior, and finally, reluctantly, Artaban.

"Very well," Melchior said. "We depart at first light. May the Wise Lord guide our steps."

CHAPTER SIX

Late Autumn / Early Winter, 7 BC
Road to Damascus, Syrian Province, Roman Empire

Dust clouded Artaban's vision as he urged his horse toward the city gates, desperately trying to keep pace with Asparak, a member of their security detail. Blood caked his sleeve where a bandit's arrow had grazed him. Behind him, the sounds of steel and screaming still rang in his ears. Tabor, the camel driver, was down, and Belshazzar was unaccounted for. They had to reach the Romans before it was too late.

Their group had extended their travel into the twilight hours in an attempt to reach Damascus that day. The final conjunction was predicted to occur the very next night, and they wanted a chance to get settled into the city and establish contact with the scholars at the temple observatory before the event occurred. Despite a host of errors, disruptions, and delays, they had managed to get within a long day's ride of their immediate destination, and everyone was ready to avail themselves of the city's amenities and a much-needed rest.

Then, when they could just begin to see the city walls in the waning light of sunset, the road dipped into a narrow wooded valley. They had been pushing the horses and camels hard, and the beasts desperately needed to refresh themselves in the stream of water that flowed through the gorge. As soon as they had dismounted, a barrage of arrows streaked into the group from multiple directions. Artaban, still on his horse, felt a sharp bite as a shaft cut through his tunic and sliced a gash in his upper arm. His horse reared and wheeled as chaos broke out all around him. He saw Tabor fall to the ground with a bolt in his chest. More arrows struck two of the guards as the security detail drew their weapons and hastily formed a defensive line.

Then Captain Vakshuvar shouted Artaban's name and pointed his sword down the road. Asparak, the only security guard still on his mount, waved for him to follow and raced off toward Damascus. The soldier charged at two ruffians who blocked the road, trampling one and slashing at the other with his blade. A final volley of shafts streaked past their heads, but they had soon galloped out of range and were on the way to get help. They could only hope the remaining guards could fend off the attackers long enough for them to return with a security force from the city.

Artaban followed Asparak as he veered away from the city gate to a watchtower off to the right. He shouted in Latin to one of the soldiers on duty. "We need the *stationarii*! Our caravan of Parthian dignitaries is under attack."

The five closest soldiers raised their spears and pointed them directly at Artaban and Asparak. "Halt!" one commanded as their horses came within a few yards of the outpost.

"Now, man. We need help now. Our caravan is under attack this very moment."

"I'll need to see your papers," the soldier demanded.

"Damn the papers!" Asparak shouted back. "Where's your *optio*?"

An officer emerged from the tower door and strode immediately up to the group of men.

"Here now, Marcus. What's the issue?"

The soldier began to respond, "*Optio*, these men—"

Asparak and Artaban both reigned their mounts in tightly as they struggled to calm the beasts after their frantic dash for help.

"*Optio*," Asparak cut the soldier off, "our caravan of Parthian dignitaries is under attack by brigands in the ravine just four miles down the road. Our security detail can hold them off for a short while, but we need a force of *stationarii* now or it'll be too late."

The officer looked them over for a long moment, locking eyes with each man. Images flashed through Artaban's mind of similar cold, calculating eyes peering out from behind another bronze helmet many years ago at their family's home, not too far from this very place, and he couldn't hold this Roman's gaze. His eyes flickered to the ground.

Perhaps it was something the officer saw in Asparak's demeanor—the recognition of truth spoken by a fellow soldier —or perhaps he assessed Artaban to actually be a scholar, despite his appearance. But for whatever reason, they gained his confidence.

"Ready the detachment," the *optio* barked. "We ride when the last man is saddled."

As the cavalrymen mounted their horses, the reality of the situation washed over Artaban, and a wave of nausea swept over him. Memories from his childhood flooded his mind. He could not believe he was seeking the aid of Romans in this city where Romans had virtually destroyed his life. He had expected an auxiliary cohort of Syrian soldiers to be stationed at Damascus, not Roman legionaries. But just the sight of the bronze helmets, the chain mail armor, and the red cloaks of the soldiers made him shudder. The force represented by these men was dangerous and untrustworthy. And yet, the dangerous force they wielded with their longswords and javelins was the only thing that might save his companions from the bandits accosting them.

"Lead on," the *optio* directed Asparak, who then dug his heels into his mount's side.

Asparak glanced back at Artaban, who had decided his presence was of no use in this fight. He was a scholar, not a warrior. But Asparak must have sensed this reticence and pointed vehemently down the road. He shouted to Artaban, "We need every man," then galloped away.

Artaban wrestled with his conflicting emotions a moment longer, but as the last man of the cavalry troop rode out of the stable yard, he reluctantly fell in behind the rear of the formation.

As it turned out, he was not needed for the fight. The mere sight of the *stationarii* cohort charging down the hill caused the rogues to flee. But Asparak was correct in a different way. Though the Romans turned the tide of the battle, they then pursued the thieves into the night, leaving the caravan members to gather their scattered animals and tend to their own wounded.

Tabor, their substitute caravan master, had bled out from the arrow to his chest. After bandaging the superficial wound on his own arm, Artaban helped wrap Tabor's body and secure it to one of the mules. Three of the guards had also been injured. One had received a cut on his thigh that was relatively minor, but the other two would need extended care in Damascus. Thankfully, the magi had all come through unscathed, save for Artaban's minor scrape. And Belshazzar eventually emerged from a well-concealed position among some rocks near the stream.

Artaban walked over to Captain Vakshuvar as he finished directing the recovery efforts. The soldier shook his head, his weathered face troubled. "In twenty-three years of military service," he muttered, "I've never seen bandits coordinate like that. Professional timing. Good intelligence about our route and numbers. Military-grade equipment." He picked up a discarded sword from the ground and assessed the blade. "Either we've got very bad luck, or someone's investing serious resources to stop this mission."

"Who do you think was behind this?" Artaban asked.

"Hard to say," he replied. "This sword is standard issue for a Roman auxiliary unit. But if the Romans planned this attack, that begs a bigger question."

"What do you mean?"

"Why would a Roman cohort come to our aid if the Romans are determined to turn us back?" He hesitated for a moment. "Actually, I can't figure out how you convinced them to muster out to begin with. If I was a garrison commander, I would never send out a troop based on the word of two random travelers. That's just begging to ride into an ambush."

"Well, I certainly didn't convince them," Artaban said. "Asparak did all the talking."

"Hmm," he muttered. "In any case, it sure seems like someone's watching our backs. Maybe the old man is right about his god…" He left the thought unfinished as he straightened up and scanned over the scene. "We were outmatched here. If those soldiers hadn't shown up, we'd all be dead."

The remark struck Artaban, and he unconsciously fingered the bandage on his arm.

"How's that wound?" the captain asked.

"I'm fine," Artaban replied. "It's not deep."

"Well, it's probably a good reminder of just how dangerous this business has become," he said, then turned and trudged back up the hill toward the horses.

Exhausted and bloodied, the group reassembled themselves and slowly plodded the remaining distance to Damascus. The city gates were closed and barred by the time they finally arrived, so they had to set up camp outside the walls, but within sight of the watchtower where the *stationarii* were garrisoned.

They had made it to the next waypoint on their journey, but at what cost? Artaban grappled with the thought that the success of their mission might eventually result in even more peril, not only for themselves but also for their kingdom. If these conjectures about a coming messiah were true, and the Roman authorities discovered the real purpose of their journey, the Emperor's fury might descend on all of Parthia, just as the cavalry soldiers had fallen on the highway robbers this night. But for Parthia, there would be nowhere to run from the wrath of Rome.

Having not erected his tent for the night, Artaban eventually fell into a restless sleep under the very stars that had led them down this treacherous road. The final conjunction was at hand. On the evening of the morrow, those same stars would either point them onward or bring this whole reckless endeavor to a merciful end.

"In the name of Ahura Mazda, the Wise Lord," Melchior intoned with his hands lifted to the sky. "We come to lay the body of our brother Tabor to rest, that the purity and sanctity of the earth may remain undefiled."

In the early light of dawn, Artaban and Gondophares had carried Tabor's body into the stone circle, which the men of the security detail had hastily constructed. They had laid him out on a makeshift sky stone where the beasts and the elements would purify his body by scavenging and decomposition.

Melchior's resonant voice continued the litany. "This flesh is now lifeless, but the soul has gone to the *Chinvat* Bridge, where it shall be weighed by the Righteous Judge. If his thoughts were good, his words were true, and his deeds just, may he be welcomed into the House of Song, and dwell in the Light of Ahura Mazda forever. If he bore sins, may the prayers of the righteous and the mercy of the Holy Immortals intercede on his behalf. We commit this body to the Circle of Silence, to be cleansed by the birds of the sky, who fulfill their sacred duty without enmity or malice. Let this act preserve the earth from corruption and honor the wisdom of the Holy Creator. May light prevail over darkness. May truth prevail over the lie. And may the soul of Tabor find peace on the path prepared for him."

As the assembled group stood in reverent silence, paying tribute to their fallen comrade, Artaban was tormented by the memory of how his own mother and father had been denied the honor of this simple ceremony at their deaths not too far from this very place. He didn't even realize the others had completed their silent prayers and walked away until he felt a slight tug on his sleeve and heard Gondophares whisper, "It's time to leave."

They had camped for the night on a hilltop within sight of the watchtower from which their saviors had sallied forth to rescue them on the road the previous evening. Early in the morning, their small retinue had risen and shaken off the weariness of the previous night's horrors. Before turning their attention to the city, they had paused to honor Tabor in the Zoroastrian way. But now, their mission called them onward.

Artaban pulled his travel cloak tighter against the morning chill, wincing at the pain in his arm, and peered down upon the sprawling contours of Damascus. After weeks of arduous travel across the Syrian countryside, sleeping under stars, rationing water, and constantly watching for bandits, the sight of the ancient city's walls brought a mixture of relief and apprehension.

He glanced around and noticed the strain on all their faces. Without Tadmor's expertise, they had relied on Tabor's limited knowledge of the routes and the kindness of other travelers they encountered. There had been a host of unexpected obstacles, some nearly catastrophic, that had delayed their progress and threatened to abort their mission altogether.

They had made several wrong turns that cost them precious time, approached wells with empty water skins only to find them dry, and confronted corrupt officials who demanded illegal taxes and bribes.

On one occasion, they had taken a few steps into a wadi just moments before a flash flood raged through the dry stream bed, drowning one of the pack mules that could not be pulled back in time and creating an impassable river that took two more days to recede.

Several members of the party, including Belshazzar and Gondophares, had fallen ill with a sickness that brought vomiting and diarrhea for nearly a week. It eventually claimed the life of Burzoe, their steward.

Once, they had narrowly escaped a skirmish between three warring villages and, on another occasion, faced accusations of theft from a merchant caravan they'd camped beside on the outskirts of Bambyce.

It was a miracle they had made it this far, and the attack the previous night threatened to push them all over the edge. Artaban himself was more than ready to abandon the ill-fated mission and return to Parthia. Surely the king would not fault them for terminating the effort, considering all the hardships they had faced.

Now, the city stretched out before them like a jewel set in an emerald oasis. The Barada River, fed by the melting snows of the Anti-Lebanon Mountains, nourished a verdant valley dotted with olive groves and fruit orchards. Despite his weariness, Artaban could see why Damascus had been called the "Pearl of the East." Yet beneath his appreciation of the city's beauty lay a gnawing dread he could not shake.

Damascus had flourished under Roman rule as a crucial junction where multiple trade routes converged—the Via Maris from Egypt, the King's Highway from Arabia, and the great east-west routes connecting the Mediterranean with Mesopotamia and the distant Silk Road. Caravans stretched along the avenues leading to all the city's gates, their heavily laden animals and closely guarded wagons bearing testimony to the city's commercial importance.

As their small party drew nearer to the gates, Artaban marveled at the diversity of travelers who shared the road. Nabataean merchants led strings of camels loaded with precious frankincense and myrrh from southern Arabia. Greek traders drove oxcarts filled with amphorae of wine and olive oil. Jewish pilgrims walked alongside their donkeys, making their way to or from Jerusalem. And everywhere, the bronze glint of Roman armor flashed as legionary patrols moved with practiced efficiency.

Captain Vakshuvar rode up alongside them. "The men are tired, Magus Melchior. We've been pushing hard for ten days to reach Damascus before the conjunction. Perhaps we should find lodging first and then seek out these contacts that Volusius mentioned."

"Agreed," the old sage responded. "You can find help for your wounded men while we contact the scholars at the temple observatory." He glanced back to their rear, then added, "Any more word on the watchers who have been trailing us? Could they have been behind the attack?"

Whenever their caravan had traveled through towns or villages, Captain Vakshuvar always sent a man back to see if their visit had engendered any undue attention or if anyone was making inquiries about their activities. It was part of his standard security protocol. Ever since they had crossed over into

Roman territory, some anonymous man or men had been discreetly questioning various merchants and traders about their group. But Captain Vakshuvar had been unable to identify who they were or why they were trailing the magi.

"No more word since Adraa," Vakshuvar replied. "Same situation there with someone asking a lot of questions. We've still never determined who it could be. Maybe someone in the Roman government, since it started at the border. Or maybe it *was* the bandits trying to figure out our vulnerabilities and identify the best opportunity to strike. We'll keep our eyes and ears open, though it'll be more difficult in a city this size and with several of my men out of action."

"I understand," Melchior said. "We appreciate your efforts to keep us all safe."

As they joined the slow-moving queue approaching the eastern gate, Artaban studied the massive stone archway above them. This was the famous Bab Sharqi, the eastern gate of Roman Damascus, where the Straight Street began its mile-long journey across the heart of the old city. Roman engineering had transformed the Aramaean settlement into a model of urban planning, with straight roads, public baths, and impressive temples.

A Roman centurion and his clerks managed the steady flow of traffic entering the city. Tax collectors examined cargo manifests while customs officials searched selected wagons for contraband. The process moved efficiently, but Artaban couldn't help feeling exposed as they drew nearer to the checkpoint.

"Papers and declarations," the Roman official demanded when their turn came.

Melchior produced their travel documents—the letters of transit they had obtained at the Euphrates crossing, along with the authorization from Lord Vahman. The official studied them carefully, occasionally glancing up to appraise the members of their party.

"Parthian magi," he noted. "Purpose of visit?"

"Scholarly consultation," Melchior replied in fluent Greek. "We seek discourse with learned men regarding ancient astronomical observations and prophetic writings."

After routine questions and the payment of fees, the officials waved them through. The moment they passed under the stone arch, Artaban felt as though a weight had settled on his shoulders, and he absentmindedly fingered the bandage on his arm. The wide avenue stretched before them, its stone pavement worn smooth by centuries of foot traffic, hooves, and cart wheels. Shops lined both sides, their wooden awnings providing welcome shade for pedestrians. The air filled with a cacophony of sounds—merchants hawking their wares, the clatter of looms from textile shops, the ring of hammers from metal smiths, and the constant chatter of people conducting business in a dozen different languages.

They found lodging at a respectable inn called the "Merchant's Rest," located on a side street not far from the city's center. The innkeeper, a heavyset Greek named Apollodorus, proved welcoming once he saw their Persian gold coins. He provided clean rooms and a secure stable for their animals.

As the others settled their gear and tended to the wounded guards, Melchior approached Artaban. "Walk with me," the old sage said simply. "Simur needs some air, I think. Perhaps you could use some too."

The starling ruffled his feathers on Melchior's shoulder and squawked, "Brack. Fresh air. Good for the soul."

Artaban was not really in the mood to talk or explore. He

mostly wanted to be alone for a while to sort out his thoughts. But he acquiesced to Melchior's promptings and followed the old man out the door. They made their way out into the street and casually strolled toward the city center.

"Artaban, my son, what troubles you?" Melchior asked.

Artaban shrugged. "Nothing, wise *Usted*. All is well."

"Hmm," Melchior muttered under his breath.

They walked on for several paces, the paving stones of the Decumanus Maximus hard beneath their feet compared to the dusty dirt road they had walked on for weeks.

Finally, Melchior broke the silence. "Do you remember when we studied the movements of Shīr, the Lion, during your training?"

"That was a long time ago, Master."

"But you remember that particular subject with somewhat more clarity than many others, do you not?"

Artaban waited several moments before replying, his thoughts dull with the memories. "I do."

"My mind is not what it once was, but I seem to recall your consternation at discovering the importance that Romans attach to the occasions when the sun passes through Shīr."

Artaban jerked his head toward the nearby Temple of Apollo. "You mean because Caesar Augustus credits his conquest of the East to his god of the sun and of the Lion?"

"Each ancient culture interprets the signs in the heavens in its own way. The same omen might have much different significance to us, to the Greeks, or to the Romans. It's important to understand the various perspectives, because such signs can prompt the movement of either olive branches or spears here on the earth."

"I know this well, Master," Artaban replied.

"Yes, I believe you do. And yet," Melchior went on, "this particular subject troubles your mind even still. I noticed the set of your jaw as we passed by the Roman guards at the Sun Gate when we entered the city. What is it about Romans that causes you to gnash your teeth in their presence?"

"I have no love of Rome," Artaban replied, "but I have great respect for its power." He focused his attention on the bustling crowds that thronged about them as they progressed up the street toward the center of the ancient city. "Listen to them," he said, then paused for a moment. "These are men and women of the East, and yet they speak Greek and Latin and build enormous monuments to Roman gods." He shook his head in disgust. "Rome dominates them. It robs them of their culture and their identity. And they don't even care."

Melchior gestured toward a moderately sized observatory on the left side of the street, adorned at its crest with a row of eight-pointed star rosettes arrayed over cypress trees. "Even so," he countered, "Ahura Mazda, the One True God, maintains a venerable position in this place."

Artaban averted his eyes from the shrine that Melchior pointed out and clenched his teeth. The older man must have noticed his reaction.

"A magus must detach himself from how he wishes things to be and see things as they are. We cannot allow our hopes, dreams, worries, or fears to cloud the night sky and obscure the signs of heaven. Only with clear vision can we rightly understand the guidance of our God." He came to a stop and stared straight into Artaban's eyes. "Your enmity towards Rome appears to run deeper than a concern over the clash of empires. Does something more personal cast a pall over your mind's eye? Do private passions rule your heart?"

Artaban tore his gaze away from the penetrating stare of his old mentor. Almost unconsciously, his eyes came to rest on the temple observatory that now lay just over the older man's shoulder. His thoughts were directed inward, and a few heartbeats passed before he realized what he was looking at.

Melchior must have seen him grimace. Without even turning, the wise sage apparently knew what had caused his reaction.

"Ah, the temple," Melchior raised a hand and stroked his beard. "I know well your zeal for our faith. But I suspect that's not the root of the issue. There's something deeper here, something deep inside your heart."

The old man tilted his head to the right, and Artaban felt the compassion that radiated in the warmth of his expression.

"My son, a wound festers in the dark like mold in a damp cellar. But bring it into the sun, and it begins to dry, to breathe, to heal. Pain concealed becomes rot. Pain revealed becomes a scar. And scars are but the beginning of full restoration."

Artaban took a deep breath. The two men stood alone, like an isolated island amid an ocean of strangers. The milling crowd faded into the background of his awareness, and it was, to Artaban, as if only he and his old *usted* remained.

"My father," he began, "served in that temple. I was just a boy, but I vaguely remember it being built—or modified, at least. I think they were reconfiguring an existing structure."

"You were here during the occupation?"

Artaban nodded. "Yes. When Parthia had taken control of Syria and Palestine from the Romans."

"I didn't know that. You never mentioned this during your training. You must've been very young."

"I was about seven summers old. My father had been a novice advisor in the Court of King Orodes when he was planning the invasion of this province."

"I remember," Melchior said. "The Great King wavered on whether to launch that invasion. I was a senior apprentice to Master Tirdād, who has now sadly passed to be with the *avashan*. He was tasked to search the heavens for a sign that the God of Light would bless the campaign with success. And then, when the moon hid the face of the sun—"

"I know," Artaban cut in. "My father was a strong voice in

the Court, arguing that the eclipse was a sign of Ahura Mazda's favor. He helped convince the Great King's advisors to endorse the invasion plan and to advocate for the offensive. When the army was successful, my father gained great favor with King Orodes. He was given a prestigious assignment at a new temple observatory to be established here in Damascus."

Melchior reflected on Artaban's words for a moment, and his expression slowly turned grim. "Then you were here when the Romans returned..." his voice trailed off.

Artaban took a deep breath, and the images from his childhood flooded his mind. He remembered falling asleep beside the fire in the courtyard of their home, his head cradled in the crook of his arm to cushion it from the rough bricks. The night was crisp and clear, and he stared into the sky, trying to identify the clusters of stars his father had taught him, until his lids grew heavy and he slipped away into a peaceful slumber.

Suddenly, he jolted awake to the sight of an immense golden eagle glaring in the sun. A gentle breeze wafted ashes from the smoldering fire into a swirling column about the raptor, filling the air with a musky odor, and making it appear as if the bird arose from the caldrons of the underworld. Iron-shod sandals clattered on the cobbles as soldiers in chain mail shirts and bronze helmets surged through the courtyard, bypassing him on their way to his father's chambers.

A powerful voice bellowed, "Nazar of Ctesiphon, Royal Astrologer to King Orodes of Parthia, you are charged with inciting rebellion through false prophecy against the authority of Rome."

Several soldiers broke from the ranks, brandishing short swords, and hacked away the woolen curtain covering the entrance to his father's sleeping chamber. Moments later, they wrestled his father through the doorway, his mother wailing in his trail. Sympathetic cries of fear echoed out of the adjoining rooms where his younger brother and sisters were roused by the commotion.

Artaban shook the memories from his mind as he finished relaying the tale to Melchior. "They hung him on a cross outside the Eastern Gate and burned his scrolls at his feet. It took over three days until he breathed his last breath." A shiver crept up Artaban's spine. "They held us back with swords and spears as he cried out for water through sun-parched lips. My mother refused to leave his side. Eventually, she collapsed from exhaustion and despair at a soldier's feet. He kicked her, but she didn't rise." Artaban pressed on his forehead, trying to push back the throbbing pain brought on by the horrible memories. "She never rose again."

Melchior grasped Artaban's shoulder and steadied him with a firm but compassionate hold. "I'm so sorry, my son. I can't begin to imagine the horror of that day, or the pain those memories have brought back. I'm beginning to understand your contempt and your fear of those who would do such a cruel thing."

"The truly sad part is that Rome felt no hatred of my father. They did not loathe him, nor fear him. They felt nothing at all. His torture was just a public spectacle to make a point. Rome had returned. Rome was back in power, and no challenge to Roman authority would be tolerated."

Melchior still held his shoulder in his grasp and squeezed it gently. "The impersonal imperatives of nations have very real and personal consequences. Armies leave a host of innocent victims in their wake. But kings and prophets and soldiers alike must one day face the *Chinvat* Bridge. Those who murdered your parents have fallen to their doom in the House of Lies, while your mother and father have crossed that bridge and ascended to the House of Song. Take comfort in the knowledge that our Great God is the ultimate judge of men's souls."

Artaban shifted free of Melchior's steadying grasp. The

swirling crowd flowed back into his awareness, and he merged back into the stream of people heading toward the city center.

"Sometimes I wonder," he thought out loud. "My father interpreted omens on behalf of our God, and yet that same God did not come to his aid."

"You doubt the righteousness and justice of Ahura Mazda?" Melchior's tone took on a slight edge.

"I often wonder whether we understand his messages as clearly as we suppose. When we interpret the signs in the heavens, do we truly discern his will, or do we but hear what we want to hear?"

Melchior caught up with Artaban, so they walked side by side. "If you have such doubts, why then did you pursue the training to become a magus? Why did you come to me at the House of Knowledge?"

Artaban shrugged. "My uncle followed our family to Damascus. He was no court official or temple priest—just a humble shepherd. After my father died, he took us into his home and moved us back to our family lands outside Ctesiphon." Artaban chuckled to himself. "My uncle encouraged me to follow in his footsteps and become a shepherd. He had no wife and no sons to pass along his trade to. He said I could hear the voice of our God more clearly in the stillness of open pastures than in tracking the motions of the stars through the sky."

"There may be wisdom in his words," Melchior conceded. "Any yet?"

"And yet I was tormented by my father's fate. I was driven to understand where he had gone wrong and how he had led our kingdom to such calamity. My uncle eventually gave up and turned his attention to my little brother. But he had salvaged my father's shadow stick and armillary rings from the wreckage of our home here. Once he understood I was set on my path, he gave them to me with his blessing."

"You have them still?" Melchior asked.

"They are very precious to me. I even brought them on this journey. I thought they might be useful."

"Perhaps in more ways than just determining the alignment of the stars," Melchior suggested. "Your father might have been wrong in his interpretation of the eclipse, or he may have been correct. We may never know. But he is not to blame for the Roman retribution on our kingdom or on your family. You are your father's son, but in this saga, you can neither vindicate him nor bring justice upon his oppressors."

Melchior motioned for Artaban to stop, indicating that he had more to say, but Artaban just pressed on down the street without pausing. And the old sage let him go.

In the fading distance, Artaban could hear Simur's raspy cackle. "Brack. Can't change the past. Must let it go."

CHAPTER SEVEN

Late Autumn / Early Winter, 7 BC
Damascus, Syrian Province, Roman Empire

T he final conjunction blazed overhead as the four magi stood on the flat rooftop of the Dar-e Nur temple observatory. At this late hour, the sounds of the bustling city had faded into a low murmur. The stillness of the evening, the gentle chill, and the canopy of stars, shining like diamonds sewn into black velvet, made the magi's long vigil feel more like worship than toil.

"There," Melchior breathed, pointing toward the western sky. "The fulfillment of the ancient prophecies."

In the constellation of *Ea*, three brilliant lights drew together in a celestial dance that had not been witnessed for perhaps a thousand years. *Marduk* and *Ninub* burned with unusual intensity as they merged into one brilliant light, while *Nergal* hung nearby like a crimson jewel.

Belshazzar's charts and instruments lay spread across a small table, weighted down against the evening breeze. "The almanacs were precisely correct," he announced with undisguised awe. "All three Wanderers converge within *Ea* exactly as predicted. This is the final confirmation we needed for our mission to proceed."

Gondophares gazed at the sky with a look of reverent wonder. "I still can't believe we've witnessed it with our own eyes. Surely this validates all our conclusions. A divinely appointed king must certainly have been born."

"Brack," Simur chirped from his perch atop the starling's small travel cage. "A rare sign. A potent sign."

But Artaban stared at the celestial display with growing dread rather than wonder. "Look around you," he said, gesturing toward the city spreading below them. "Roman standards fly from every watchtower. Roman soldiers patrol every street. Roman law governs every transaction in the marketplace. And we stand here plotting to honor a prophesied king who will supposedly overthrow all their power."

"We plot nothing," Belshazzar shot back. "We simply seek to honor a newborn king and to ensure that Parthia ends up on the right side of any impending change in the political landscape."

"Think about what we've already endured," Artaban continued, his voice taut with frustration. "The Chancellor tried to stop us at the border. Our caravan master was arrested for crimes we knew nothing about. We've been detained by the authorities, waylaid by the forces of nature, and nearly killed by bandits. Good men have died because of this mission—Tabor and Burzoe." He lifted his hands in a gesture of exasperation. "And for what? To deliver gifts to a child who may or may not even exist, all based on our interpretation of movements in the stars?"

"Artaban," Gondophares interjected, "you speak as if our hardships negate the signs in the heavens. But consider the alternative. What if we abandon our commission now, just as the final conjunction confirms our interpretation? What if the very obstacles we've faced are tests of our faithfulness to our divine calling?"

"Or what if they're warnings?" Artaban countered. "What if the great Ahura Mazda is trying to turn us back from a path that will bring destruction not only on ourselves, but our entire kingdom?"

Belshazzar tapped his finger slowly and deliberately on the astronomical charts. "You speak like a man who has lost faith in the power of the Wise Lord. This conjunction is unprecedented —a sign that appears only once in a millennium. The Hebrew prophecies speak of exactly such a time. How can you witness this with your own eyes and still doubt?"

"I acknowledge the exceptional rarity of the conjunction," Artaban replied. "And I agree it must have great significance."

"But..." Gondophares prompted.

"But I have concerns about our interpretation." Artaban spread his hands wide in the air. "We noted the triple conjunction and interpreted it to mean a divinely appointed king would arise."

"A reasonable assertion," Gondophares declared.

"Perhaps," Artaban went on. "Then we saw that *Nergal* would join the final convergence and concluded that this divinely appointed king would arise out of Syria or Judea."

"Again," Gondophares responded, "a very reasonable contention, based on centuries of tradition."

"Ah, but that's where we strayed from solid foundations into rampant speculation," Artaban said, raising a finger and pointing it at his two fellows. "Based on that supposition, we consulted the writings of the Hebrew prophets—prophets, I might add, who do not share our faith or acknowledge Ahura Mazda as the One True God."

He pressed on before anyone could interrupt him. "Those writings did not even mention signs in the heavens or interpreting celestial omens. They only talked about a Jewish messiah, whom *we* then correlated with our own *Saoshyant*. Don't you see the weakness in that train of reasoning?"

"A weakness, perhaps," Gondophares conceded, "but not necessarily a flaw."

"Okay," Artaban pressed forward. "Then where are the Parthian prophecies that would support this conclusion? Surely, we should be able to identify some writings of our own prophets that would confirm such a momentous event in human history. So where are they?"

Artaban's question received only blank stares in reply.

After a long, awkward moment, Belshazzar responded, "Well, we know the *Saoshyant* will be the last great deliverer who will usher in the final battle between truth and falsehood. That battle will culminate in the resurrection of the righteous dead and the purification of the world."

"Come, Belshazzar," Artaban said, his voice tight with frustration. "Think of what you're saying. You know very well that our own prophecies speak of *three* great saviors, and the *Saoshyant* is the last of all. Yet clearly, the first two have not thus far appeared. How can we suddenly leap over those first two saviors and declare that the *Saoshyant* has now arrived, all based on ancient writings by followers of a foreign god?"

Belshazzar stood abruptly, knocking over his wine cup. "Because the signs are undeniable! This conjunction—"

"The signs could mean anything!" Artaban slammed his palm on the table, making the astronomical instruments jump. "My father read signs too, and Rome crucified him for it."

"Enough," Belshazzar exclaimed. "I won't let the ghost of your father's failure rob me of fulfilling my father's calling."

The stark words hung heavy in the air.

Melchior set down his stylus carefully. "Artaban," he said gently, "your father's death was tragic. But that doesn't mean—"

"Doesn't it?" Artaban's voice cracked. "We're risking everything—our lives, our kingdom—on interpretations that could be completely wrong."

The old sage reached across to clasp Artaban's trembling hand. "Then we pray we've served faithfully, even in error. But if we turn back now when heaven itself cries out…" He let the implication hang unspoken.

"Our interpretation of this omen," Artaban insisted, "is based almost entirely on the writings of the Hebrew prophets. Do you not see how we left behind the certainty of our own traditions and ventured onto the dangerous ground of conjecture?"

"But the timing and location align perfectly with the predictions about the Jewish messiah," Belshazzar insisted. "And though Daniel was a Hebrew prophet, he also served the Babylonian and Persian courts. The influence of his knowledge and actions is felt within our own culture down to this day."

Artaban placed his hands firmly on the table, leaned forward, and emphatically insisted, "This venture is not merely an interesting academic exercise. The actions we take as a result of our speculation may well provoke the ire of Rome. And I've seen what happens when Rome perceives a threat," he said sharply. "I've seen the crosses and the pyres. I've seen the cold, calculated cruelty with which they eliminate any challenge to their authority."

"Brack. Old wounds," Simur observed quietly, and the small bird's insight cut through the tension like a blade.

Melchior raised his hands to still the rising tempers. "Brothers, we stand at a crossroads more significant than any we have yet faced. Each of your perspectives has merit, and all deserve careful consideration."

He moved to stand beside the table where the star charts lay, positioning himself on the other side of Artaban and subtly easing the three men closer together.

"Artaban's concerns are not born of cowardice but of hard experience. Rome's power is indeed real and immediate. If the authorities discover we seek a king prophesied to rule over all nations, the consequences could be severe."

"But Master," Gondophares protested, "surely—"

Melchior held up a hand. "Let me finish. You, Gondophares, and Belshazzar also speak truth. We have witnessed signs in the heavens that are too portentous to ignore. King Phraates himself, the divinely appointed ruler of our realm, recognized the significance of these signs when he commissioned our venture."

"At least our Great King heeds omens from the heavens," Gondophares said. "Not all rulers do. Sometimes the greatest tragedies aren't those revealed by the stars, but the preventable suffering that follows when authorities ignore wise counsel."

Melchior stroked his beard thoughtfully as he gazed up at the brilliant conjunction. "The question before us is not whether the signs are real. They clearly are. The question is whether we have the courage to follow where they lead, despite the very real dangers Artaban has identified."

"And what if following these signs leads to the same fate that befell my father?" Artaban asked quietly. "What if our interpretation proves to be as mistaken as his?"

Melchior lifted his hands in a gesture of resignation. "Then we pray for the divine mercy and protection of our Great God for an error made with purity of intentions." Then his voice took on a sober tone. "But if we turn back now, when the heavens themselves cry out that momentous events are unfolding, we will face his judgment for our faithlessness."

"The prophecies of Daniel speak of kingdoms rising and falling," Belshazzar added, his voice now more measured. "If Rome's time is indeed coming to an end, would it not be wiser to align ourselves with the rising power rather than the falling one?"

Artaban turned to stare directly at his colleague. "And if the prophecies are wrong?" he reiterated, clenching his fists at his sides. "These Hebrew seers must surely have been inspired by the Prince of Darkness. They do not follow the Father of Light. So what happens if we've been deceived by the Father of Lies? What if this child we seek, assuming he even exists, is nothing more than another failed pretender to David's throne? Rome has crushed dozens of would-be messiahs. What makes this one different?"

"The stars," Gondophares said simply, pointing skyward. "No mere pretender has ever been heralded by such signs."

"Brack. Faith and fear," Simur squawked. "Both have risk. Both are needed."

Melchior nodded at the bird's insightful wisdom. "Simur speaks truly. Faith without prudence is recklessness. Prudence without faith is dread. We must walk the narrow path between the two."

For several minutes, the four men stood in contemplative silence, each wrestling with the magnitude of the decision before them.

Finally, Melchior spoke with the quiet assurance that comes only from a lifetime spent in pursuit of truth. "My friends, we debate as if this decision were ours alone to make. But did we choose to discover the triple conjunction, or was it revealed to us? Did we seek out the Hebrew prophecies, or were they placed in our path? The great Ahura Mazda does not work through coincidence. He has woven together threads from across centuries—Babylonian calculations, Persian wisdom, Hebrew visions—into a single tapestry that points to this moment, this child, this destiny."

The conjunction blazed overhead, indifferent to their human deliberations, while the great city below echoed silent proclamations of Rome's authority and power.

The old sage's words grew heavy with conviction. "We have been chosen not merely to witness history, but to participate in its turning. Artaban, your father died because his focus fell on earthly kingdoms. But we do not ride to honor Parthia or to defy Rome. We ride to kneel before a king of kings, whose kingdom shall have no end. To retreat now would be to declare that we fear Caesar's legions more than we trust in the Lord of Creation himself."

"And if the Romans discover our true purpose?" Artaban asked. "If they learn we seek a king prophesied to rule over all nations?"

"I understand your concerns about Roman retaliation," Gondophares said calmly, "but consider the alternative. What if this child is real, and we do nothing? What if our silence condemns ordinary families to suffer through upheavals they could have prepared for?" His voice carried the weight of personal experience. "I've seen what happens when those with knowledge fail to act on it. The consequences always fall hardest on those with the least power to protect themselves."

Belshazzar looked around the group. "I say we continue to Jerusalem. The signs could not be clearer."

"I agree," Gondophares said without hesitation.

All eyes turned to Artaban. He gazed once more at the brilliant conjunction, then down at the Roman standards visible atop the city's watchtowers. When he finally spoke, his voice was heavy with resignation.

"I have voiced my concerns, and they remain unchanged. This path leads toward great danger, not only for us but also for our kingdom. Yet I swore an oath to King Phraates, and I will not abandon my companions when they choose to honor that oath." He paused, then added quietly, "May the Wise Lord preserve us from the consequences of our actions."

"Then we are decided," Melchior said. "We depart for Jerusalem as soon as we can arrange safe passage and resupply our caravan." He looked up once more at the celestial display. "The stars have spoken. Now we must follow where they lead."

As they prepared to leave the rooftop observatory, Artaban

cast one final glance at the conjunction blazing overhead. The signs were undeniably magnificent, but he could not shake the feeling they were walking into a trap that would destroy them all. His father's astronomical instruments, carefully wrapped in his pack, seemed to weigh heavier than ever—a reminder of how costly it could be to trust in messages written in the stars.

As they gathered up their charts and prepared to leave, a middle-aged man with a slender frame, dark hair, neatly trimmed beard, and deep-set eyes approached them. He wore the gray and midnight-blue garb of the temple's senior scholars, with the sash of an astronomer tied neatly around his waist.

"Magus Melchior," he began.

"Do I know you?" The old sage asked.

"Please forgive the intrusion. I am Baruch, of the senior order here at Dar-e-Nur. I have an urgent message from Lord Vahman."

"Lord Vahman?" Melchior asked, but the man silenced him with a quick gesture.

He glanced cautiously around at the other astronomers who had gathered at the observatory to witness the rare conjunction in the sky. "We must talk," he said, "but not here. Please follow me to a place where we can converse in private."

He turned and led them toward the stairs that descended from the rooftop observatory to the main levels of the temple.

Artaban tugged lightly on Melchior's sleeve. When the old man looked back, Artaban shook his head slightly and then gave a quizzical look intended to convey suspicion. In response, Melchior waved off the caution and pointed for them to follow Baruch.

This temple was not even close to the scale of the Bīt

Mummu in Babylon, yet the path the man took seemed just as convoluted to Artaban as any in the catacombs of that grand edifice. Their descent far exceeded the height of the observatory, so they must have proceeded well below ground level. Finally, the stranger exited the stairway, navigated a maze of corridors, and opened a creaky wooden door braced with iron bands that led into a room dimly lit by an oil lamp.

"Now we will be well away from listening ears and prying eyes," Baruch said. "We can speak freely here."

The dank feel and musty smell told Artaban they must either be in a storage area or a study alcove adjacent to the temple archives. But there were no shelves, no supplies stacked against the walls, and no table upon which to lay scrolls or clay tablets.

"You mentioned a message from the Royal Astronomer," Melchior prompted.

Baruch nodded. "We received an urgent communique from Lord Vahman several days ago indicating that your party was scheduled to wait in the city until the conjunction of *Marduk* and *Ninub* before proceeding to Jerusalem. We watched the gates, searched the inns, and even inquired among the caravans camped outside the walls, but could not locate your group. So we waited for you to show up here to observe the conjunction."

"Yes," Melchior responded. "We encountered many delays along our route and arrived only this morning. I'm not surprised you couldn't locate us. What message do you have for us from Lord Vahman?"

"The tone of the dispatch was rather urgent, and we were cautioned to handle the matter discreetly." Baruch replied. "I am afraid your party is at substantial risk. It seems the Chancellor, with support from some of the Great Houses, has contrived to waylay you here and prevent you from leaving the city. I was instructed to bring you immediately, and with utmost discretion, to a secure location where arrangements can be made to facilitate your onward journey to Jerusalem."

"The Chancellor works deliberately against the will of the Royal Astronomer?" Melchior asked in surprise.

"As I understand it, he defies the very will of the king himself. Did not the king commission this expedition to seek out and honor the child king of Judea?"

"Hmm," Melchior muttered. "Such is the nature of palace intrigue, I suppose. I've always endeavored to remain apart from such affairs, focusing instead on the will of our Great God as revealed in the heavens and the sacred writings. This news should shock me, but I suppose it does not."

Artaban noticed that Melchior never actually answered the question about their mission being chartered by the king. Perhaps he thought the comment had been rhetorical.

Melchior took a deep breath and looked back up from what must have been internal musings. "Can I see the message?"

"Certainly," Baruch replied. "It has been decoded. We have both the original and the transcript at the safe house. We assumed you would want to read the entire contents for yourself."

"So you trust the messenger, then? You believe the dispatch to be reliable?"

"It is beyond suspicion. The Royal Astronomer maintains a robust communication network between the observatories throughout the kingdom and into neighboring regions. It's necessary for much of this correspondence to remain private, as you might suspect. This message arrived with Lord Vahman's official seal, and the code is virtually impossible to break or falsify."

"Forgive my interruption," Belshazzar broke in. "You've said 'we' in several instances. Who else knows about this situation? The master of the observatory? The chief priest at the temple?"

"Unfortunately, Master Melchior's comments about the nature of politics are all too true. The Royal Astronomer has found it necessary to recruit a small cadre of people he can trust here in Damascus to report on the activities of the facility and to handle, let's say, special situations."

"First, Rostan. Then Volusius. Now this," Gondophares muttered. "I'm beginning to wonder who we can trust."

"Rostan?" Baruch asked.

Artaban saw Melchior give Gondophares a quick, very subtle glance, cautioning him to silence.

"Just someone we encountered back in Parthia who claimed to represent the king," Melchior commented, cleverly using the truth to disguise itself. "What are we to do now? Wait here?"

"No," Baruch replied. "The temple is undoubtedly under the watchful eye of the Chancellor's agents. We need to get you to a safe house not far from here. We have begun the coordination necessary to effect your clandestine departure from the city."

"Shouldn't we go to the inn first?" Belshazzar asked. "We will need to get our animals and supplies."

"I'm afraid you don't appreciate the gravity of the situation," Baruch said soberly. "If you're discovered by the Chancellor's men, you may be detained indefinitely."

"Are you trying to say our lives are at risk?" Artaban asked, dumbfounded.

"We can't discount the possibility," Baruch replied. "The potential ramifications of your mission are substantial and wide-ranging. There are very powerful stakeholders with much to gain or lose. And as I understand the situation, very few people know of your interpretation of the heavenly signs or of this expedition. The most effective way for all this to go away might be for you and your party to simply disappear."

"But we serve the—" Gondophares began, but was cut off by Simur.

"Brack," the bird squawked loudly. "Secrets are dangerous things."

The men stared at each other for a moment in stunned silence at the implications of Baruch's declaration. Finally,

Melchior said, "I'm sure the Royal Astronomer will watch out for our well-being. I know Lord Vahman well, and he's someone we can trust completely."

Gondophares addressed Baruch. "What about the other members of our party? Will one of your people bring them to the safe house?"

"Unfortunately, it won't be possible for your entire party to escape without notice. We'll send new horses and fresh supplies out of the city with a trade caravan. We have also arranged for a modest security detail. Each of you will be secreted outside the walls by different means. Then you can rendezvous with each other and the security detail about a day's journey down the road to Judea. The guards will have your mounts and supplies."

Artaban was taken aback by this turn of events. Though he had been conscious of the risks involved in angering the Romans, he suddenly realized how naive he had been about the opposition from within their own country. He was astonished to think that their own people might want them dead. It made him wonder if the obstacles they had faced on the road had been random chance after all.

"What about the gifts?" Belshazzar asked.

"Gifts?" Baruch prompted.

Melchior inserted himself before Belshazzar could respond. "We brought certain items to present as gifts to the child king. We will need to retrieve those items and take them with us."

"Ahh, I see," Baruch said. "It would be far too dangerous to procure anything from the inn. Your rooms are undoubtedly being watched. I'm sure we can provide some suitable replacements and arrange for them to be at the rendezvous point with the supplies."

All four magi muttered objections among themselves until Baruch asked, "Is there a problem?"

"These gifts are very specific items. They are of modest value but have much deeper symbolic meaning. They have also been crafted and packaged to reflect their Parthian origin. I'm afraid these specific items are critical to the success of our mission."

Baruch considered the issue for a moment and then replied. "Okay, I'll discuss the matter with my colleagues and see what can be done. Now, if you would please follow me, I'll get you to the safe house."

"Would you give us a moment to confer among ourselves?" Melchior requested. "We need to determine if there are other important issues that must be addressed for this plan to be successful."

"I'm afraid time is of the essence," Baruch said, shaking his head. "I must get you out of the temple while the astronomers and priests are still focused on the conjugation and before the morning staff arrive. We'll need to facilitate your exit from the city before the Chancellor's agents discover you're missing. You'll need as much time as possible to get a head start on them toward Jerusalem."

"We're leaving tonight?" Artaban blurted.

"You must all be outside the city walls before midday if you are to evade the Chancellor's men."

"How do we get out of the temple without being seen?" Gondophares asked. "There's only one exit from the observatory. We must have been spotted leaving the platform a while ago, and I saw only three exits from the temple itself."

"Follow me," Baruch answered. As they left the small room and proceeded down the corridor, he explained further. "This temple was built on top of a more ancient holy site. It was originally an Aramean sanctuary dedicated to Hadad, which was then later converted by the Seleucids into a temple of Zeus. We rebuilt it as a Zoroastrian temple and observatory during the Parthian occupation. It's possible to access the original catacombs, which connect to a wider network of passages under this ancient part of the city."

He led them down two more passageways, lined with doors

on both sides, and into a storage room filled with an array of discarded items stacked on shelves—dusty oil jars with Greek inscriptions, broken astrolabes, fragments of marble statues, amulets made from animal bones, and various tools. Baruch strode through the room to a small, decayed wooden door. He reached behind one shelf, removed a loose stone, and inserted his hand into the cavity. A moment later, Artaban heard a soft thunk, and the door swung open, whereupon Baruch removed his hand and replaced the stone.

"I apologize for the tightness of this next passage. It isn't terribly long. But you will each want your own lamp, as it is quite dark and narrow until we get to the main network of tunnels. I'll ask the last man to close the door behind us."

He took some small oil lamps from a nearby shelf, lit them from his own, and handed one to each of the four magi. Then he called for them to follow him and disappeared through the door.

Artaban was last to enter the passage, and he closed the door behind him as instructed. He was almost instantly overcome with a wave of panic. He had never been comfortable in confined spaces, and he suddenly felt as if the walls were closing in on him. The passage was really more of a man-made tunnel, barely wide enough for him to walk forward without rubbing his shoulders on the walls, and so short he had to stoop. He could see the curved pick marks from where the passage had been hewn out of solid rock.

The tunnel was much longer than Artaban expected, despite Baruch's earlier assurances. Artaban, anxious to get to the other end of the cramped space where he might again breathe freely, stopped counting at five hundred paces, and yet the passage stretched on. Finally, the lamps ahead of him came to a stop at another small, ancient wooden door. Baruch knocked five times, paused, and then knocked three times more. A moment later, the door swung open, and they emerged into a larger, circular space with four exits at odd angles from each other.

A stout man in leather armor with a full beard and a sword strapped to his hip looked them over briefly and then turned to head down the passage on the left without saying a word.

"This is Koren," Baruch said in a hushed tone. "He helps with security. He will lead us the rest of the way to the safe house."

At least this passageway was more spacious, and Artaban's anxiety abated to a small degree. He still didn't like being led through a dizzying array of corridors to an unknown location by men they barely even knew. But, as with the mission in general, he was being dragged along with very little ability to control his own destiny. He had felt trapped by circumstances almost the entire time—compelled by the king to be part of the group, then always outnumbered by the opinions of his three companions. Now, he was forced to participate in a perilous escape plan because it was literally impossible to walk away. He found himself having to rely on faith that their Great God was, in fact, guiding their path. It was an unfamiliar and uncomfortable mindset for him to adopt.

After another seemingly interminable walk through underground passages that twisted, turned, and forked in various directions, Artaban had lost all sense of their location. He could not have navigated back to the observatory if his life depended on it. Eventually, they came to what appeared to be an underground catacomb, with crypts lining both walls. Halfway down this long corridor, they turned into a side passage that ended at a medium-sized room. It was well lit with oil lamps, and shelves of clay tablets lined the walls.

Baruch motioned toward a low table surrounded by cushions, set with fresh fruit, bread, and cheese.

"I'm sure you're tired and somewhat disconcerted by the sudden turn of events. Please refresh yourselves and take your rest, while I go check on the preparations for your exit from the city. You have a very long day ahead of you."

"Where are we?" Artaban blurted, no longer able to contain his growing frustration. "It looks like we wandered into a crypt."

"That's very close. This is an ancient Assyrian administrative vault, built after the conquest of Damascus by Tiglath-Pileser III over six hundred years ago. When they occupied the city as a provincial capital, the Assyrians used this underground vault to store sensitive bureaucratic records and to bury prominent government officials."

"When you talked about a safe house, I somehow imagined a building above ground," Artaban said.

"Ahh. I can understand your confusion," Baruch replied. "Rest assured, this is the ideal location for us to stage your escape. We're actually situated very near the city walls. A couple of you will be able to leave without even going through a gate."

"How?" Gondophares asked excitedly. He appeared to actually enjoy this intrigue.

"You'll see," Baruch replied, flashing a conspiratorial smile. "Now, please get some rest while I coordinate with our team on the next steps. This is an intricate plan, and the timing is critical. Please be patient. I'll return shortly with your individual escorts. They'll have everything you need—clothing, money, food, and information on how to proceed."

"We're trusting in you, friend," Melchior said, "as an agent of Lord Vahman to lead us through this perilous situation. May the Lord of Light guide our steps and illuminate the path ahead."

Baruch bowed slightly. "Though I'm certain this location is safe and you won't be discovered here, I'll take the added precaution of closing the door. Rest assured, Koren will be guarding the passageway." He gestured to an alcove recessed into one wall. "There are some pots available if you need to relieve yourselves before I return."

With that, the two strangers exited the room and closed the

door behind them. Artaban could hear their footsteps echoing down the corridor.

"Well, brothers," Melchior said, settling his aged bones gently onto one of the cushions. "I suggest we avail ourselves of our host's hospitality and get some sorely needed rest. It's been an eventful night, and the coming day promises even more turmoil. Shall we..." he concluded, reaching for a cluster of grapes.

"I have a bad feeling about this," Artaban intoned. "I don't trust these men and their schemes."

"Neither do I," the old sage replied.

"What?" Artaban exclaimed. "You don't trust them?"

"Baruch was clearly lying," Melchior said in a matter-of-fact tone.

"Lying about what?" Gondophares joined the conversation. "About the dispatch from Lord Vahman? About the plot to detain us here and derail our mission?"

Melchior shrugged. "I suspect the plot is all too real. There are powerful men who oppose our mission. But yes, the story of the dispatch was undoubtedly a fabrication. There probably was an urgent message, but I expect it came from the Chancellor himself, not the Royal Astronomer."

"How do you know?" Belshazzar asked. "He knew a great deal about our mission, and I didn't hear any factual errors that would show he was not telling the truth."

"It wasn't what he said," Melchior replied. "His demeanor gave him away." The lips below his mustache stretched into a wry smile. "When you've instructed as many students as I have, you develop a sense of when people are not being completely honest. I'm confident that Baruch is just such a man."

"If you didn't trust him, then why did you allow them to lead us into this labyrinth?" Artaban said in exasperation.

Melchior finished his grapes and reached for a fig. "I trust in the Lord of Truth to overthrow the twisted plots hatched by the Father of Lies."

"Twisted plots?" Artaban exclaimed as a sudden thought struck him. He leapt to his feet, rushed to the door, and began tugging at the handle. The door didn't budge. Frantically, he grappled with the latch and jerked the lever back and forth violently, but to no avail. "We're locked in," he wailed in frustration, kicking at the doorframe.

"Artaban, come, sit. Rest a while. All will be well."

Artaban ignored his old mentor. He began pounding on the door and shouting, "Help! Somebody help."

At that point, Belshazzar and Gondophares also rose and joined Artaban at the door. Instead of jerking at the handle, Gondophares began hastily inspecting the latch and trying to wiggle it loose. Belshazzar united with Artaban in calling for aid.

Melchior just sighed and tasted a piece of cheese, while Simur squawked, "Panic and fear. Brack. Poison to the soul."

After a prolonged bout of banging and shouting and fiddling with the latch, the three junior magi finally gave up and collapsed on the cushions near Melchior.

"I'm quite certain our captors locked us securely away beyond the range of helpful ears," Melchior said.

"Why?" Artaban demanded in desperation. "If you knew Baruch was lying, why did you allow him to lead us into this trap? I don't understand."

"Sometimes it's useful if you allow your enemies to believe they've succeeded."

"But they did succeed," Gondophares insisted. "We're trapped, and no one knows where we are."

"Not true," Melchior contended. "The God of Creation knows our precise situation. Have faith."

"Have faith in what?" Artaban cried. "If we didn't use the wisdom he gave us to avoid capture, why should we expect him to intervene? What could he do anyway? Haven't you always said that Ahura Mazda works through people to effect His will? Well, no living soul knows where we are, except the ones who trapped us here. Who, exactly, do you expect that our Great God will send to rescue us?"

Melchior sighed heavily. "The Master of Heaven and Earth chose us for this task. He revealed the sign in the stars to us. He showed us its true meaning. He gave us favor in the eyes of the king to sponsor this mission." The old man reached out and grasped Artaban's arm. "If the Lord of Creation called us to this duty, he will see us through to its completion."

Artaban stared hard into Melchior's eyes. "Tell that to Tabor and Burzoe. They were good men who both perished on this journey of divine will. What prevents us from meeting with that same fate?"

Melchior shrugged. "If we die, we'll cross the Chinvat Bridge and ascend to the House of Song, knowing we've been faithful to our calling. A man can hope for no better fate."

Artaban just shook his head.

"I suggest we burn one lamp at a time to conserve oil," Gondophares advised. "While we wait, at least we will have light."

"Trust in the Light of Heaven," Melchior advised, "not merely in the light of men. I recommend we turn our attention to faith and prayer."

With that, their old *usted* laid back, closed his eyes, and soon fell into a peaceful sleep. With nothing else to do, the others tried to join him in rest. But for Artaban, sleep would not come. Instead, he wrestled with his fears, the memories of his father's errors, and the wraiths from his past.

The hours ticked by, the food dwindled, and the oil in the lamps waned. Artaban's fingers fiddled with the bandage on his arm, and his dread continued to grow until every thought and inclination of his heart was consumed by fear. He feared for his life. He feared vanishing without a trace to report to his family. He feared having no legacy to leave behind in the world. And most of all, he feared losing the last vestiges of faith he had in his God. At this point, he wasn't even certain there was a Chinvat Bridge to cross or a House of Song to enter. If these things were real, and if the price for entry was genuine faith, he doubted he would possess the currency to pay his way.

He peered up as the flame in the last lamp flickered and faded until only the darkness remained.

Quietly he whispered, "Where is the deliverance of our God now, old Master?"

He could not see Melchior's face, but knew it still shone with hope, even now.

Then came sounds so faint they seemed like wraiths in the night or figments of his desperate imagination—the distant murmur of muffled voices, the rustling of feet. Slowly, ever so slowly, the noises grew until he knew they were not just fantasies or illusions.

Artaban nudged Gondophares. "Did you hear something?"

"No—" he began, but then checked himself. "Wait. Yes, I think maybe I did."

Artaban strained to see if he could recognize the voices, but they were not yet distinct enough to tell. He wondered if it was Baruch and the burly soldier coming to finish them off. He held his breath as the footsteps stopped outside the entrance and hands began fumbling with the latch. Then the door swung open, and Captain Vakshuvar strode in, with a stranger following behind. Artaban flinched as the light of their lamps filled the room.

A grin spread across Melchior's face as the old man patted him on the arm. "There, my son," he whispered, "is the deliverance of our God." Then in a louder tone, "Captain, it's good to see you."

"And you, Magus Melchior," he replied. "I trust you're well and unharmed."

"Quite well. It seems our enemies intended to abandon us here to waste away, rather than have our blood on their hands. Who is your friend?"

Captain Vakshuvar smiled. "Those contacts Volusius gave us proved to be quite knowledgeable and resourceful. They're all part of the network Rostan has cultivated over the years. Though I still can't believe we were able to find you here. The trail was pretty thin." He shook his head. "We were very lucky."

"Not luck," Melchior replied, slapping him on the back. "It's divine providence."

"Maybe so," the old soldier continued, "but for now, we have some very practical issues to contend with. We need to get out of this city unobserved and make our way to Judea. I took the liberty of sending a messenger ahead to request an audience with King Herod."

"Well done. What's the word from Jerusalem?"

"Herod's court is unsettled," the stranger replied to Melchior's question. "The commoners mutter of unjust executions, while the king's new heir is still unrecognized by the people. Scribes from a separatist sect in the desert whisper of Balaam's star and the visions of the prophet Daniel. Some believe the coming of their messiah is near. It's a volatile time, and you'll need to proceed with the utmost caution."

"And," Captain Vakshuvar added, "we still need to be wary of those who want to see our mission stopped here. I'm afraid we'll need to depart the city secretly and separately, then reassemble about a day's journey down the road toward Jerusalem. We'll leave our animals and supplies behind and receive replacements from a trade caravan that should be leaving the city right about now."

"That," Artaban interjected, "sounds remarkably like the plan our captors used to deceive us into following them."

"They weren't unintelligent men," Vakshuvar replied. "Just misguided. And they now think you're all trapped in a crypt deep in the bowels beneath the city. We'll let them continue to believe that until we're well away and beyond their reach."

Melchior clasped their captain's shoulder and nodded to the stranger. "You've served your God and your king well, my friends. We are forever in your debt."

As they all filed out of the crypt and down the passage, Artaban continued to struggle with his doubts. The fears that had plagued his mind while they were captive in the darkness would not abate so easily. Had this indeed, as Melchior implied, been deliverance from the hand of their God? Or had the intelligence network of the king merely outwitted the sophistry of the Chancellor? Was it truly a divine miracle, or simply political maneuvering that had rescued them? He had no actual way of knowing for sure. But in either case, he had been delivered from one prison only to return to the captivity of a mission he wanted no part of and a purpose in which he did not believe.

CHAPTER EIGHT

Winter, 7 BC
Jerusalem, Kingdom of Judea,
Syrian Province, Roman Empire

"My friends," Narsai began, his face grave in the lamplight of his well-appointed villa, "you have arrived in Jerusalem at perhaps the most perilous time in a generation. Tensions here are always volatile between Roman authority, Herodian ambition, temple loyalties, and oppression of the common people. But now... now the city feels like dry kindling waiting for a spark."

The elderly Parthian merchant gestured for the four magi to settle themselves on the cushions arranged around his low table, while Captain Vakshuvar stood watch near the door. One of the household servants had set out refreshments—dates, almonds, fresh bread, and watered wine. The air inside the home radiated with the mingled aromas of saffron, sandalwood, and frankincense. Silk tapestries embroidered with Parthian motifs adorned the walls, muffling the city's noise beyond their limestone arches. A soft breeze drifted in from the courtyard, rustling the leaves of a fig tree growing in the center of a carefully manicured garden.

"King Herod grows ever more suspicious of threats to his throne," Narsai continued, stroking his gray beard. "Just this past year, he executed his two eldest sons on charges of treason. Rumor says he murdered them to secure the succession for Antipater, the younger son of his second wife, though now even he finds himself under suspicion."

Artaban shifted uncomfortably on his cushion, the merchant's words stirring memories of their precarious escape from Damascus and the following two weeks of unexpected delays and dangers.

Volusius' network of contacts in Damascus, all of whom insisted on remaining anonymous, secreted the members of their party out of the city separately, using different means for each one. If any of them had been intercepted, the others would have been able to continue on with the mission.

The cook and the one remaining animal handler, who had papers of their own, left with merchant caravans. The guards were locked in an iron cage on a cart and passed off as captured warriors being transported to Caesarea to be trained as gladiators for the arena. Melchior was disguised as the scribe of a wealthy merchant traveling to Jerusalem. Gondophares was led through a broad underground chamber once used as a burial vault to a partially collapsed, Assyrian-era canal system that eventually emerged outside the city wall. Belshazzar was likewise led through the service tunnel for an active water supply channel, while Artaban himself was lowered in a basket out of a window in the exterior wall.

When they all assembled at the rendezvous point, they were supplied with the animals and provisions that had been promised, but soon discovered the gifts were missing. After questioning their escorts and racing off to intercept one of the merchant caravans, the guards eventually found the items in the possession of a trader in fine perfumes. The man claimed they had innocently been mixed up with his own inventory and said the magi should be thankful because the items might otherwise not have made it through the export customs inspections.

The journey itself had proved equally problematic. One night, south of Scythopolis, a rockslide blocked the road and delayed their caravan. Though they cleared a path with the help of local herders, they lost a full day. When they finally reached the Judean border, the officials at the toll station threatened to deny them entry unless they paid a special "fee" because of their Parthian origin. Only then did Artaban realize that animosity and mistrust of Parthians extended beyond just the Romans to the Jews as well. Finally, a flash flood critically damaged the bridge over the Kishon River in the Jezreel Valley near Megiddo, just hours before they were due to cross. All the caravans on the Via Maris, the primary trade route from Damascus to Jerusalem, had to divert through Galilee to Capernaum, then descend through the hill country to Jerusalem—a detour that cost them several days and strained their supply of rations.

As Artaban reflected on the host of obstacles they had encountered on the full journey from Ecbatana, he got a disturbing sense that greater forces than the Chancellor and the Great Houses were opposing their progress. Sure, their enemies in the Parthian Court could intimidate border security officers, direct spies to intercept them, or perhaps even pay brigands to waylay them along the route. But they certainly could not cause rockslides or floods. It would not be unusual for any one or two of these impediments to hinder a typical journey from Parthia to Judea. But for so many diverse hardships to plague a single party made Artaban wonder if something bigger and more sinister might be working against them.

His troubled thoughts eventually refocused on the current

conversation with Narsai, though the nagging suspicion lingered in the back of his mind.

"How," Melchior asked Narsai, "were you able to secure an audience with the king on our behalf? I confess I'm somewhat surprised that a Parthian merchant, however well respected, could gain such access to Herod's court."

Narsai offered a half-smile. "My dear Magus Melchior, you underestimate both the value of commerce and the power of information. I've traded in Jerusalem for over thirty years, and my caravans have enriched Herod's treasury through a great deal of taxes and tribute. More importantly, I have made it my business to understand the currents that move beneath the surface of this city's politics." He lowered his voice and spoke the next words in a hushed tone. "Our Great King often has occasion to call on my services."

"Well, you have our gratitude," Melchior said. "You've risked much on our behalf."

Narsai took a sip of wine from the silver chalice he held loosely in his hand. "Please help me understand the nature of that risk. The original message I received from our mutual friend in Ecbatana was somewhat cryptic."

"You mean Rostan?" Gondophares asked.

Narsai waved his hand and tilted his head to the side in a gesture of affirmation, but did not actually say anything. He went on, "As I said, the original letter had somewhat less, umm, detail than I would have liked." He flipped his fingers in the air. "Such is not uncommon in this business. Some things are best not written down for prying eyes to see. But now that you are here, would you please elaborate on the purpose of your audience? It will help me advise you on how to proceed."

The four magi looked at each other, and Melchior nodded slightly, a signal that he had decided to trust this man who had already proven so valuable to their cause.

Melchior drew a breath and began. "We have come in

response to an ominous sign in the heavens—a rare triple conjunction within the constellation of *Ea*. Such an event occurs perhaps once in eight hundred years. Our astronomical calculations and ancient Hebrew prophecies converge on a single conclusion—that a divinely appointed king has been born in Judea."

"The prophecies speak of one who will rule over all nations," Belshazzar added. "One whose kingdom will never end, but who will himself destroy all other earthly kingdoms."

"If our conjectures are true," Melchior concluded, "King Phraates believes it would be wise for Parthia to establish friendly relations with one heralded by such prophetic visions and heavenly omens. So we have brought some gifts to honor the infant king."

Narsai's face had grown increasingly grave as they spoke. When they finished, he sat in silence for several long moments.

"My friends," he finally said, "you have just described the very nightmare that haunts Herod's dreams. Do you understand what you are saying? You speak of signs announcing the birth of the Jewish messiah, the one prophesied to restore David's kingdom and rule over all the earth. If Herod believes you have come to acknowledge such a king..."

"Perhaps," Artaban interjected, "the signs point to the rise of the son you just mentioned, uh..."

"Antipater?" Narsai prompted.

"Yes," Artaban affirmed. "If Antipater became the new heir after the death of his older brothers, perhaps he is the one indicated by the stars. If so, then Herod need not feel threatened in any way. Would he not be pleased to know that his own son would be the king of prophecy who will elevate Judea to prominence once again?"

Narsai grunted. "Not likely. Antipater is not exactly a young man of stellar moral character. He's certainly not the kind of person whose kingship would be heralded by heavenly omens.

Herod himself now mistrusts the ambitions of this son and his conniving mother. Besides," he reached up and rubbed his temples, "the messiah is to come from the Davidic line, and Herod isn't even a Jew."

Artaban glanced at Melchior and saw uncommon lines of worry crease the old sage's brow as he digested this revelation. The concern he read on his mentor's face only multiplied his own fears. He was well aware of the risks they took in antagonizing Rome. He had been unprepared for the opposition they had faced during their journey from within the Parthian Court. Now it seemed they were in jeopardy of provoking the ire of the very man they had come to address.

"There is one more thing you must understand," Narsai continued grimly. "Herod's not only paranoid, he's also gravely ill. Some say he doesn't have long to live, which makes him even more desperate to secure his legacy and eliminate any threats to his succession. A dying king has nothing to lose and everything to fear."

"But if the prophecies are correct," Belshazzar offered, "wouldn't that be hopeful news for the Jews? King Herod is old, and his time on the throne is nearing its end. If he were to usher in the reign of the messiah, it would make him one of the most revered monarchs in history. Surely, he would rejoice to see his own people, yea even the people of all nations, throw off the yoke of Roman oppression."

Narsai laughed. "Herod doesn't despise Rome. On the contrary, Herod longs to be accepted and admired by Caesar. Pff," he said with a wave of his hand, "he probably wants to become a Roman. He's built monuments to Rome all over his kingdom—Herodium, Masada, the Antonia Fortress here in Jerusalem, not to mention a half-dozen temples to Augustus. Hate Rome? Far from it. Herod owes his very throne to Rome. When the Parthian invasion deposed him thirty years ago, it was the Emperor's legions that put the crown back on his head.

No, my friends, you will not delight King Herod with your news of a coming messiah who will rise to challenge the might and power of Rome."

Artaban leaned forward urgently. "Then what do you counsel? Should we abandon the audience and depart Jerusalem immediately?"

"No," Narsai shook his head. "To leave now would only arouse Herod's suspicions and likely result in your arrest before you could reach the city gates. He would wonder why envoys from Parthia with an entourage of security guards and support staff would venture this far, then cancel an audience and depart with no explanation. No, you must appear before him as scheduled, but with extreme caution."

"Brack," cackled Simur, "No turning back."

"What about the common people?" Gondophares asked their host. "When powerful changes come, ordinary folk sometimes sense the trouble first. And they're the ones who'll pay the highest price if we guess wrong about what's coming."

"Hmph," Narsai grunted. "The common people are like tinder waiting for a spark. They chafe under Rome's yoke. They resent legionaries patrolling their streets. They suffer from the taxes levied by their own king and his imperial overlords. And they distrust Herod."

"We've heard that word circulates about the coming of a messiah?" Gondophares pressed. "How do people on the streets react to such rumors?"

Narsai took a long drink of wine from his chalice before answering. "People who feel oppressed always wish for a deliverer, I suppose. And there are ever those who would seek to capitalize on such hopes and fears. But you are correct that these sentiments have risen to a fevered pitch in recent days. Fringe sects and would-be prophets all clamor about the long-awaited messiah and his vengeance on Rome." He waved it off as so much nonsense.

"What of these zealots I've heard about?" Vakshuvar asked from his post by the door.

"They represent another very dangerous complication. Instead of waiting for a deliverer from God, they've taken matters into their own hands. Their skirmishes with the Roman patrols erupt almost daily, though those are mostly in the villages and countryside beyond the city."

"One more thing," Vakshuvar said, stepping closer. "I'm almost certain I saw the Roman garrison commander from the border at Zeugma earlier today near the palace complex. His name is uh…"

"Varro," Artaban interjected.

Narsai perked up at the mention of the name. "Lucius Aelius Varro?"

"Yes, that's the one," Vakshuvar replied. "You know him?"

Narsai nodded. "He's a bit of a sycophant. He abhors his post at the far reaches of the empire, despite the fact that he extorts money from every trade caravan that crosses the border. He's always trying to ingratiate himself with the Roman legate or anyone else with the power to get him reassigned to a more desirable station."

"Well, he ordered us to be detained for several days at the border," Vakshuvar added, "and personally questioned everyone in our group. He ended up arresting our caravan master, a man named Tadmor, on charges of tax evasion and fraud."

"Tadmor's a fool," Narsai said, shaking his head. "Why did you hire him if—"

"This Centurion Varro," Captain Vakshuvar cut in. "Why would he be here in Jerusalem? It seems a bit too coincidental."

"You say he questioned you at the border?" Narsai asked. "Did you tell him why you were traveling to Jerusalem?"

"Of course," Melchior answered. "It was specified in our letters of introduction and transit from the Royal Astronomer."

"Did you tell him about the signs you observed in the stars?"

Narsai asked, the tension in his voice rising. "Did you tell him about your speculations? Did you say anything about a Jewish messiah?"

Melchior looked at his fellow magi, and they all shook their heads.

"We didn't mention the messiah explicitly," Melchior replied, "though we did say, as our letters indicate, that we traveled to consult with Jewish scholars about the interpretation of certain prophecies in the Hebrew scriptures which could be related to the conjunctions we observed."

"When I spoke with the centurion," Artaban added, "he appeared to be uninterested in our theological and astronomical issues. He was much more focused on whether we were transporting any trade goods."

Narsai frowned. "If Centurion Varro thought there was anything about your visit he could use to curry favor with the legate or King Herod, he would most certainly try to exploit it."

"That could explain the shadow we've been dragging since the border," Vakshuvar said, glancing at Melchior.

"Shadow?" Narsai prompted.

"I always send one of my men back to villages we pass through to see if anyone has taken special notice of our party. Ever since we crossed into Roman territory, there's been a trail of discrete inquiries about us among the merchants and tradesmen we've dealt with. Unfortunately, we've never been able to get a good description of the men asking the questions."

"It's very possible that Varro sent men to trail you," Narsai concluded.

"We were ambushed by bandits outside Damascus," Gondophares interjected. "Do you think—"

"No," Narsai cut him short. "Varro wouldn't want you killed. He'd want to determine more specifically what you were here for and see if there would be something he could use to his advantage. Once you arrived in Jerusalem, he may have decided to take matters into his own hands. Perhaps he discovered something he wants to alert King Herod about. Or maybe he wants to observe what happens here and report back to the Roman legate in Antioch. In any event, that just complicates your situation all the more."

"Then how do you suggest we proceed?" Melchior asked.

"You walk a blade's edge," Narsai warned. "You must present yourselves not as political envoys, but as scholars seeking to understand the signs you have observed—as devout men following a celestial mystery. Emphasize that you travel under the patronage of the Royal Astronomer, not the king. Express uncertainty about the meaning of the conjunction and ask for Herod's permission to confer with his wise men on the matter."

"But what about our true mission?" Belshazzar asked. "If the newborn king announced by the signs in the heavens is not one in Herod's household, then who could it be? And where might we find him?"

The four magi first looked at each other, then collectively shifted their gaze to their host.

Narsai shook his head. "I'm a merchant, not a scholar or a prophet. I'm afraid you'll have to seek answers to those questions elsewhere. I've arranged an audience with King Herod, as my contacts from our king requested. But that's all I can do."

"And what of the gifts?" Gondophares asked. "Should we offer them to King Herod instead of taking them to the boy king, if we ever do find him?"

Narsai sighed. "I forgot you mentioned gifts. What are they?"

"I'm to give a small amount of gold," Gondophares replied. "Magus Belshazzar will offer frankincense, and Magus Melchior will present myrrh. They're tokens, really, and not in such quantities to be of any great value."

Narsi's eyes narrowed as he considered the information. He glanced quickly at Artaban as if to inquire why he would make no offering, but then returned his attention to Gondophares.

"The monetary value is of no consequence whatsoever," he declared. "But the symbolism is most concerning. Those specific gifts confirm the messianic focus of your mission." He lifted his hands in a gesture of incredulity. "Gold for a king, frankincense for a priest, myrrh for a prophet—the three roles the messiah is prophesied to fulfill. Any scribe in the court would recognize the significance immediately." He stroked the worry lines on his brow. "You must not allow King Herod to learn of these gifts, or you shall certainly disclose your true purpose and risk his wrath."

"Brack. Too much truth," Simur squawked, echoing the merchant's concern.

He stood and walked to the window, parting the curtain to glance toward the southern skyline where Herod's palace rose in the distance. The sky was tinged with twilight, and the city's lamps flickered like grounded stars.

"When is the audience?" Artaban asked quietly.

"Tomorrow, two hours after sunrise," Narsai responded. "You'll be escorted to the palace by the king's guards. That's both an honor and a precaution. I will not attend with you," he said, turning back. "Four foreign sages will attract enough scrutiny as it is. My involvement would only complicate matters. And you must not bring your guards or attendants. You four alone will face the king."

"We'll speak with care," Melchior assured him. "But we will not lie."

"Of course not," Narsai said dryly. "Just speak the truth *selectively*."

He offered a final nod, then turned to a small table and unrolled a parchment bearing the official mark of the palace. "This is your writ of passage. Memorize the names listed on it and show it to the guards at the western gate of the palace compound."

Melchior stood, his aged frame somehow radiating dignity

and determination despite the grim circumstances they faced. "We're grateful for your wisdom and your courage in arranging this audience. Whatever comes, we'll trust in the providence of our God of Light and Truth."

As the magi departed Narsai's house and trudged through the dark streets of Jerusalem toward their lodgings, Artaban found himself picking off the last bits of the scab from the wound on his arm. He couldn't shake the feeling they were walking into a situation far more dangerous than any they had yet encountered. Tomorrow, they would face a king who had already proven he would kill to protect his throne. And if their suppositions were indeed correct, somewhere in this ancient land, a child lay sleeping, unaware that his very existence had set in motion events that would determine the fate of kingdoms.

The stars glittered above the inner courtyard, their light filtering through the fig leaves that danced in the night breeze. The distant murmur of Roman sentries calling out the watch from the Antonia Fortress drifted across the upper city, a constant reminder of the Empire's watchful presence. Artaban stood near a carved limestone column, arms folded, gazing into the garden's shallow pool. The reflections of the stars rippled on its surface—distorted, uncertain.

Their traveling party had finally settled into their accommodations for the evening. One of Narsai's business contacts had arranged for them to lease a private guest house in the Lower City that would allow for the security and discretion they needed.

Behind him, the sound of soft footsteps announced Melchior's approach. The elder magus joined him in silence, Simur perched characteristically on his shoulder.

"You've been restless since we arrived," Melchior said.

"Hmm," Artaban mused. "I guess I'm concerned about how we'll address King Herod tomorrow," he replied without looking up. "I see many paths leading forward, but none to a good end."

"Tell me about these paths, my son. How do you appraise our situation?"

A silence hung in the air for a long moment before he finally replied. "If we tell the king about the signs we have seen in the stars and what we think they mean, he will no doubt believe we intend to sow the seeds of rebellion. We all heard from Narsai how paranoid Herod is. A monarch who would kill his own sons would surely do the same to envoys from a rival kingdom."

"Perhaps," Melchior said.

"Or worse," Artaban went on, "he might just pass the information to the Romans and give them an excuse both to execute us and to launch an invasion of our country." He turned to face his mentor. "Such a course could risk not only our own lives, but also those of our wives, our children, our king, and our people."

"We do indeed bear a heavy burden. What other options do you see?"

Artaban took a deep breath and exhaled slowly. "We could follow Narsai's counsel and withhold the true nature of our mission." He shrugged. "Claim to be merely traveling scholars, commissioned by the Royal Astronomer to consult with experts on the Jewish scriptures about the meaning of various kinds of heavenly omens."

"Okay," Melchior replied. "Is such a path without its own risks?"

Artaban sighed and looked back down at the black depths of the pond. "No." He shook his head slightly. "No lie, however small, ever stands on its own. The pathway of deception is never a straight route. Every fork in the road requires new and more elaborate fabrications until you become lost in an unending maze of deceit that ultimately leads back to the point of origin, albeit with much greater consequences."

"That is the general lesson history teaches those wise enough to inquire. But what, specifically, might that mean in this present situation?"

"Hmm," Artaban murmured. "It's probably not possible to trace every strand in the web. But some implications are easy enough to predict. We couldn't confer in earnest with our Jewish counterparts without eventually disclosing our true interests. Their astronomers have undoubtedly observed the same convergence in the heavens, though without a full knowledge of its rarity and import. But if we wanted to learn anything new about the identity of the messiah and where we could find him, our underlying intentions would reveal themselves soon enough. Our motivations would then appear even more sinister when reported to the king, wrapped in a cloak of lies and deceit. And the reprisal would be even more severe."

"That's a fair assessment, I'd say," Melchior remarked. "So where does that leave us? Is there no other course?"

Artaban thought for a moment, then pointed to the reflection of the stars in the pool. "*Marduk* and *Ninub* have now diverged and turned their separate ways. The omen has come and gone, and events in this world continue on as if nothing has occurred at all. Perhaps," he mused, "we could present our gifts to Herod as tokens of Parthian friendship and simply allow the moment to fade."

"Ah," Melchior pointed up to the night sky. "But behold, *Nergal* still rises within *Ea*. The promised king has surely been born. The sacred flame has been kindled, and it will not be quenched. All may appear normal for now." He tossed a small pebble into the pool that landed in the midst of *Nergal's* reflected image. "But the stone has been cast, and the ripples will spread to the ends of the earth."

Artaban straightened and faced his old *usted* squarely. "Okay. So what exactly do you propose?"

"Brack," Simur squawked from his perch on his master's shoulder. "No good options. Still must choose."

"One critical thing was missing from each of your assessments, my son."

Melchior's face was soft with compassion. His eyes held no malice. There was no accusation in his tone. Just the genuine concern of a wizened sage for a devoted disciple. Still, Artaban felt himself bristle at the allegation.

"And what's that?" he asked with a harder edge in his voice than he intended.

"You never mentioned Ahura Mazda, our Wise Lord," Melchior said. "What about his will in this matter? How might he use his infinite power to intervene in the situation? He called us to this task, did he not? Shall he not guide us through to its end?"

"Like he guided my father?" Artaban asked, unable to mask the sarcasm in his tone.

Melchior sighed. "Artaban, what happened to your family was an unspeakable tragedy. I can't begin to imagine the pain you've experienced, but—"

"Not just my family," Artaban cut in. "My father's interpretation of the signs in the heavens and his advice to King Orodes led directly to his death. But it also brought the retribution of Rome on our entire kingdom. It's why that tyrant, Herod, is on his throne even now."

Melchior placed his hand gently on the shoulder of his younger protégé. "I think you give your father more credit than he deserves, and place far too much responsibility on his shoulders. He was a very junior advisor to the Court at the time. He may well have been vocal in his opinions, but the king was ultimately responsible for the decision to wage war. And kings are often quick to heed the advice they already want to hear."

"But my father was sincere in his faith. He earnestly believed he was interpreting the signs correctly. Yet he was wrong, and Ahura Mazda allowed him to err."

"Ahh," Melchior said, stroking his beard. "So the actual issue is one of faith. You find it difficult to believe that a god of truth, righteousness, and justice could allow such a calamity to befall his worshippers and one of his beloved sons."

"Yes," Artaban replied without hesitation. "Yes, I find it difficult to believe." It felt good somehow to say the words out loud. "What if…" he hesitated momentarily, pondering how to phrase the issues he wrestled with in his mind. "What if there are no signs in the stars at all? What if they aren't really heavenly spirits, dancing to the will of a supreme god?" It struck him that his words would be considered blasphemous to a man of faith like Melchior, but still he pressed on. "What if they're just inanimate objects tracing paths across the sky that never alter? After all, we were able to predict the precise time and nature of this conjunction. If the Wise Lord dictates their motions to convey special messages about events in our world, how could we predict them so precisely?"

"An interesting thought," Melchior replied, seemingly unperturbed by Artaban's egregious proclamation. "Or, perhaps, the Lord of Light uses the movement of the stars as an intricate clock with which to choreograph the events in our world."

"Brack," quipped Simur. "Perfect timing."

"Perhaps," Melchior suggested, "both the Parthian conquest your father advocated and Rome's reprisal were necessary steps leading to this king's arrival."

"What do you mean?" Artaban asked.

"What if your father's interpretation was correct after all? What if his personal sacrifice supported a greater good?"

"I don't understand."

"Don't forget the cosmic conflict," Melchior reminded him. "We serve the Father of Truth, but there is also a Father of Lies.

The battle they wage for control of the cosmos is ultimately fought within the hearts and minds of men. Perhaps the confrontation between Parthia and Rome is just a mirror of the greater struggle that has raged throughout time and eternity. But," and he jabbed his finger toward Artaban to emphasize his next point, "we know how that war ends. The *Saoshyant* will come and lead the forces of light and truth to the ultimate victory over darkness and lies. Perhaps—just perhaps—that time has come, and this Jewish messiah will be the Promised One we've all hoped for."

"But what does that have to do with my father?"

"When Parthia invaded Syria thirty years ago, how did we defeat the Roman forces?"

"Lots of reasons, I suppose," Artaban replied. He was intimately familiar with the history of those events. He had poured over the records, trying to understand where his father had gone wrong. "I guess it came down mostly to a combination of factors—Roman disunity, strategic surprise, local support, and the superiority of our Parthian cavalry."

"Okay," Melchior replied. "Be more specific."

Artaban chafed with irritation. He didn't understand what this had to do with his father's failed interpretation of heavenly omens or the situation they found themselves in now.

"Fine," he replied, and began a monotone rehearsal of the facts. "The Romans were engaged in a civil war between Antony and Octavian that diverted their military forces away from their eastern provinces. Parthia allied with the Roman defector, General Quintus Labienus, who rallied support from local Syrian militias and some disaffected Roman garrisons. We leveraged the speed and flexibility of Parthian light cavalry units and horse-mounted archers to achieve quick and decisive attacks on unprepared Roman outposts. The end result was the rapid capture of Damascus, Antioch, and eventually Jerusalem."

"Exactly," Melchior said with an expression of satisfaction on his face.

"I still don't understand," Artaban shot back, his voice edged with annoyance. "What's your point?"

"Could we achieve that same kind of victory today?"

"Not likely," Artaban said. "After their recapture of the Syrian province, the Roman position here is stronger than ever."

"So what would it take for Parthia to successfully invade Syria and capture Jerusalem again?"

Artaban threw up his hands in exasperation. "We couldn't do it. Not without…" and his speech slowed dramatically. "Not without divine intervention."

"Or—" Melchior began, but Artaban finished his thought.

"Or the coming of the *Saoshyant*."

"That," Melchior stated emphatically, "is precisely my point. We didn't need the help of our Great God to conquer Syria in your father's day. And it's only because of the first invasion that the Roman position is stronger now than ever before." He shook his head and sighed. "Even the best of men only reach out to God when they're beyond the limits of their own capabilities."

"Brack," Simur emphasized. "Extreme times. Extreme measures."

"So, I have to ask," Melchior prompted his friend, "would your father have been willing to sacrifice his life in this world to prepare the way for the *Saoshyant* and to earn eternal glory on the other side of the *Chinvat* Bridge?"

Artaban mulled the question over in his mind, but made no reply.

"And," Melchior went on after a long moment of silence, "if your father were here now, even knowing his own fate, what would he counsel you to do?"

Artaban knew the only right answer to that question, but could not make himself form the words.

The old sage patted him affectionately on the shoulder.

"To answer our original question," he said. "We are servants of the Lord of Light and Truth. When we stand before King Herod on the morrow, we shall address him in the only way we can—with openness and honesty about what we have observed and what we believe it means. If that provokes his wrath, we will trust in the God who called us to this task. He will guide us to its end."

As his mentor turned to walk away, Artaban heard Simur's succinct assessment. "Brack. Fear fades. Faith endures. Truth will set you free."

Artaban tensed as they passed through the gate into a vast colonnaded courtyard. He caught his first view of the monumental palace in the reflection of a long rectangular pool, flanked by trimmed hedges, rows of date palms, and carefully manicured beds of winter flowers—cyclamen, anemone, and marigolds.

As Herod's chief steward escorted them wordlessly down the tiled pathway, Artaban gaped in wonder at the immense gleaming white limestone walls of the palace, trimmed in gold. The scale and grandeur echoed the power of Rome, while the architecture itself reflected Hellenistic influences—slender, fluted columns with ornate capitals surrounding geometrically arranged gardens interspersed with fountains and statues posing in elegant or heroic postures. Meanwhile, symbols of Judean heritage and faith were scattered throughout the grounds as well. Sculptured lions, pomegranates in stone reliefs, decorative friezes depicting olive branches, and menorah-style lampstands lined the covered walkways.

The courtyard swirled with color and rank. Scribes in plain white robes whispered beneath the arcade, scrolls tucked under their arms, while a scattering of temple priests, clad in black hooded cloaks, cast watchful eyes over the milling crowd. Judean nobles gathered in small groups around the various fountains, debating in low voices, as barefooted slaves in short tunics moved briskly between the guests, their heads bowed. There were even a few Roman officials, dressed in traditional togas, mingling among the Judean and Idumean gentry.

As they processed through the midst of this eclectic mix of nobles and government officials, the Parthian magi caused quite a stir. They wore their formal regalia, which they had kept carefully packed away during the long journey. Robes of crimson and indigo rippled in the breeze, gold sashes gleamed across their breasts, and the conical caps of Zoroastrian scholars crowned their heads.

The lords and ladies of Herod's court smiled at them in pleasant acknowledgement as they passed by, many turning to whisper among themselves in low murmurs. Some of the men in this crowd would, no doubt, attend their audience with the king, to bring a first-hand account of the interview back as gossip to share with their less-privileged acquaintances.

The magi mounted the twelve steps that led from the sunken garden to the entrance of the monumental palace. Its doors loomed before them, tall and unyielding. They were crafted from cypress heartwood, their surfaces clad in hammered bronze sheets that caught the morning light like fire. Rows of rounded studs reinforced the seams, and engraved lions prowled across the lower panels, bordered by pomegranate vines twining up toward the lintels.

The soldiers flanking the entry wore short red cloaks over dark tunics, their bronze helmets reflecting the bright light of the rising sun. Each wore a Roman-style *gladius* at his hip and clutched a spear in his hand. Artaban didn't have the same visceral reaction to these soldiers as he did to the Roman forces they had encountered so often along their route. Though these men represented a threat to their lives, especially considering the message the magi bore to their king, the nature of the danger seemed different somehow. His pulse did not quicken as much in their presence, nor did he feel the same queasiness in his gut.

At a gesture from the steward, a sentry opened the doors, and they stepped into the entrance hall. The corridors of the upper palace seemed unnaturally silent. Other than a few more guards, Artaban saw no one at all. A filtered golden light slanted through narrow clerestory windows high above their heads, casting long, angular shadows across the polished limestone floor. The silence, the light, even the precise geometry of the stones beneath their feet, seemed calculated both to impress and to set them at ease. Artaban could not shake the feeling they were stepping into a trap with a serene facade and a sinister core. He unconsciously ran his fingers over the scar that was left behind by the wound on his arm, a constant reminder of the very real dangers they faced.

"You understand the protocol?" the chief steward asked as they paused before the inner doors of the audience chamber?

"Yes," Melchior replied, and the rest of them nodded.

Artaban's heart raced as the immense bronze doors creaked open. This confrontation with a paranoid king could very possibly end in their death. Despite the rules of court etiquette, he could not prevent himself from glancing up briefly through the open portal at the royal hall. His eyes took in a similar mix of Roman, Greek, and Jewish motifs that mirrored those of the courtyard. The sight both awed and amazed him.

He was awed by the grandeur of the hall. The vaulted ceiling towered overhead to a height of at least twenty men. Elaborate frescoes covered the walls, depicting scenes from what must have been Jewish and Roman history. The marble floor was decorated with elaborate mosaics in geometric designs and was lined on both sides by a Hellenistic-style colonnade. Herod's throne sat perched at the top of a dozen steps, flanked by two golden lions. The whole grand edifice was clearly crafted to convey an overwhelming impression of wealth and power. And it was quite effective.

The four magi moved forward in measured steps, following the protocol the chief steward had explained to them. At the prescribed distance, they prostrated themselves on the marble floor, remaining there until given permission to rise.

"Your Majesty," announced the steward, "I present Melchior of Babylon, Belshazzar of Nippur, Gondophares of Sakastan, and Artaban of Ctesiphon—magi of the Parthian realm, who seek an audience with your royal person."

After a long moment, Herod's voice cut through the silence. "Rise and speak."

The four men stood, and Melchior stepped forward as their spokesman. "Your Majesty, we bring greetings of friendship from the Court of Phraates, Sovereign of Parthia. May the favor of the Wise and Righteous God rest upon your house and your realm."

From this closer perspective, Artaban could view the royal assembly in more detail. Herod leaned back almost casually on his those, as if bored by another day of formalities he would rather have skipped. A priest in an extremely elaborate ensemble stood at the king's right side. Artaban wondered if Melchior knew the symbolism of the various articles of clothing the holy man wore. A short, squat man with a stern expression stood to the king's left, with a scribe seated at a desk off to one side, stylus in hand. Two guards stood rigidly at attention on each step, and a gallery of nobles formed three tiers of seats that angled out from both sides of the dais.

Herod inclined his head. "You have traveled far. Parthian scholars are welcome in Jerusalem. What cause brings you to the City of Peace?"

Artaban tensed. This was the moment of truth. After his

conversation with Melchior, he knew his old master would be forthright about their mission. But how would this suspicious and volatile monarch respond to an implied challenge to his authority, especially when surrounded by such an array of court officials and within the hearing of Roman ears? He fought to suppress an involuntary shudder.

"Great King, we have witnessed a sign in the heavens. A conjunction of extraordinary rarity has occurred, which our calculations tell us happens perhaps once in eight centuries. The wandering stars *Marduk* and *Ninub*, which your astronomers call Jupiter and Saturn, have met three times within the constellation of Pisces. They were joined in their final convergence by *Nergal*, the red Wanderer known to you as Mars."

A murmur rippled through the small assembly of courtiers, and Artaban noticed the scribe quickly scratching notes on his wax tablet.

"And what," Herod asked with studied casualness, "do your traditions say of such a sign?"

Melchior paused for a moment before responding. Artaban sensed the old sage take a deep breath before answering.

"Your Majesty," Melchior continued, "our ancient records speak of great kings rising when the supreme Wanderer and the royal star meet within the constellation of wisdom and new beginnings. But this rare triple conjunction suggests something far more significant—the birth of a ruler destined to alter the balance of earthly powers."

Artaban watched Herod closely. The king's expression remained impassive, but he sat up straighter on his throne. "Where exactly do you expect this new king to be born?"

"Your Majesty, in seeking to understand this omen, we consulted the writings of ancient seers, including the Hebrew prophet Daniel, who served in the courts of Babylon and Persia. His visions speak precisely of the time when a divinely appointed king would arise to establish an everlasting kingdom. We assumed," Melchior added with careful diplomacy, "this newborn king might be found within Your Majesty's own household, perhaps a son or nephew whose lineage traces back to the royal house of David, as the prophecies require. This is why we appear before you now, Mighty King. We saw his star in the East and have brought tokens of friendship from the Parthian Court to honor him."

For the first time, Herod smiled, but the expression was thin and cold.

"You honor my house with your conjecture," he said. "Yet no such birth has taken place in our royal family."

At this, Herod's advisor, the squat man with calculating eyes, leaned over to whisper urgently in the king's ear. Herod waved him back with visible irritation.

"Show us the gifts you have brought to this auspicious child," Herod commanded.

The senior three magi lifted up the small, ornately carved boxes they each held. Gondophares opened his first, revealing a quantity of gold coins bearing the image of King Phraates. Belshazzar's box contained costly frankincense from the southern trade routes, while Melchior's held precious myrrh, its fragrant resin carefully preserved in sealed vials. Amid the lavish opulence of the palace, Artaban realized these tokens must have appeared trivial in the eyes of the Judean sovereign and his court.

Artaban felt Herod's eyes briefly settle on him, expectantly. He bowed his head and cast his eyes to the ground in a rush of embarrassment and shame. He alone bore no gift for the infant king.

At that moment, Artaban heard a muffled exclamation from the priest who stood at Herod's right hand.

"What is it, Simon?" Herod demanded.

"My Lord King," the priest replied, "I believe these gifts have been carefully selected, not for their value, but for what they represent."

"Go on," Herod prompted curtly.

"Gold signifying the wealth of a king," Simon replied. "Frankincense for the holy intercession of a priest, and the oil of myrrh for the anointing of a prophet."

Herod's advisor stiffened, and Artaban heard a collective gasp from the gallery.

Simon summarized his assessment in a tone of awe. "These are meant as tribute for the Messiah."

Herod paused for a moment to allow the emotions of the crowd and the murmuring to settle. He regained his composure and maintained a stoic expression.

"Is this true, honored Magus? Is it your belief that this newborn king is the promised Messiah of the holy scriptures?"

The entire court seemed to hold its breath in anticipation of the reply. Artaban likewise fell still, every muscle tense, as if a single misstep might bring the weight of the empire crashing down upon them. Both the Judean court and the Romans would be listening intently to Melchior's reply.

"Indeed, Your Majesty," Melchior confirmed. "It is the conclusion we deduced from the signs in the heavens and our very limited knowledge of Hebrew prophecy." He went on quickly before he could be cut off by the king. "But our under-standing of the Jewish scriptures is admittedly inadequate. And so we appear before you now as scholars and not diplomatic envoys. We've come to consult with your own experts on the soundness of our analysis. If it proves true, we would likewise be eager to know where the child could be found, that we might present our gifts as tokens of friendship with him and rejoice with you over the arrival of your long-awaited messiah."

The fire has been lit, Artaban thought to himself. *It cannot now be extinguished.*

There was no longer any doubt as to the purpose of their

mission to declare the birth of the Jewish messiah. If that fact would incite Herod's rage or provoke the wrath of Rome, there was nothing they could do to stop it now. Their fate was in the hands of the political powers of this world. If there truly was a god in heaven, they would need His intervention to navigate their way out of this snare of their own devising.

An agitated muttering rippled throughout the gallery as Melchior finished his declaration. The title "messiah" seemed to echo off the stone walls like a forbidden word. Then the sharp crack of a staff striking marble cut through the noise. The steward stepped forward and raised his hand.

"Silence before the king!" he intoned. "Let the court attend to His Majesty."

The gallery hushed. Even the guards shifted subtly, their spears tapping once against the floor in a rhythm of warning. Herod said nothing, and his face retained its dispassionate air. His advisor again bent to whisper in his ear. The king thought over the words for a moment and then turned to address the priest.

"Simon, you have experts in the law at hand who can address these issues, correct?"

The priest's reply was steady and confident. "Yes, Lord King. Eliezer ben Zadok and Hillel the Elder have both written extensively on the prophecies of the Messiah. They are representatives of the Sanhedrin here at your court."

"Send for them," the king ordered. "We shall settle this matter here and now."

"Certainly, Lord King." He gestured to a scribe in the background, who promptly exited the audience chamber. "If it pleases Your Majesty, the lords of the court would certainly consider a scholarly discussion of this nature to be somewhat tedious. Perhaps they can be dismissed at this time and later informed of the outcome."

A murmur arose from the gallery, which was promptly quelled by two sharp raps of the steward's staff.

The king locked eyes with the priest, and an unspoken agreement seemed to pass between them. A moment later, the king spoke. "Clear the court," he ordered. Then glancing at the four magi, he added, "Our Parthian guests shall remain."

After three more cracks of the steward's staff on the floor, the nobles rose and began exiting the gallery. Meanwhile, Herod conferred in hushed tones with the priest and his advisor, and the four magi were left standing in the middle of the audience chamber without leave to move, sit, or speak among themselves.

Momentarily, the king glanced around the hall, then gestured for the senior military officer to approach. The soldier went down on one knee at the base of the dais and bowed low.

"You and the guards are dismissed. There is no threat here."

"By your command," he said, then bowed again, backed away from the king, and ordered the soldiers out of the hall.

The king continued to confer with his counselors, and the magi continued to wait for what felt like an interminable amount of time. Artaban wondered if this was some subtle form of retribution for the trouble they had caused. Based on this monarch's recent actions—executing his own sons as traitors to the crown—he was unlikely to receive news of the messiah as anything but a threat to his power, despite his apparent indifference. Artaban's apprehension grew along with the aching pain in his legs. His mind wrestled with the question of why everyone had been ushered out of the hall. Clearly, Herod wanted no witnesses to what would come next.

Finally, Artaban glimpsed motion at the far side of the great room, and two men strode toward the throne. As they drew near, Artaban could see their features more clearly. The first, robed in white linen and bound with a sash embroidered in crimson and gold, looked similar to the priest, Simon. The other, a lean man with a silver-streaked beard and sharp eyes, wore a blue-gray cloak that fell in clean folds from his shoulders. Artaban guessed he was a senior scholar or scribe. The two men approached the king, knelt, and bowed low.

King Herod glanced at Simon, who gave a slight nod in return.

"Rise," the king commanded, and waited for them to get to their feet. Then he waved his hand toward Simon, who took up the dialog.

"These distinguished magi have come on behalf of King Phraates of the Parthians. They purport to have seen signs in the heavens, which they believe may point to the birth of a great king. After consulting the writings of the prophet Daniel, they concluded this child would, in fact, be our promised Messiah. His Majesty, King Herod, would like to know if their conjecture is true. Do we have reason to believe the Messiah has indeed come? Hillel, how do you read Daniel's prophecies in this regard?"

The man in the garb of a scholar inclined his head briefly, then replied. "My Lord King, the visions shown to Daniel by the Most High God portray the dominion of the Messiah quite vividly. His kingdom will indeed grow to fill the whole earth. One vision, brought from the throne of heaven by the archangel Gabriel, outlines a timeframe when we can expect the Messiah to appear. Unfortunately, the beginning point for that prophetic time period remains a matter of great uncertainty. The predicted time could be soon, or it could be as much as forty years in the future. The wisest of your loyal scholars debate this issue even now."

The king allowed his guard to slip briefly and cast an irritated glance at his high priest, as if angered that he was first hearing this news from Parthian astronomers rather than his own advisors.

"So it could be now?" Simon clarified.

"It is… possible, Lord King."

The men always directed their responses to the king, regardless of who asked the questions.

"What about these signs in the heavens, Eliezer?" Simon asked the priest. "Have our watchmen observed any such omens?"

"Your Majesty," he replied, "I assume our learned guests refer to the meeting of Jupiter and Saturn, which occurred just a few weeks past."

Simon inclined his head toward Melchior.

"Indeed," Melchior confirmed. "Just such a conjunction has occurred thrice within the past year, all within the constellation of Pisces. During this latest encounter, they were joined also by Mars." Melchior had used the Roman names for the heavenly bodies, which would be more familiar to the Jews than their Parthian equivalents. "We estimate such a sequence of events transpires only once in a thousand years."

Artaban chanced a look at the priest and could see a momentary look of shock in his expression.

"The words of the rogue prophet, Balaam, recorded in the books of Moses, might possibly refer to such an extraordinary event," Eliezer said with awe in his tone, and then quoted from memory, "'I see him, but not now. I behold him, but not near. A star will come out of Jacob. A scepter will rise out of Israel.' Many of our scholars believe this speaks of a heavenly sign that will announce the Messiah's birth."

An icy chill ran up Artaban's spine when he heard these words, and his entire body tensed, his fingers clenching at the folds in his robe. In all their research, they had never discovered any prophecy about a star or celestial event that might tie so directly to the conjunction they had observed in the heavens.

"So you're saying the scriptures confirm the assertions of our Parthian guests?" Simon asked.

"It is a matter we should commit to further study and prayer," Eliezer replied.

"Is it likely to be true?" Herod broke in with an edge of tension in his clipped tone.

Eliezer shrunk back slightly. "It is… possible, Your Majesty. I can make no more definitive claim."

The king again shot a look of annoyance at Simon before returning his attention to his scriptural experts. "If the Messiah has, in fact, been born, where should we look to find him?"

There was a long moment of silence before Hillel apparently mustered the courage to speak.

"That is more certain, Sire. The scriptures are much clearer about the location of the Messiah's birth than about its timing."

"Where?" the king prompted.

"Your Majesty," Hillel replied, "the prophet Micah declared, *'But you, Bethlehem Ephrathah, though you are small among the clans of Judah, out of you will come for me one who will be ruler over Israel, whose origins are from of old, from ancient times.'"*

Eliezer nodded in agreement. "Indeed, Your Majesty. King David himself was born in Bethlehem, and the Messiah must come from David's line."

"Bethlehem," Herod muttered, regaining his composure. "I see. Is there anything else?"

The two scholars looked at each other briefly, then Eliezer replied. "No, Your Majesty. Much has been written about the work of the Messiah, of course. But there is nothing more about the timing or location of his birth."

The king relaxed back on his throne. His eyes narrowed, and he appeared to be pondering the information he had just heard. After several long moments, during which no one else uttered a word, Herod finally turned to address Simon.

"I require from you and your scribes a complete accounting of what your sacred writings say concerning the Messiah. Tell me who he is, by what signs he may be known, what actions he will take, and the manner in which he will establish his kingdom on this earth. I want every prophecy, every detail that might aid in his identification. You will present your summary to me in one week's time."

"As you will, Lord King."

"And Simon, I need information I can use. No speculation. No debate. I want clarity, not commentary."

"Of course, Your Majesty. It will be done."

"And now, leave me," the king said, dismissing them with a wave of his hand. "I will have a private word with our guests."

"My Lord?" The royal advisor asked with a confused expression. He had remained silent throughout the whole academic discussion.

"Go," Herod commanded sharply.

"As you wish, Lord King."

The men all bowed and backed away from the throne.

Artaban's pulse quickened. His mind raced with the implications of what the Jewish scholars had revealed. It took several moments for him to realize they were all alone with the king. He feared what might come next. At least there were no soldiers present to execute them or to haul them away to a secret prison cell.

To Artaban's surprise, the king's expression softened.

"My friends," he began. "I'm somewhat disconcerted by the fact that we must learn such significant news from foreign dignitaries, such as yourselves, rather than from our own wisest scholars. Even so, we're grateful to you for bringing us these glad tidings."

"You honor us with your words, Your Majesty," Melchior replied.

"We adjure you to complete your journey. Go to Bethlehem. Find the infant Messiah, and honor him with the gifts you have brought from your king."

Artaban could scarcely believe what he heard. He had expected rage from this man, who everyone said was mad. Indeed, his recent actions had demonstrated that fact without dispute. And yet now, he appeared to receive the news of a coming messiah who would displace his own kingdom with enthusiasm.

"We entreat you to share the news no further among the people of Judea. If it is true, then our royal court should be the first to greet this long-awaited king and welcome him to our land. I myself am eager to honor him with gifts of eternal friendship, as your own King Phraates has commissioned you to do."

"Your Majesty," Melchior replied, "these sentiments come as great encouragement to ones who have journeyed so far on such an uncertain quest. We are most grateful for your assistance and approbation."

"How long has it been then," the king inquired, "since you first saw this sign in the heavens?"

"Magus Belshazzar first discovered the omen in our almanacs over a year ago. And we witnessed the first conjunction almost eight months ago."

"So the child has walked among us for all that time without our knowledge?" Herod asked in surprise. "Our greetings are long overdue."

"We are uncertain, Lord King, whether his birth was marked by the first conjunction or the last. Perhaps your own scholars can shed more light on that issue."

"In any event, our hospitality to such a one is long overdue. Go now with my blessing. And when you have located the newborn Messiah, please return and tell me where he can be found, that we may honor him with a welcome worthy of such a king."

The magi, receiving their dismissal, backed away from the throne, and left the grand hall.

As they were escorted from the building, Artaban reflected on the final session with the king. Despite his reactions to the reports from his own scholars, which appeared to be ones of agitation and scorn, his open acceptance of the news they brought seemed genuine enough. He certainly said all the right words. Still, Artaban could not reconcile this attitude with the long history of Herod's paranoia. He was also deeply bothered by the incongruity between Herod's relationship with Rome and the news of a coming Messiah who would ultimately cause that empire's fall.

They eventually exited the palace doors and emerged into the light of day—a physical illumination that seemed to bring with it a new clarity of perspective. As they crossed the upper courtyard, Artaban's eyes drifted eastward, to where the sun ignited the golden roof of the great Temple, rising above the city like a holy flame. The contrast struck him. There, the prayers of a nation ascended to their Creator God. Here, the schemes of a paranoid king festered behind veiled doors. Though Herod claimed to honor the God of Israel, his throne faced away from the sanctuary. From this Roman-style palace, the Holy Temple was just another silhouette against the eastern sky.

CHAPTER NINE

Winter, 7 BC
Jerusalem, Kingdom of Judea,
Syrian Province, Roman Empire

The oil lamp cast restless shadows across the whitewashed walls as Artaban knelt beside his travel chest, placing garments inside with slow, deliberate motions that mirrored the struggles occurring in his mind. Through the narrow window of their lodging, the sounds of Jerusalem settling into evening drifted up from the streets below—vendors closing their stalls, distant trumpets announcing the evening sacrifice in the temple, a donkey braying somewhere in the dark. The weight of the day's events pressed upon him like the shadow of his father's cross darkening his childhood memories.

His fingers returned to the healing wound on his arm, pressing, testing, measuring the pain. Each touch was a reminder that Tabor had died on that Damascus road, and that he himself had nearly perished, all for a mission he'd never fully believed in. Now he was finally choosing to walk away.

From behind, soft footsteps crossed the portico. "You seem to be in great haste, my son," came Melchior's gentle voice. The old sage stood in the doorway with Simur perched on his shoulder, the starling's bright eyes taking in the scene with characteristic acumen. "Bethlehem is but a short journey from here. We can prepare at first light and be there well before midday."

Artaban didn't look up from his packing. His fingers moved to the small bundle containing his father's astronomical instruments—the shadow stick, armillary rings, and calipers that had somehow survived the destruction of their home in Damascus decades ago. They felt heavier tonight than ever before.

"I won't be going to Bethlehem," he said quietly.

The words hung in the air between them like the smoke of incense. Melchior stepped into the small chamber, his movements slow and deliberate.

"What do you mean?"

Artaban closed the lid of his chest and began fastening the leather straps. He forced himself to meet his mentor's eyes— those patient, knowing eyes that had seen him through years of study and struggle at the Bīt Mummu.

"I found a caravan headed east at dawn, merchants from Palmyra returning along the winter trade routes to the Euphrates. I'll join them and make my way home from there."

Melchior settled his aged frame onto a low wooden stool near the table. The lamp flame flickered as he moved, sending new patterns of light and shadow dancing across the walls.

"What of our mission?" he began. "Surely you don't mean to abandon it now. We've come so far, endured so much..."

"My mission is complete," Artaban said blandly. "King Phraates charged me to serve as his voice of caution in this endeavor, and I have done that as well as I could. At each step of this journey, I raised the concerns that needed to be considered.

I questioned our interpretation of the omens. I warned of the dangers from Rome. I urged prudence when others counseled haste." He gestured toward the window, beyond which lay the sprawling city with its Roman garrison and Herodian palace. "Today we appeared before Herod's court and delivered our message. The king now knows of the signs in the heavens and the birth they supposedly foretell. By now, the Romans must surely know as well. My role in this matter is finished."

"Brack," Simur squawked, ruffling his dark feathers. "Running away. Running away."

The bird's words stung more than Artaban cared to admit. He turned back to the travel chest and tugged unnecessarily at the leather straps, as if testing the security of their hold. In truth, he was measuring the soundness of his own motivations.

Melchior stood in contemplative silence for several moments, his weathered hands folded at his front. When he finally spoke, his voice carried the wisdom of decades spent observing both the heavens and the human heart.

"There's more to this than duty discharged, I think. Tell me, Artaban, what truly troubles you? What drives you to flee from companions who have become brothers and from a quest that has consumed the better part of a year?"

Artaban's movements became more agitated. He unbuckled the straps, opened the lid, and then began pulling items from the trunk and repacking them, as if the mere act of organizing his belongings could somehow organize the chaos in his mind.

"To be honest, Master, I don't think I ever truly believed in our cause. I never planned on joining this expedition to begin with. I was shocked when King Phraates directed me to go with you. From the very beginning, I feared the retribution of Rome more than I trusted in the omens of heaven. I'm not even sure there is a god who directs the course of the stars above or the events on this earth below."

The admission hung between them like a personal betrayal.

Artaban had never spoken the words aloud before, though they had haunted his thoughts throughout the long journey from Ecbatana. He was surprised at how much lighter he felt having finally given voice to his doubt. At the same time, he was terrified by what that admission might mean. Melchior had been his mentor in a life of faith and service to Ahura Mazda.

Melchior leaned forward slightly, his voice taking on the tone he had used in the teaching halls of the Bīt Mummu when guiding his struggling students toward understanding. Artaban turned and looked deeply into his mentor's eyes. Instead of the condemnation he expected, he saw only a deep compassion.

"Take heart, my son," Melchior said, placing a hand on Artaban's shoulder. "Every true magus eventually confronts a crisis of belief in one form or another. It's a necessary part of the faith journey. Without it, one might wonder if his devotion was genuine at all."

"Even you?" Artaban asked.

Melchior smiled softly and gave a gentle nod. "Yes. Of course. Especially me."

"How?" Artaban prompted.

Melchior exhaled a long, slow breath. "Years ago, when pestilence swept through Babylon, it carried away my wife and my youngest son. I had charted the heavens faithfully. I had prayed at the fire altar daily. Yet still the plague came. I asked myself over and over, what use was a god who could not protect those who served him?"

Artaban searched his mentor's face, seeing pain etched into the lines of memory. "And what answer did you find?"

Melchior sighed, stroking his beard. "At first, none. Only silence. For months, I abandoned everything—my studies, my prayers, my faith. I convinced myself that the stars were merely distant fires and that our ceremonies were empty rituals. But over time, I came to see that the struggle between light and darkness touches every soul. Suffering is not proof of our God's absence, but proof of the enemy's fury." He fixed Artaban with a steady gaze. "The question is not whether sorrow comes, but whether we will stand with the Father of Truth in spite of it."

Artaban lowered his eyes, his chest tight. "That's a hard road."

"Yes, it is. But it's also the road that leads to life. And," Melchior looked deeply into his eyes, "it's the path you're on this very moment."

"Then what's your counsel to me now, Master?"

"Consider all we have witnessed. The conjunctions all occurred exactly as predicted. We found confirmation in the Hebrew prophecies. We escaped from Damascus when all seemed lost. And we learned from King Herod's own scholars that their ancient texts speak of precisely such signs announcing their messiah's birth."

Artaban felt his hands unconsciously clench into fists. "I admit, the Jewish prophecies seem to fit what we've observed in the heavens. But we haven't yet seen the child. Even if we do find an infant in Bethlehem, how can we truly know that he's the promised messiah? How could we tell the difference between the King of Kings and any other Jewish infant? What proof will there be that we're witnessing the fulfillment of prophecy rather than just seeing what we're hoping to see?" Artaban slammed the lid to his trunk shut with more force than he intended. "Worse yet, what if word of our visit reaches Roman ears? What if our presence in Bethlehem is seen as Parthian interference in a Roman province? The consequences could destroy our kingdom."

"Sometimes," Melchior replied with a calm steadiness in his voice, "proof comes only after the step of faith. And sometimes, never at all in this life."

Artaban's jaw tightened. "Faith," he repeated, as if testing the word and finding it bitter.

"The true issue is not the signs, my son," Melchior said, his tone warm but resolute. "It's not Herod, or Rome, or even the child. It's whether *you're* willing to trust the One who called you to this journey. Fleeing to Damascus won't resolve the questions that plague your heart. They'll only follow you across the desert and back to Ctesiphon, growing larger and more burdensome with every step you take."

"Brack," Simur's shrill voice cut through the air. "Trust in the Lord."

The starling's words pierced the dark clouds in Artaban's mind and sent a shiver down his spine. For perhaps the first time since he had known the little bird, he suddenly wondered where its jarring comments actually came from. Most of the time, Simur just parroted phrases he'd learned from his master. But there were other times, like just now, when his short outbursts seemed to come from a wisdom even greater than Melchior's own. Could some other force be speaking through that bird? Speaking to *him*...

Artaban shook his head to clear his thoughts and continued lashing the straps on the trunk. "I envy you," he said to his old *usted*, "that you found your way back to faith. I want to believe. It's just..."

Before Melchior could respond, Gondophares burst through the doorway without bothering to knock, his usually composed demeanor replaced by urgent excitement. His dark hair was disheveled, and his eyes shone with an intensity Artaban had rarely seen.

"Master Melchior! Artaban!" he gasped, struggling to catch his breath. "You must come to the roof immediately. There's something you must see."

"What is it?" Melchior asked. "What's happened?"

"Just come!" Gondophares insisted, gesturing frantically toward the stairs that led to the building's flat roof. "Belshazzar is already up there. He's been checking and rechecking his charts, and he says it's impossible, but—" He stopped himself short, as if struggling to find the right words. Eventually, he gave up and pled, "Please, Master, just come and see for yourselves."

The urgency in Gondophares' voice was unmistakable, tinged with an awe that bordered on fear. Artaban had known the man for over fifteen years and had seen him maintain his composure through sandstorms, bandit attacks, and audiences with kings. Whatever had caused this sudden agitation must have been extraordinary indeed.

The three men climbed the narrow stone steps to the rooftop, the scuff of their sandals echoing in the confined space. As they emerged onto the flat roof, Artaban took a refreshing breath of the cool evening air, and it lifted his spirits a little.

Above them, the familiar constellations spread across the dark canopy of heaven. The moon was new, leaving the stars to burn in all their brilliance against the black tapestry of night. *Ea* hung in the western sky exactly where it should be, its distinctive pattern easily recognizable to trained eyes. The Wanderers, *Marduk*, *Ninub*, and *Nergal*, had continued their choreographed dance since the final conjunction, gradually separating as they followed their predetermined paths.

Belshazzar stood near the eastern parapet, his astrolabe in his hands and several charts spread on a small table beside him. He gaped in astonishment as he pointed toward the constellation of *Ea*.

"There," he said, his voice filled with a mixture of awe and disbelief. "Do you see it?"

Artaban followed his gaze and felt his breath catch in his throat. Where the triple conjunction had occurred just weeks ago, a new star blazed with brilliant light. It outshone every other celestial body in the sky and seemed to pulse with an inner fire.

Most remarkable of all, it appeared to be growing larger as they watched, as if moving steadily closer to the earth.

"By the sacred flame," Artaban whispered. "What is that?"

"It's not on any of our charts," Belshazzar said, his voice barely a whisper. "I've checked and rechecked against every map in our records. This star is not documented anywhere. We all watched *Nergal* move out of this region just two nights ago, leaving no Wanderers within *Ea*. I'll swear by Ahura Mazda that this light did not exist just one night ago. And," he turned toward them, his face drained of color, "it's located exactly where the last conjugation occurred."

Gondophares moved to stand beside Artaban, both men staring up at the impossible star. "Could it be one of the hairy stars?" he asked.

Melchior stepped forward, his aged eyes studying the phenomenon with a marked intensity. "No," he said slowly, his voice filled with growing wonder. "The hairy stars have tails streaming behind them. This appears to be a single point of light, and it doesn't move across the sky."

"And see how it brightens as we watch?" Artaban whispered.

"Yes," Melchior concurred. "This is no ordinary celestial Wanderer."

As if to confirm his words, the mysterious star seemed to pulse brighter still, its radiance casting faint shadows on the rooftop around them. The light was warm and golden, unlike the cold silver radiance of the moon or the distant twinkle of ordinary stars. It seemed almost alive, as if some sort of intelligence dwelt within its luminous depths.

"What do you think it could be?" Artaban found himself being drawn into the mystery—his declarations of doubt and his plans to flee back to Parthia fading from his mind. The sight of this unexplainable star had driven away all thoughts of departure, replacing them with wonder and a growing sense that they stood on the threshold of something truly momentous.

Melchior stood in silent contemplation for several long minutes, his weathered face upturned to the sky. "I believe," he said almost reverently, "that our Great God has sent us a heavenly messenger to guide us to the promised king. The Jews would call it one of the *malakim*, an angel clothed in light. The conjunction pointed to the time and place of the messiah's birth, but this…" He gestured toward the brilliant star. "I believe this will lead us to his very door."

"Brack," Simur chirped from his perch on Melchior's shoulder. "A sign from heaven."

They stood in awed silence for several moments, watching as the star continued to brighten and grow larger still. It seemed to beckon them toward some specific destination. Artaban found himself thinking of the ancient stories of *yazatas*—divine messengers who sometimes took physical form to carry out the will of Ahura Mazda. Could this be such a being?

Finally, Belshazzar broke the silence, his voice filled with new determination. "We should leave for Bethlehem tonight. Now, while the star shines so clearly and shows us the way. If this truly is divine guidance, we dare not delay or risk losing it."

"Travel in the darkness?" Artaban asked, though his tone lacked the conviction of his earlier objections to Belshazzar's other suggestions. "The roads can be treacherous at night, and there are still bandits in the hills."

"The star provides all the light we need," Gondophares said. "Look how it illuminates the rooftop around us. And if our God has sent this sign, do you think he would abandon us to brigands on the final stage of our journey?"

"We should travel light and swift," Belshazzar added, his mind already racing ahead to practical considerations. "Just the four of us and two guards for protection. We should take only the gifts and what we absolutely need for the journey. The rest of our party can follow tomorrow with the baggage train."

Artaban felt himself caught between his long-held skepticism and the overwhelming evidence of his senses. The star, whatever it was, defied every natural explanation he could conceive. It was too bright, too timely in its appearance, and too perfectly positioned to be coincidence. Yet accepting its supernatural origin meant admitting that everything he had doubted might actually be true.

"I'll come with you," he heard himself say to Melchior. "This... development... changes everything. I think I'll postpone my return to Parthia."

Melchior turned to him with a smile that seemed to mirror the radiance of the star above. "I'm glad, my friend. Very glad indeed. Your presence has always been a blessing to our company, even when—no, especially when—you've challenged our assumptions."

The decision made, the magi moved with surprising speed for men who had spent the day in tense negotiation with the royal court. Within the hour, they had gathered their precious gifts of gold, frankincense, and myrrh, along with water skins, travel cloaks, and the minimal provisions needed for a short journey. Captain Vakshuvar chose one of the guards to accompany them and left his lieutenant to coordinate the rest of the company's movement the following day.

As they prepared to mount their horses in the stable yard, Artaban found himself handling his father's astronomical instruments with unusual care. He had almost left them behind, but something compelled him to bring them now. Perhaps it was fitting that these tools, which had failed to protect his father from Roman wrath, might yet witness the birth of a king who would challenge Rome itself.

The mysterious star hung before them like a celestial beacon as they rode out of Jerusalem's gates, its light so bright it made the road as visible as if it were day. Then a sudden thought struck Artaban, and it forced him to look back in surprise. No one else in Jerusalem seemed to be aware of the strange light. He didn't recall seeing anyone gathered together in groups and pointing to the sky as they had done. Even the guards at the gate appeared to be oblivious to the phenomenon as they cautioned the group about the hazards of traveling outside the city at night.

As they made their way along the ancient road toward Bethlehem, their voices carried softly on the night air, mingling with the steady clip-clop of their horses' hooves.

"What do you think it is?" Gondophares asked, his eyes fixed on the brilliant light that seemed to hover just ahead of them, always at the perfect distance to illuminate their path without blinding them.

Belshazzar adjusted his grip on his horse's reins. "We've all studied the stars in the heavens for most of our lives," he replied thoughtfully. "We've observed the Wanderers in their courses, tracked the progression of eclipses, and calculated the movements of the constellations. But I've never seen anything like this. It moves too deliberately to be natural, yet it's too substantial to be an illusion."

"The *yazatas* of our faith sometimes guide travelers in this way," Melchior said quietly, his eyes fixed on the light ahead. "I'm convinced that we're being led by divine will."

Artaban rode in silence for several minutes. He hesitated to give voice to his thoughts. The presence of this star challenged all of his doubts. He wanted to attribute the vision to some kind of natural phenomenon, but he could not come up with a viable option. With every step they took toward Bethlehem, he became more and more persuaded that it must be of divine origin.

But if that were the case, he had a larger issue of faith to contend with. The Hebrew scriptures had provided the clues they needed to identify the birthplace of the Promised One, not the sacred writings of their own faith. Melchior had originally suggested that any truths which appeared in Jewish prophecies were shadows of the pure revelations of their own Great God, Ahura Mazda. But if this light was indeed a divine messenger sent to lead them to Bethlehem, exactly as predicted by the Jewish prophecies, then which truth was the pebble, and which others were the ripples in the pond?

Captain Vakshuvar, who had been riding at the rear of the line while the other guard patrolled ahead, edged up closer to Melchior.

"Someone's trailing us," he said, just loud enough for them all to hear.

"Herod's men?" Melchior asked.

"It's hard to tell," Vakshuvar replied, "but I don't think so. They look like they're equipped with Roman gear. Maybe Varro or his men. I don't think they're an immediate threat. Probably just watching us." He looked back for a moment. "But it's odd..." his voice trailed off.

"What's that?" Melchior asked.

"Look how they move, like their horses are stumbling about in the dark. And they seem oblivious to the fact that we can see them plainly in the light from this... this... star, or whatever it is. Anyway," he concluded, "I would expect them to make more of an effort to remain concealed."

"Maybe," Melchior suggested, "this illumination is meant for our eyes only."

Captain Vakshuvar slowly shook his head. "One thing's for sure," he marveled, "it's like nothing I've ever seen before." He paused for a moment and then went on. "I tend to be a practical man. I'm perfectly happy confronting the point of a spear or the edge of a sword, but I prefer to leave the spiritual things to people like you." He took a deep breath. "And yet, this is… I don't know what to say." He shook his head again. "Maybe even I might have to start believing in…" His voice trailed off, and he shrugged before slowing the pace of his horse and falling back a few paces to the rear of the line.

As they followed the winding road through the Judean hills, the star appeared to descend lower in the sky and to grow brighter still. By the time they crested the last hill and saw the sleepy little village spread out below them—a modest collection of stone houses clustered around ancient olive groves—the celestial light had positioned itself directly over one particular dwelling.

The house was unremarkable in every way except for the column of golden light that bathed it in radiance. It was built of stone, with thick walls and small windows, shuttered against the chill of the night. Nothing about the structure suggested it housed anyone of particular importance.

"It stopped," Belshazzar whispered in amazement, bringing his horse to a halt on the hillside overlooking the town.

The star hung motionless above the house like a lamp suspended from heaven itself. Its light illuminated every detail of the building below while leaving the surrounding structures in relative shadow. No other dwelling in Bethlehem was so marked or so clearly distinguished from its neighbors.

Artaban glanced back to see Captain Vakshuvar slide off his horse. He landed on his feet and squared his shoulders, staring straight ahead with his eyes fixed on the star. His hand momentarily moved to his sword hilt, the gesture of a soldier facing a threat he couldn't understand. Then, slowly, he removed his helmet and stood bareheaded under the impossible light, his weathered face showing the wonder of a practical man confronting the divine.

"Look at this place," Gondophares said in awe.

"What do you mean?" Belshazzar asked.

"It's not a palace," Gondophares whispered, his voice filled with reverence. "It's just a normal, everyday home. I guess the King of Kings will grow up as part of a regular family. And yet," he marveled, "Rome itself will eventually bow before his throne."

Artaban still had his eyes on the captain of their guard. He saw the professional soldier struggling to process what he was witnessing and knew they were both experiencing some of the same doubts and fears.

"Whatever we find in that village," Vakshuvar finally said, "apparently it's important enough for heaven itself to light the way."

Artaban turned and gazed down at the little home, bathed in light from what must surely be a divine messenger, his mind struggling to process the implications. If they were correct and this star truly marked the birthplace of the Jewish messiah, then they were about to meet the child who would somehow fulfill the ancient prophecies—a child who would establish a kingdom that would never be destroyed, and who would rule over all nations.

"We should wait until morning," Melchior said, practical wisdom tempering his excitement. "It'd be unseemly to wake a family in the middle of the night, especially if there is indeed a newborn child within. Appearing at their door like thieves in the night would hardly be appropriate for foreign emissaries bearing gifts."

In their haste, they had brought no tents or shelters. The little village was asleep, with all doors barred for the night. So the four magi tied their horses to trees and lay down on the ground, covered by their cloaks, while the guards took turns standing watch.

But sleep proved impossible for Artaban. He wrestled with

his doubts and fears as he lay staring up at the brilliant star, which maintained its vigil above the house in Bethlehem, its light unwavering and constant.

The questions that had plagued him throughout their journey returned with renewed force. Faced with such a miracle, how could he doubt that the signs they observed in the heavens were indeed a sign from God? If the stars and the ancient prophecies had together led them to the birthplace of the Promised One, what did that mean for his lack of faith? And who would that Promised One turn out to be—the *Saoshyant* of their faith, or the Jewish messiah?

The implications were staggering. If the Hebrew prophecies were true, this child would establish a kingdom that would consume all others. Rome, for all its power and cruelty, would fall before him. The oppressed would be lifted up, and the mighty would be brought low.

But what of Parthia? What of their own kingdom and people? Would they be counted among the righteous nations that welcomed this new king, or would they be swept away with the rest of the old order? Their mission here might determine not just their own fates, but the destiny of their entire nation.

And what of his own heart? He had come this far clinging to doubt, using skepticism as armor against painful memories and a fear of Rome. But the armor that protected against such disappointment also blocked out hope. If he continued to hold faith at arm's length, how could he truly experience whatever miracle awaited them in that humble house below?

Perhaps faith was not the absence of doubt, but the willingness to act in spite of it. Perhaps the gift he could bring was not gold or incense or myrrh, but something far more precious and far more difficult to offer.

As the hours passed and the star continued its silent vigil, a strange peace settled over Artaban's troubled thoughts. The fears that had driven him to pack for a return to Parthia seemed less urgent now, less important than the mystery unfolding before them. Whatever happened in the morning, whatever they found in that star-lit house, he would meet it with an open mind and a willing spirit.

The night deepened around them, but the star shone on, bright and eternal—a beacon of hope in a world grown dark with oppression and despair. And in the heart of one doubtful magus, the first fragile shoots of genuine faith began to take root at last.

CHAPTER TEN

Winter, 7 BC
Bethlehem, Kingdom of Judea,
Syrian Province, Roman Empire

" Ⅰt's gone." Gondophares nudged Artaban, rousing him from an uneasy sleep. "The star is gone."

Artaban rubbed his eyes and looked up at the sky, tinged with the glow of the rising sun. He stretched to shuffle off the weariness of a night filled with troubled sleep.

"But it was real, wasn't it? Not just a dream?"

A smile spread across Gondophares' face. "Oh yes, my friend. It was quite real."

They woke the others, who needed no coaxing to leave the warmth of their cloaks and face the chill morning air. All were eager to approach the house illuminated by the divine messenger and see the infant king they had traveled so far to find.

"Captain Vakshuvar," Melchior addressed the leader of their faithful guard detail. "I know you're as eager to see the child as we are. But I think it would be wise not to arrive in force for our first encounter."

"As you will," Vakshuvar replied, clearly using his discipline as a soldier to restrain his own disappointment.

Artaban could tell the miraculous appearance of the star had been as compelling to the hardened warrior as it had been to the four scholars.

"Perhaps I should stay behind as well," Artaban suggested, "to keep the group small. Once you've found the boy, there'll be plenty of time for additional introductions. I'm sure the rest of our company will also be anxious to meet him."

Melchior smiled. "A skeptic to the very end, I see." His eyes held a mixture of affection and understanding. "Your role among us has been as important to the success of this mission as any other. You've earned the right to see this young child, who is destined to rule over empires. And yet," he sighed, "we shall honor your wishes, if that's your true desire."

Artaban felt his shoulders sag and pulled them back to hide his reaction. He had hoped his old master would insist that he accompany them. He knew his own statement had been prompted by a mix of shame and bravado. But he was unwilling to back down now.

"It is," he muttered and turned away. "I'll come with Captain Vakshuvar and the rest of the company, after they arrive."

"Very well," Melchior replied. "Shall we go?" he prompted, ushering Belshazzar and Gondophares toward the road.

Of the three magi, only Gondophares looked back at Artaban with a questioning look. Artaban met his gaze for an instant and then dropped his eyes to the ground.

After the trio had plodded a hundred paces down the dusty path, Simur came fluttering back and perched on Artaban's shoulder. The bird pecked at Artaban's ear, and he swatted in annoyance to shoo it away. But the little starling persistently evaded his defensive gyrations and continued to assault his ear. After another pitched round of jabs and parries, Simur finally retreated to a nearby branch and squawked, "Brack. Face your fear."

Artaban's head jerked around, and he found himself staring directly into one of the bird's round, unblinking eyes. Simur tilted his head, keeping his eye trained on Artaban's own for a couple of heartbeats, then flew away, back toward his master.

Artaban shook his head. This was ridiculous. The annoying little bird was right. Though the king had praised him as the group's "voice of caution," he was really just using his doubt as a shield. He feared belief, for all of its terrible implications. If the Parthian God was real, what did that say about his father's tragic failure? What did that mean in the face of Rome's brutal reprisal on his kingdom and on his own family? How could a God of justice and truth allow such pain and sorrow to afflict his most faithful followers?

Yet Artaban could not deny the testimony of his own eyes. Yes, the stars in the distant heavens, like *Marduk, Ninub, and Nergal*, did trace regular, predictable paths across the sky. Maybe there were omens in those patterns, or maybe there were not. But what he witnessed last night—when one of those very stars came down from the firmament and touched the earth below—must surely have been a miracle from God. There could be no other explanation.

A new resolve grew in his heart and stiffened his spine. At some point, he would eventually have to reconcile his under-standing of God with these nagging questions about truth and justice. But those were issues for another day. In this moment, with the overwhelming evidence bearing down on his mind, he had to acknowledge the reality that a god—some god—did exist. And that God was now reaching into the affairs of men in a real, tangible way. Beyond that, for some unfathomable reason, this God had chosen to involve him, a broken, wounded, prideful skeptic, in his plan to usher the prophesied King of Kings into a chaotic, dysfunctional world.

"Master," Artaban cried out. "Master, wait. Forgive my foolishness. I do want to come, very much. I want to meet this baby boy, and to welcome him as a friend."

The others stopped and waited for Artaban to join them. Melchior nodded, his expression one of patient understanding that held no condemnation or scorn.

"I expect," he said, "that all men will be forced to confront this child in one way or another. It will be for each to choose whether to honor him or scorn him." He nodded and smiled. "I believe that you have chosen the path of wisdom."

The star had vanished with the dawn, but its final position remained etched in their memories, where it hovered over a modest stone house near the town's center. Now, in the daylight, the little house was indistinguishable from its neighbors except for the divine appointment that had marked it the night before.

The village was still waking from its slumber, and only a few people appeared outside their homes. Those who did, eyed the four strangers warily, but didn't confront them.

Artaban glanced at his fellows and thought about how they must appear to these Judean villagers. They were not dressed in the formal attire they had donned for their audience with King Herod. Instead, they wore casual clothing covered by travel cloaks, still wrinkled from a night spent on the open ground. Still, the style of their garb was distinctly Parthian and would undoubtedly appear foreign to the people of this small, rural town.

As they neared their destination, a young man with a firm

stature, disheveled hair, and an unkempt beard emerged from a side doorway, carrying an empty water jug. He looked up and appraised them with a cautious eye. As they drew nearer, he set the jug down, stood, and squared his shoulders.

"Peace be upon this house," Melchior said in the Judean tongue.

"And upon you," the man replied warily. His gaze shifted past the elder Magus to the three other magi. "You're strangers to Bethlehem." He again looked them up and down. "Who are you? What's your purpose here?"

Artaban assessed the man's expression as somewhat intimidated, but not fearful.

"We're scholars from the Court of King Phraates of Parthia. We've traveled a very long way to get here. We seek a child," Melchior said with gentle solemnity. "The one born as King of the Jews. We saw his star in the east, and it has led us to this very door. Is there a baby boy in your home?"

The man's expression slowly changed as he considered Melchior's reply. Wariness gave way to astonishment, then to cautious welcome. Something apparently convinced him they were not a threat.

"Come in," he said, stepping aside. "I'm Joseph, son of Jacob. This is my uncle's house."

Joseph turned back inside and called, "Mary, we have some… interesting visitors. I think we'll want to hear their story."

Artaban followed his companions through the door and was greeted by the musty smell of straw and the pungent odor of animals. He was surprised to see that they had entered the part of the dwelling where livestock was kept in the winter months. He glanced around, but saw no sheep or goats.

The rules of hospitality would normally dictate that visitors be welcomed through the front door into the living quarters of a home, not through a side door into the stable. Artaban wondered at this breach of etiquette, especially given the great disparity between the social class of the host and his guests. Yet, as their spokesman, Melchior showed no signs of offense when Joseph offered them places to sit on reed mats spread out along one wall.

As his eyes adjusted to the dim interior, Artaban noticed a young woman in the shadows of the far corner, nestling an infant protectively in her arms. She wore a dark wool mantle around her shoulders to fend off the morning chill and had a scarf draped loosely over locks of brown hair. She appraised the strangers warily and then shot a questioning glance at Joseph.

"Please forgive our intrusion into your home, mistress. We are men of faith and learning from the kingdom of Parthia. We've come to meet your son and to learn more of his birth."

Mary continued to look quizzically at Joseph, who hastened to add some details to Melchior's introduction. "He said they were led to our house by a star and came to find the one born as King of the Jews."

Mary inhaled sharply, then breathed a sigh of relief. She turned slightly toward them, relaxing her protective posture over the baby. Artaban guessed that very few explanations would relieve an anxious mother's concern for the safety of her child so readily. Something about that clarification must have resonated with her recent experiences, and Artaban was eager to learn more.

"My name is Melchior," their mentor said with a slight bow. "And these are my companions, Belshazzar, Gondophares, and Artaban." He gestured to each of the men in turn. "We are magi in service to the Parthian king."

"What are magi?" The woman's voice was quiet and pensive.

"Ah, forgive my use of Parthian terms. We are scholars and men of faith. We observe the heavens for signs of the divine will. Just such signs brought us here over a journey of many months."

The woman took a tentative step forward, and Joseph moved to her, placing a comforting arm around her shoulders.

"What did you see?" he asked. "What would bring you all that way?"

Belshazzar jumped into the conversation, barely containing his own excitement at the situation. "We identified a unique conjunction of specific heavenly bodies—" he began, and was cut short by a look of obvious confusion on the woman's part. "A meeting or joining together of certain stars in the sky." He brought his hands together to illustrate his point. "Our records show that such a meeting of these particular stars in this specific way only occurs about once in a thousand years."

Gondophares continued the explanation, no doubt in terms he thought might be more helpful. "Parthian magi have been interpreting such signs in the heavens for hundreds of years. After much study and debate, we concluded that this specific omen predicted the birth of a great king in the region of Judea."

"I'm somewhat familiar with the writings of the Hebrew prophets." Melchior added. "When my former students consulted me on their discovery, I suspected the signs might possibly indicate the coming of the Jewish messiah."

The young couple looked at each other with expressions that seemed to convey a sense of affirmation rather than surprise.

Melchior glanced at each of the two parents in turn and then spoke. "I had expected our assertions to surprise or bewilder you. But I see that's not the case. This is not a new notion to either of you, is it?"

"No," Joseph replied. "Not entirely."

"Please," Gondophares prompted. "Can you tell us your story? Tell us about your son and his birth."

"That might take a little time," Joseph said. "And I'm so sorry. We've been terrible hosts. Please let me offer you some refreshment."

"That's not—" Belshazzar began, but Melchior cut him off.

"It's very kind of you. We gladly accept your hospitality."

Joseph again bade them to sit on the reed mats, then filled a basin with water and passed it to them so they could wash their hands. Mary laid the baby down in a small manger and disappeared through a doorway into the home's inner courtyard. She re-emerged moments later with a jug, several clay cups, and a folded towel.

"We were just preparing some bread and milk to break our fast," she said, handing each one a cup. "It's a humble meal, but we would be honored for you to join us."

"It's *our* honor, mistress," Gondophares replied, "that we sup together with the mother and father of a king."

Artaban saw Mary's eyes drop as she poured goat's milk into the cups.

The couple took places on mats positioned across from the four visitors. Joseph opened the towel and took out two large, round loaves of flatbread. He lifted them up and murmured a prayer.

"Blessed are You, Adonai, Lord of heaven and earth. By Your hand we are fed, by Your mercy we live, and by Your grace we share these blessings with our guests."

Artaban heard Mary whisper, "Amen."

Joseph tore the loaves into pieces and distributed them to everyone. Mary also passed around a small dish of olives and another of dates. It was a simple repast, but one shared in what was becoming an amiable relationship.

As they ate together, the baby slept quietly in his makeshift bed, occasionally gurgling or letting out a faint grunt before settling again. Artaban felt something stir within him as he looked at the infant. It wasn't the sense of awe he might have expected, but something subtler and yet more profound. The child appeared entirely ordinary, wrapped in simple cloth and sleeping peacefully. There were no trappings of royalty, no gilded cradle or silk curtains embroidered with lions. There were no nursemaids attending him or soldiers standing guard. Only a peasant girl, a common laborer, and a manger bed. And yet the stars in the heavens above had proclaimed this child to be the King of Kings.

"Tell us please," Artaban felt compelled to ask, "what's the child's name?"

Mary smiled softly, as if recalling a fond memory, and finally replied, "His name is Yeshua."

"Yeshua..." Melchior muttered. "Or Jesus in the Greek, correct?"

Joseph nodded.

"Interesting," Melchior mused. "A curious meaning, 'to rescue.' Is he named after someone in your family? Or does it perhaps recall the ancient forefather who once led your people into the Promised Land?"

"No," Joseph replied. "There's no one in our family with this name." He looked at Mary with a raised brow, and she urged him to continue. "An angel appeared to me in a vision shortly after I discovered Mary was pregnant. The angel said, 'You shall call his name Jesus, for he will save his people from their sins.'"

Artaban shifted uneasily as questioning looks passed between his companions. The father's account of a heavenly messenger certainly supported their conclusion that the boy's birth was divinely ordained. But it also raised a host of other questions. Why here and not in Parthia? Would the great Ahura Mazda raise up a deliverer among the followers of a foreign religion? And what did it mean that this boy would save his people from their sins? Wasn't the messiah prophesied to deliver the kingdoms of the world from the tyranny of Rome?

"When was he born?" Belshazzar finally asked.

"He's just about a month old now," Mary replied.

"How many days ago?" Belshazzar reiterated. "How many days exactly?"

As Mary pondered the question, Joseph spoke up. "Twenty-six days."

The four magi stared at one another for a long moment. Joseph apparently noticed their astonished expressions and asked, "What's wrong?"

"Nothing," Melchior said. "Nothing at all is wrong."

"You see," Belshazzar elaborated. "That is the exact day of the final conjunction of the stars we told you about earlier."

"That can't be a coincidence," Gondophares muttered, almost breathlessly. "It must confirm our understanding of the signs."

Just then, baby Jesus woke and began to cry. Mary immediately rose and went to him. She picked him up, cradled him in her arms, and began rocking him gently as mothers do.

"Could you perhaps go back and tell us more about the birth of your son?" Melchior requested. "Joseph, you said a heavenly messenger visited you. Was there anything else unusual about how this young child came into the world?"

Mary and Joseph again shared a knowing look. Something that appeared to be an unspoken consent passed between them.

Joseph began, "Well, we weren't exactly married when all this happened. We were betrothed, but..."

Mary picked up the story. "Before Joseph and I were married, the angel Gabriel appeared to me in a vision—"

Artaban gasped. "Gabriel!" He exclaimed, looking at Melchior. "The same angel that explained the prophecies to Daniel?"

"Indeed," Melchior confirmed. "I doubt that's a coincidence. It must be a connection between the prophecy and its fulfillment almost four hundred years later."

Artaban marveled as the pieces of the puzzle continued to fall into place. He vaguely heard Melchior ask Mary to continue her story.

"Well, as I was saying, Gabriel told me some incredible

things." She shook her head. "No, some unbelievable things. He said I would soon conceive and give birth to a son, even though I had never been with a man. When I asked how this could be, he said the Holy Spirit would overshadow me and that the baby conceived in my womb would be called the holy Son of God."

"Wait," Belshazzar broke in. "Are you saying that Joseph isn't the boy's father?"

"I'm not his natural father," Joseph replied. "But I love him as my own and will try to raise him the best that I can."

"Then how…" Belshazzar's question trailed off in the air.

"It's a miracle of God," Mary said. "My parents were very angry when my pregnancy began to show. They didn't believe my explanation."

"Neither did I at first," Joseph added. "I was very hurt by what I thought was a cruel betrayal. Yet, I respected Mary's father and didn't want to bring dishonor on their family. So I had planned to divorce her quietly." He took a deep breath and then continued. "But then an angel of the Lord spoke to me in a dream as well. He told me the baby in her womb had been conceived by the Holy Spirit."

"And you're certain of all this?" Belshazzar asked, the doubt revealing itself in his tone.

"I know it sounds incredible," Joseph replied. "But this was no ordinary dream. Believe me, when an angel of the Lord appears to you, it's an experience like nothing else you've ever known. I'm absolutely sure of what I saw."

The infant stirred, then gave a soft cry. Mary shifted, drawing him close, and quieted him with the tender instinct of a mother.

"That's a remarkable story," Melchior said. "It certainly affirms our suspicions about the identity of your child."

"Oh, that's not all," Joseph said. "There's more."

"What do you mean?" asked Gondophares.

"We're not actually from Bethlehem. I work as a carpenter in a village called Nazareth."

"That's up by the Sea of Galilee, isn't it?" Gondophares asked. "I think I remember the name from when we passed through that region."

"It is," Joseph said. "Right before the baby was due, Caesar ordered a census. He issued a decree for everyone in the province of Syria to be counted and taxed. The decree required everyone to return to their place of birth. So Mary and I traveled here from Nazareth, because I'm originally from Bethlehem."

"Is that why you're staying in the stable of your uncle's house?" Gondophares asked.

"Yes," Joseph said. "When we arrived in Bethlehem, the living quarters here were all full. But Uncle Tobiah arranged for the sheep and goats to be sheltered in other homes and made this space available to us."

Mary still rocked the baby back and forth, holding him close to her heart. "Yeshua was born right here," she said, gesturing toward the manger. She paused for a moment and then added, "Now that I think of it, I suppose I shouldn't be surprised that shepherds would be the first to come see him."

"What do you mean?" Gondophares asked.

"Shortly after Jesus was born," Joseph explained, "while Aunt Hannah was still helping Mary to recover, eight shepherds came to our door asking about a newborn baby. They told us angels had appeared to them with news that the Messiah of the Lord had been born in the city of David. And they found us here, just as the angels said they would."

Belshazzar sat upright when he heard this account. "What exactly did they say? Did they actually refer to your son as the messiah?"

"I'm not sure of their exact words, but yes, they did call him the Messiah of the Lord."

The four magi looked at each other in astonishment. This was independent confirmation from heavenly messengers of the conclusions they had reached so many months ago from the signs in the stars. Belshazzar immediately continued with a follow-up question.

"How did they find this specific house? Did a star from heaven or an angel lead them here?"

"I'm not sure," Joseph shrugged. "I never thought to ask. I suppose this house was the only one in the village with a lamp lit at the time. Our little boy decided to come in the very middle of the night." He reflected for a moment and then said, "I guess I could ask you the same question. How did you find us here?"

"King Herod's scholars told us the messiah would be born in Bethlehem," Gondophares replied, "but a star came down from the sky and led us here from Jerusalem all throughout the night. It came to a stop and shone brightly right over this house. Didn't you see it?"

Mary and Joseph exchanged a worried look.

"You had an audience with King Herod?" Joseph finally asked.

Melchior addressed this concern. "When we came from Parthia, all we understood was that a great king would be born in Judea. We assumed it would be a new baby in King Herod's household. As representatives of King Phraates, we were granted an audience with the king. But, as you know, the newborn king was not from within Herod's family. When we told him of the signs in the heavens, he called upon his experts in the Hebrew scriptures. They said the prophets of old predicted Bethlehem as the birthplace of the messiah."

The concern on Joseph's face grew darker. "I'm not sure that's such a good thing. King Herod can be unpredictable and cruel. He's already killed his two oldest sons because he thought they were plotting against him. I don't know how he would react to news about a Messiah. And rumors about Jesus are already circulating around Jerusalem."

"Why is that?" Gondophares asked.

"Eight days after Jesus was born, we took him to Jerusalem for his circumcision, like the Law requires. At the temple, we encountered an old prophet named Simeon."

"Simeon?" Melchior asked.

"He's an elderly man who has spent all his time at the temple," Joseph replied. "He came up to us and asked to hold the baby. He said God had promised he wouldn't die until he'd seen the Lord's Messiah. Then he took Jesus in his arms and started praising God, saying his eyes had seen the salvation of Israel."

"There was a prophetess there too," Mary added, "named Anna. She must have been over eighty years old. When she saw our son, she started thanking God and telling everyone nearby that this was the child who would redeem Jerusalem."

"Many people heard our conversations with Simeon and Anna," Joseph said. "Apparently, rumors spread around Jerusalem that the long-awaited Messiah had finally come. But until now, no one has come looking for him here."

"Hmm," Melchior murmured. "After the scholars told us what the scriptures had to say about the messiah, King Herod dismissed everyone from the audience chamber. In private, he encouraged us to find the child and then report back to the court once we had located him."

"Oh, no," Mary exclaimed. "Please don't do that. I'm afraid of what King Herod might do to my baby. Even if he doesn't plan to hurt Yeshua, I don't want him to grow up in the palace."

Joseph nodded in concurrence. "I think that's why God placed Jesus in our care—so he could grow up as a normal boy and not as a political tool of the royal court."

"We understand," Melchior said. "I think your concerns are valid. I thought our appearance before King Herod had progressed in an unusual manner. We'll honor your wishes and be cautious about revealing the boy's whereabouts."

All this time, Artaban had listened intently to the story of the baby's birth, feeling the ring of truth in what Mary and Joseph had said. There was no artifice in their telling, no attempt at elaboration or drama, just the simple recounting of events that had forever altered their young lives. And the accumulation of testimony—the angelic visitations, the shepherds, the prophets in the temple, the star itself—created a tapestry of evidence that even his skeptical nature found increasingly difficult to dismiss.

"I believe," Melchior declared, "your story confirms the speculations we formed many months ago, when we first discovered the exceptional signs in the heavens. I, for one, am fully convinced that your son is indeed the messiah predicted by the prophets of the Hebrew scriptures. Furthermore, I believe he may also be the long-awaited *Saoshyant* of our own faith tradition." He looked around at his fellow magi and received nods of affirmation. "And so," he continued, "we bring gifts of friendship and honor from ourselves and from the Parthian Court of King Phraates."

Belshazzar rose, reached into his travel bag, drew forth a casket of carved cedar, and held it out before Mary and the baby.

"In the courts of Parthia, gold is the sign of kingship. It adorns the throne, the diadem, and the scepter. To lay gold at a child's feet is to confess his right to rule. Today I present gold to this baby boy, for though he rests in swaddling clothes, I see upon him the mark of divine authority. May the nations one day know that a king was born here in the City of David."

Mary took a sharp breath and looked up at Joseph.

"What is it?" Melchior asked, seeing her reaction.

"It's just…" Mary began. "Well, the angel Gabriel told me, 'Your child will be great, and the Lord God will give him the throne of his father David.'"

Belshazzar laid the small chest of gold before the infant and said, "I offer this on behalf of my father, who carried this calling faithfully until his death, trusting that I would complete what he began." He looked up with tears in his eyes. "He would rejoice to see this day. The stars that marked his birth have led me here."

Next Gondophares stepped forward, carrying an alabaster jar. He uncorked it, and the fragrance of frankincense filled the chamber, sharp and sweet.

"In our temples, frankincense rises in smoke before the Almighty. It symbolizes prayer, intercession, and the bridge between earth and heaven. I bring this not as tribute for an earthly monarch, but for one who will serve as priest of the Most High—one who will intercede for the people of Israel and of all nations."

Mary's eyes widened, and she nodded slowly. "When we brought Yeshua to the temple, Simeon said he would be 'a light of revelation to the Gentiles, and glory for Israel.'"

Melchior then rose, drawing forth a small sealed vial. The bittersweet scent of myrrh soon mingled with the incense.

"Myrrh is the anointing oil of prophets. With this gift, I acknowledge Jesus as a prophet who will speak the word of God with truth, but also as one destined to suffer the persecution that has been the common fate of the prophets of old. For true service to the Lord lies in sacrifice. May this offering testify that even in sorrow, God brings hope."

Joseph's brows furrowed, but Mary whispered, "The angel also told me, 'A sword shall pierce your own soul.'" She shook her head slowly. "I don't know what that means, but I thank you for your words of encouragement in the Lord."

All eyes then turned to Artaban.

His heart thundered. For months, he had borne no gift, only doubt. But the signs in the stars and the testimony of this couple had left him with a new sense of resolve. Now the moment had come, and he knew what he had to do.

Slowly, he drew from within his cloak a bundle of leather wrappings. With trembling hands, he unrolled them, revealing his father's old instruments—the shadow stick, the armillary rings, and the worn bronze calipers once used to trace the heavens.

"These," he said hoarsely, "belonged to my father, who studied the stars before me. They are the tools with which I have sought to serve Ahura Mazda and the King of Parthia. They have been my life's devotion, the measure of my knowledge, and the symbol of my calling." He swallowed hard. "I bring them now and lay them at the feet of your child."

He placed the instruments on the ground before Jesus.

Mary looked at him with quiet wonder. "Why would you give us such personal things?"

"Because…" Artaban said, his voice breaking. "Because they have led me here. And here their purpose ends. I once thought wisdom lay in the stars, but I see now it is in the hand of the God of Israel. I give up my service to other thrones and take an oath this day to serve this child, Jesus, as the Messiah of the one true God. My life, my skill, and my loyalty are his."

The words rang in the stillness like a vow before heaven itself.

Artaban bowed low, pressing his forehead to the earth. And as he did, a strange peace flooded his soul. The bitterness of Rome's cruelty, the grief of his father's execution, the years of doubt all seemed to lift, replaced by a certainty stronger than calculation and brighter than the stars.

Melchior laid a hand on his shoulder, his eyes moist. "Wisely spoken, my son."

Jesus made a soft sound—not quite a cry, but a gentle vocalization that seemed almost like a response. Mary looked down at her son with wonder, then back at Artaban with tears streaming down her young face.

As Artaban remained kneeling, Jesus suddenly reached out with one tiny hand, his fingers grasping at the air between them. Without thinking, Artaban extended his own hand, and the infant's impossibly small fingers wrapped around his thumb with surprising strength.

In that moment of connection, something profound shifted within Artaban's heart. All his intellectual reservations, all his careful skepticism, all his fears about the consequences of belief, simply melted away in the face of this perfect simplicity. This was not the overwhelming divine presence he might have expected, but something far more powerful—the gentleness of infinite love made manifest in human form.

The morning sun had climbed higher, sending stronger beams through the small window and illuminating the scene with golden light. The astronomical instruments lay gleaming on the floor beside the gifts of gold, frankincense, and myrrh—an offering both humble and precious, representing not just the wisdom of the East but the evidence of a changed life. In that moment, Artaban understood what the angels and prophets had meant when they had called Jesus a savior.

Jesus released Artaban's thumb and settled back into his mother's arms with a contented sigh, as if his acknowledgment of the gift had sealed some eternal bond. The room fell into a peaceful silence, broken only by the distant sounds of Bethlehem awakening to another day—women drawing water from the well, donkeys braying, and children playing in the streets.

But within this humble dwelling, history had pivoted on the axis of divine revelation, and four travelers from a distant land had discovered that the greatest journey is not measured in miles but in the transformation of the human heart.

CHAPTER ELEVEN

Winter, 7 BC
Bethlehem, Kingdom of Judea,
Syrian Province, Roman Empire

Artaban blinked his eyes as hushed voices roused him from the soundest night of sleep he had experienced in months. He rolled to his knees and poked his head outside his tent to see Melchior, Belshazzar, and Gondophares conferring in low tones around a morning fire. Their expressions were grim.

Hastily wrapping a cloak around his shoulders and slipping sandals on his feet, he moved to join his companions. As he approached, all three eyed him expectantly, as if waiting for him to say something.

Seeing their expressions of anticipation, Artaban shrugged and said, hesitantly, "Peace to you this morning."

Gondophares furrowed his brow. "Did you have any peculiar dreams while you slept?"

Artaban puzzled over the strange question and finally replied. "No. Actually, I slept quite soundly. Why do you ask?"

"Because," Belshazzar interjected, prodding the fire with a stick, "we three all received nearly identical visions of warning not to return to Jerusalem."

"I fear the king intends to harm the child," Melchior added in a grave tone.

Artaban looked at them in astonishment. "You saw visions? From God in heaven?"

"They must surely have come from Ahura Mazda himself," Gondophares confirmed. "We all three dreamed of a messenger in shining light with the same instructions. 'You must not betray the child to Herod, but return to Parthia by another way.'"

"The same message to each of you?"

"Yes," Belshazzar replied. "We expected you to have had a similar encounter. I wonder why you didn't?"

"As do I," Artaban murmured, muddling through the possibilities in his own mind. "Have any of you ever seen such a vision before?"

They all looked at each other and then shook their heads.

"In all my years," Melchior said, "I've never had such an experience. But I have no doubt it was a genuine revelation from the throne of heaven. It was most certainly no ordinary dream. And corroboration from three separate sources undoubtedly assures its authenticity." He looked at Artaban with a lifted brow. "And you saw nothing?"

"No, nothing at all."

Belshazzar frowned. "Why would our Great God speak to us, yet remain silent to you?"

Artaban had no answer, and the question gnawed at him like a worm in rotting wood. Had the Wise Lord withheld his voice because Artaban had sworn allegiance to the infant king? Had his oath to the child severed him from the God of his fathers?

Simur sat perched on Melchior's shoulder, preening his

feathers in the early light. "Brack," he suddenly squawked, "A message in the silence."

Artaban stared at the bird, which went back to its preening, and wondered what sort of message it might be.

"Well," Belshazzar concluded, "even without additional confirmation, the message was clear. We should pack up our camp and leave this place as soon as possible. We've completed the task we set out to accomplish. Our job here is done. We should heed the warning of the dreams and report back to our Great King about all we've learned."

"Agreed," Gondophares offered.

Melchior stretched out his hands. "We should certainly depart before the day is out. To linger could put the child at risk. But," he added, "I believe we have an obligation to Mary and Joseph to pass this warning on to them as well. Let's go do that now before any time is lost."

After briefly returning to their tents to ready themselves, they met on the road for the short walk to the little house that had so recently been illuminated by the star from the heavens. They approached the stable door and knocked. Moments later, the door opened, and Joseph appeared looking a bit tense. Artaban peered over his shoulder into the house and could see that it was in disarray.

"Joseph, my friend, you seem distraught. Is something amiss?" Melchior asked.

"Please come in," Joseph motioned them into their temporary quarters.

The living space was in a mess. A pack, several cloth bags, and a few woven baskets were positioned along one wall. Piles of blankets, small hand tools, and cooking utensils lay in another area, and some basic food items were assembled on a nearby table. Joseph muttered an apology for the chaos and turned away to begin carefully placing items in the leather backpack. Mary sat with her back toward them, hurriedly sorting through another pile of cloaks, sandals, and headscarves, while Yeshua slept peacefully amid the turmoil in his manger bed.

"Are you preparing to leave?" Melchior asked.

Joseph paused only long enough to nod. "Yes. An angel of the Lord spoke to me in a dream last night. He told us to flee to Egypt and wait there until we are instructed to return."

Artaban heard Belshazzar and Gondophares draw sharp breaths. Joseph's vision no doubt confirmed their own revelations. Again, Artaban agonized over the fact that he alone had not received a message of warning from God.

Suddenly, Mary stopped her work and turned to face them with tears in her eyes. "King Herod is searching for my baby to put him to death."

Joseph immediately stopped packing and rushed to Mary, taking her in his arms. "That's not going to happen, Mary. We'll get away. The Lord wouldn't have warned us if He wasn't going to help us escape."

Melchior knelt next to the couple and placed a hand on the shoulder of each. "Joseph is quite right, Mary. The blessing of the Almighty is on your son. The message written in the stars is clear. Your child is destined to be a mighty king. Not Herod, nor even the Emperor of Rome, could thwart the divine will of God. I'm certain you'll be safe if you follow the guidance you've received."

Gondophares stepped nearer to the couple and said, "We were also given instructions from heavenly messengers not to disclose the child's identity to Herod. Do you see how our Great God has already taken measures to ensure your safety?"

Joseph looked up with an expression of shock on his face. "You were visited by an angel of the Lord?"

Gondophares nodded. "Myself, Master Melchior, and Belshazzar all had the same dream. We were told not to go back through Jerusalem, but to avoid Herod and return to Parthia by a different route."

Joseph glanced briefly at Artaban. Though he didn't ask the question, Artaban knew what he was thinking. "Why not you as well?" And then suddenly Artaban understood. Simur had been right, after all. There was a message in the silence, and it spoke to him more loudly now than if a host of heavenly angels had appeared in the sky.

"Joseph, Mary," Artaban said, "I would be honored to accompany you on your journey, if you'll have me."

"What?" Belshazzar exclaimed.

Artaban glanced around at his companions. "I understand now why I didn't receive a vision like the rest of you. You were all warned to return to Parthia by a different path. But, you see, I'm not supposed to return to Parthia at all. I'm meant to go with Joseph and Mary to Egypt. Simur's little quip was actually quite insightful. There was indeed a message in the silence after all."

Belshazzar shook his head vehemently. "You'd only draw unnecessary attention to them," he argued. "A Parthian magus traveling with two Judean refugees… It would put the child at even more risk. They'll be better off staying as inconspicuous as possible."

"Not necessarily," Artaban countered. "I could present myself as an indentured servant. That's actually true after all. I've pledged my life in service to the boy. So there's no deceit in assuming that identity."

He turned his attention to Joseph. "I think I can be of great help to you on your journey. I speak several languages and am familiar with the customs of many Eastern cultures. Besides," he added, feeling a wave of empathy for the couple wash over him, "sometimes it's just nice to have a friend along in uncertain times."

"Why?" Mary asked tentatively. "Why would you leave your home, your family, and your work to flee with us into an uncertain future? I don't understand."

Artaban's smile reflected the genuine warmth he felt in his heart for this simple family. "I made an oath to serve your son all the days of my life. That's no small thing. But it's also more than that. I truly *believe*, perhaps for the first time in my whole life. I believe in a God above, who sees us, and hears us, and knows our sorrows. And I believe *that God*, the God of Israel, has called me to serve Him in this way."

Artaban reached out a hand toward Joseph, who grasped his forearm in return.

The young father looked long and hard into Artaban's eyes and then nodded. "We'd welcome your help and friendship," he said, his voice cracking. "But not as a servant... as a brother in the Lord."

Artaban clasped Joseph's arm more firmly and smiled in return. An unspoken understanding seemed to pass between them. This went deeper than just a pledge of service. It marked the beginning of a bond they would share for life.

"Ahem," Belshazzar cleared his throat. "Joseph, could you please excuse us for a moment? There's an issue we need to discuss among ourselves." He bade the other magi to join him outside the door.

As soon as they were alone, Belshazzar's face darkened. He immediately turned on Artaban. "You would abandon your faith?" he exclaimed. "You would turn your back on Ahura

Mazda and our sacred traditions for these followers of a foreign God? And what about your duty to our Lord King?"

Such an accusation would have sparked a response of outrage from Artaban in times past. But for some reason, he remained perfectly calm. He realized that his decision represented a challenge to all that Belshazzar held most dear. An argument in such circumstances was one he could never win.

"Do you remember Master Melchior's analogy of the stone thrown into the pond?" Artaban asked, his voice steady and even.

"Of course I do," Belshazzar shot back. "That's precisely the point. Why would you turn away from the truth of the stone to chase a mere shadow?"

"Are we so certain of where we've placed our faith?" Artaban asked. "The ripples spread outward from the center, but sometimes it's not always clear which truth is the source, and which are merely the echoes."

Melchior raised an eyebrow. "Go on, my son," he prompted.

"Perhaps," Artaban continued, "what we've witnessed in this house was not the shadow of our truth, but the one reality that casts all shadows. Perhaps the Wise Lord I have served all my life is actually just a faint reflection of the true God who spoke through the Hebrew prophets, who sent His angel to Mary, and who guided us by His star." He paused, looking each of his companions in the eye.

"This is madness," Belshazzar protested. "You abandon everything for an uncertain future with strangers in a foreign land."

Melchior stepped forward and raised a hand. "Peace, Belshazzar. Every man must follow the convictions of conscience he receives from the Lord of heaven. Artaban's choice is not the same as mine, but I can see the hand of providence in it."

The old sage turned to Artaban, his eyes bright with both pride and concern. "But I caution you, my friend, to be mindful of the enemy. Just as you've been convinced that the God of heaven is real, remember there's also an adversary who works against the forces of good."

As those words struck him, Artaban felt pieces of a vast puzzle suddenly clicking into place. His eyes widened as revelation flooded through him.

"All the obstacles we've faced," he breathed. "The Chancellor's schemes in Ecbatana, the missing scrolls, the delays at the border, the ambush on the Damascus road. Every hindrance that delayed our progress..." He let his voice trail off, leaving the conclusions unspoken.

"What are you saying?" Gondophares asked.

"Each of them seemed like a separate misfortune," Artaban replied, his voice growing stronger. "But what if they were all centrally orchestrated by the enemy? What if they were all intended to prevent us from reaching the child in time? And then, when we finally made it to Herod's court, the enemy's strategy changed. Instead of continuing to block our path, he made the wicked king appear reasonable and friendly, so he could use us to find and kill the newborn Messiah."

Gondophares eyed his friend warily, considering the idea. Eventually, he said, "I'd never thought about it that way. But I must admit, what you say has the ring of truth."

Melchior nodded. "And yet the Lord of Heaven overruled it all. Each obstacle became an occasion for His deliverance."

"You mean like that stranger who got us through customs at the Parthian border?" Artaban asked, recalling the mysterious encounter. "Or Volusius, who showed up at just the right time and convinced that Roman bureaucrat to let us proceed?"

"Those were all Rostan's men," Belshazzar grumbled. "They were part of his network, not angelic messengers."

"In my experience," Melchior interjected, "the Wise Lord often works his will through the hands of men."

"And what about our rescue in Damascus?" Gondophares

added. "That seemed almost too convenient. Mind you, I was more than happy to see Captain Vakshuvar arrive—"

"Right!" Artaban cut in. "I thought so too. But looking back, it must have been a miracle of God that they ever found us, buried in those catacombs."

"If you reflect on all the difficulties we faced," Melchior suggested. "I think you'll see the hand of the Almighty in each resolution. I believe the Wise Lord called us to this mission and that we've been under his divine protection every step of the way."

"Then what about Tadmor?" Belshazzar argued. "Why did we lose our caravan master at the most critical stage of our journey? And the bandit attack outside Damascus—"

"But we're here, aren't we?" Artaban cut in.

"And Tabor is dead," Belshazzar shot back.

"You're absolutely right," Melchior said. "Though our Great God is mighty and righteous and just, the enemy is a powerful foe with a host of devoted followers in this world. This is a war, and the stakes are all too real."

He turned to look Artaban straight in the eye. "Remember this, my son. The battle you've entered is far greater than any worldly confrontation between Parthia and Rome. It's a struggle between light and darkness, truth and the lie. And that child," he nodded toward the stable door, "is at the center of it."

Simur fluttered his wings. "Brack," he cawed. "A child of light. Kingdoms will fall."

The magnitude of it all—the intricate weaving of prophecy and circumstance, of human choice and divine providence—left them all momentarily speechless. Artaban's chest tightened, not with fear, but with awe. To think that the cosmic conflict, which had raged since the dawn of time, now turned upon the fragile life of a child, and that he, Artaban son of Nazar, was called to guard him.

Just then, Joseph stepped through the doorway.

"Please excuse the interruption," he said. "But, Artaban, we hoped to leave by midday. If you plan to come with us, you may need to get ready."

"I'll accompany you," Artaban confirmed. "But you might delay your departure until evening. It might be wise to travel under cover of darkness, at least until we're well away from Bethlehem. Herod's soldiers may already be watching the roads."

Joseph thought for a moment, then nodded. "Yes. That's probably wise. I'm thankful for your counsel already, and we haven't even left yet."

"We," Belshazzar added, "should also be on our way. I suggest we begin our preparations as well."

As the sun climbed higher, the Parthian company prepared for their northern route home while Joseph's small family made ready to flee. Artaban moved between both groups, helping his former companions secure their belongings while gathering the supplies he would need for the Egyptian journey.

The emotional farewells were brief but profound. Years of friendship and shared scholarship could not be easily severed, yet each man understood the necessity of their different paths.

Belshazzar, despite his earlier protests, clasped his colleague's forearm warmly. "May your God, whatever name you choose to call him by, watch over you on this journey."

"He will," Artaban replied with quiet confidence. "He already has. Blessings to you on your travel home."

"Here," Gondophares said, holding out a scroll case. "I purchased some maps of trade routes from a merchant in Damascus. Maybe they'll be helpful to you."

Artaban accepted the case and pulled his colleague into a

brotherly embrace. "You're a dear friend and a fine scholar. Our Great King and our people are fortunate to have the benefit of your service. Safe travels to you."

Finally, Artaban turned toward his old mentor.

"Take this," Melchior said, pressing a small object into Artaban's hand.

Artaban opened his fingers to see a signet ring engraved with a star and a scroll. He gaped in astonishment.

"Master, your signet... I can't..." he breathed.

Melchior gently wrapped Artaban's fingers back around the ring. "I have no sons to pass on my legacy to," he whispered. "Only my students at the Bīt Mummu. I hope and pray that I've been able to convey some small amount of knowledge and wisdom."

"Master..." Artaban began, but was stilled by the old man.

"You, Artaban... You remind me of myself when I was young. Skeptical, impulsive, insightful..." he shook his head and took a deep breath. "But you also have a courage and determination that make me very proud. This ring bears the symbols of learning and revelation. They represent the triumph of light and truth over darkness. May they forever be a reminder of the great path to which you have been called, and," his voice cracked, "of the spiritual father who loves you as a son."

Artaban had no words to say. Instead, he leaned in to the old man's embrace in an effort to conceal his own tears. They held each other for a long moment in the farewell Artaban had yearned to share with his own father but never could.

As the Parthian caravan departed northward toward Damascus, Artaban stood watching until they disappeared over the horizon. When evening came, he helped to load the family's few possessions onto a small donkey, while Mary settled the infant Jesus in a makeshift carrier.

"Are you sure about this?" Joseph asked him as they prepared to depart. "You're leaving everything behind—your country, your friends, your future."

Artaban looked down at the sleeping child in Mary's arms, then up at the first stars beginning to appear in the darkening sky. "My father died serving an earthly kingdom that will eventually fade into the mists of time. And I..." He paused, searching for the right words. "I've spent my life studying the heavens, searching for signs that God is real. Now I've found that sign in your son. My future is here."

Mary smiled at him with the serene confidence of one who had already said yes to an impossible calling. "We're thankful to have you with us, Artaban of Parthia. Perhaps God has been preparing you for this moment all your life."

They waited until dusk deepened. Then, under the hush of night, they slipped quietly from Bethlehem. No torches betrayed their progress, only the whisper of sandals on stone, the soft bray of a donkey, and the rustle of cloaks.

As they set out on the southern road, Artaban glanced up at the constellations he had studied since childhood. The same stars that had guided them westward from Ecbatana now shone overhead, brilliant and eternal. Yet this night, he looked at them not as omens to be interpreted, but as distant lights kindled by the same hand that had formed the child sleeping peacefully in his mother's arms.

Behind them, Bethlehem grew small and dark, while ahead lay Egypt and all it implied—exile, uncertainty, and the unrevealed purposes of the God who establishes kingdoms and causes them to fall. The infant king they protected would start his life far away from his prophesied throne, yet Artaban had no doubt that heaven's plan would unfold exactly as ordained. And he felt both honored and overwhelmed to play some small part in that grand design.

As they walked through the cool night air, following the ancient road toward Gaza and the border of Egypt, Artaban found himself humming an old Parthian traveling tune that seemed somehow appropriate to the occasion. The words of the song were a prayer of gratitude for the mysterious ways of the Most High God, who could transform doubt into faith, tragedy into hope, and the ending of one journey into the beginning of another.

Artaban lifted his eyes to the heavens. One star shone brighter than the rest, lingering low on the horizon. Despite his years of study, Artaban could not recall its name. Yet somehow he knew, deep down inside, it was a reflection of the true Light of Heaven, which would forever guide their way.

THE BIBLE PASSAGE

Matthew 2: 1-18 (NKJV)

1 Now after Jesus was born in Bethlehem of Judea in the days of Herod the king, behold, wise men from the East came to Jerusalem, **2** saying, "Where is He who has been born King of the Jews? For we have seen His star in the East and have come to worship Him."

3 When Herod the king heard *this,* he was troubled, and all Jerusalem with him. **4** And when he had gathered all the chief priests and scribes of the people together, he inquired of them where the Christ was to be born.

5 So they said to him, "In Bethlehem of Judea, for thus it is written by the prophet:

6 *'But you, Bethlehem, in the land of Judah,*
Are not the least among the rulers of Judah;
For out of you shall come a Ruler
Who will shepherd My people Israel.'"

7 Then Herod, when he had secretly called the wise men, determined from them what time the star appeared. **8** And he sent them to Bethlehem and said, "Go and search carefully for the young Child, and when you have found Him, bring back word to me, that I may come and worship Him also."

9 When they heard the king, they departed; and behold, the star which they had seen in the East went before them, till it came and stood over where the young Child was. **10** When they saw the star, they rejoiced with exceedingly great joy. **11** And when they had come into the house, they saw the young Child with Mary His mother, and fell down and worshiped Him. And when they had opened their treasures, they presented gifts to Him: gold, frankincense, and myrrh.

12 Then, being divinely warned in a dream that they should not return to Herod, they departed for their own country another way.

13 Now when they had departed, behold, an angel of the Lord appeared to Joseph in a dream, saying, "Arise, take the young Child and His mother, flee to Egypt, and stay there until I bring you word; for Herod will seek the young Child to destroy Him."

14 When he arose, he took the young Child and His mother by night and departed for Egypt, **15** and was there until the death of Herod, that it might be fulfilled which was spoken by the Lord through the prophet, saying, "Out of Egypt I called My Son."

16 Then Herod, when he saw that he was deceived by the wise men, was exceedingly angry; and he sent forth and put to death all the male children who were in Bethlehem and in all its districts, from two years old and under, according to the time which he had determined from the wise men. **17** Then was fulfilled what was spoken by Jeremiah the prophet, saying:

18 *"A voice was heard in Ramah,*
Lamentation, weeping, and great mourning,
Rachel weeping for her children,
Refusing to be comforted,
Because they are no more."

Thanks for reading to *The Fourth Magi*. If you enjoyed the story, please leave a review on **Amazon** or **Goodreads**. Reviews are a great way to help readers like you discover good books to enjoy, and they are a nice way to say thanks to the author.

FREE OFFER

Get **free access** to **exclusive Bonus Content** to include…

- **A timeline of the events** in the story as they integrated with the **actual dates** of the **real conjunctions** of Jupiter, Saturn, and Mars that occurred in 7 BC.
- Summaries of the scholarly articles published in *Biblical Archaeology Review* that explore the nature of the star of Bethlehem in more detail.
- **Images** of the statue from Nebuchadnezzar's dream in Daniel Chapter 2 and the beasts of Daniel 7.
- A discussion of **frequently asked questions** about the Magi's visit to Jesus such as these:
  - When **Herod** decided to have the **babies** in Bethlehem **executed**, why did he choose the ones that were **two years old and younger**?
  - How could a star in the sky lead the Magi to **a specific house** on the earth?
  - Did anyone in Jerusalem or Bethlehem see the star?
  - **How many Magi** came to visit Jesus?
  - What Old Testament prophecies point to the time or location of Jesus' birth?
  - And more…

Visit **books.bryancanter.com/magi** to claim your free copy today!

IF YOU LIKE HISTORICAL FICTION...

Check out *Daughter of the Gods: A Novel of the Picts*

Summer, 367 A.D. In a land of **mystery** and **enchantment**, in an age of **Celtic gods**, **Highland warlords**, **Roman legions**, and **powerful druids**, a young Pictish healer finds herself embroiled in an **epic struggle between gods and men.**

The Celtic tribes of the Scotland and Ireland conspire to assault Hadrian's Wall and drive*<Click or scan to **read more**>*

eBook | Paperback | Hardcover | Audiobook

ABOUT THE AUTHOR

Bryan E. Canter is an author, independent publishing consultant, and retired Army officer with overseas tours in Iraq, Korea, and Okinawa. He has degrees in engineering physics, religious studies, and tele-communications. His love of literature prompted him to complete a Masters-level "great books" program at St. John's College.

As an international speaker and educator, Bryan has addressed large groups and conducted training seminars in venues across the USA, Nicaragua, India, Scotland, the Middle East, and Japan.

Bryan helps authors navigate the complex world of independent publishing as a book and audiobook publishing consultant for My Word Publishing. Additionally, he is an Amazon Ads specialist with the Successful Writer Marketplace.

Bryan lives full-time in a motorhome with his beautiful wife, Dawn, visiting historic sites and enjoying the amazing natural beauty of the United States. They especially enjoy hiking together to high mountain lakes in the Western ranges, and Yosemite is their favorite place of all.

Connect with Bryan on his website: bryancanter.com